He didn't look like a skulking criminal...

With his wind-tousled hair, two-day beard and crinkly sun lines at the edges of his eyes, he reminded her of a world-weary philosopher. Albeit a handsome, sexy one.

He turned his head and caught her watching him, and, embarrassed, she whipped around and gazed out the windshield at the driving rain. A hurricane was coming, he'd said. A deadly hurricane. Were they really in extreme danger, or was it a ruse to get her to accompany him? Terror floated in her brain, battling common sense. Would he have saved her, only to kill her?

Out of the corner of her eye she saw her cabin, Sunny Haven. There she'd be safe. Safe from the blinding rain and shrieking wind. Safe from nerves that jangled like downed power lines. And safe from this stranger. But where could she go to be safe from her attraction to him?

Dear Reader,

When a woman's alone, who can she trust, where can she run...? Straight into the arms of HER PROTECTOR. Because when danger lurks around every corner, there's only one place you're safe—in the strong, sheltering arms of the man who loves you.

You told us how much you loved the HER PROTECTOR promotion last year, so we've brought it back! And you'll love these *brand-new* stories of women in jeopardy and in love—with the only person who can keep them safe.

Since childhood, author Judi Lind has loved cozying up and watching storms, the rain pelting outside while she was safe and warm inside. But what if inside wasn't safe, either, she asked herself. What if you were cut off from the world while danger stalked closer and closer? That was the starting point for *Storm Warnings*.

I know you'll enjoy this and all the books in the HER PROTECTOR series!

Regards,

Debra Matteucci
Senior Editor & Editorial Coordinator
Harlequin Books
300 East 42nd Street
New York, NY 10017

Storm Warnings
Judi Lind

Harlequin Books

TORONTO • NEW YORK • LONDON
AMSTERDAM • PARIS • SYDNEY • HAMBURG
STOCKHOLM • ATHENS • TOKYO • MILAN
MADRID • WARSAW • BUDAPEST • AUCKLAND

For my mother, Lois Cooper, the strongest woman I've ever known. This story is about picking up the pieces and starting over. A feat you've accomplished so many times, always with courage and grace.

ISBN 0-373-22433-8

STORM WARNINGS

Copyright © 1997 by Judith A. Lind

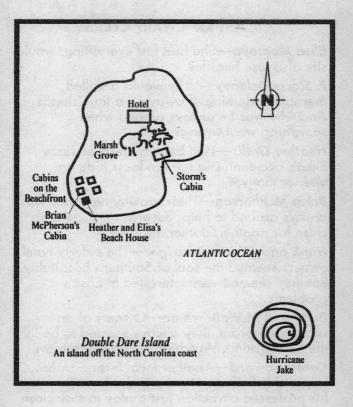

Hotel

Marsh Grove

Cabins on the Beachfront

Brian McPherson's Cabin

Heather and Elisa's Beach House

Storm's Cabin

ATLANTIC OCEAN

Double Dare Island
An island off the North Carolina coast

Hurricane Jake

CAST OF CHARACTERS

Elisa Montoya—She had lost everything; would she also lose her life?

F. Storm Delaney—Why would a skilled therapist hide himself away on a tiny island? And why was he always around when something went wrong?

Heather Gellis—Had been a lifesaver since Elisa's accident. Did her kindness hide an ulterior motive?

Brian McPherson—Their brawny neighbor was always around to help. But was he sticking so close for another, darker, reason?

Hank and Miriam Danziger—The elderly hotel owners seemed the soul of Southern hospitality. But they seemed *very* interested in Elisa's problems.

Betty and Mark Bowman—Owners of an island restaurant, they always seemed to be in the background. Watching Elisa's every move.

Carey Howard—Another local businessman. He quickly became Heather's shadow. Or was his professed attraction just a ploy to stay close to Elisa?

David Welton—The New York attorney had represented Elisa's former boyfriend, now deceased. So why had he traveled hundreds of miles to deliver a document that could have been mailed?

Prologue

Double Dare Island, North Carolina

The month of August melted away—hot, sticky, somnam-
bulant. After Labor Day, the islanders said, the tropical
breezes would finally arrive, cooling the land and, more
importantly, lowering the ocean temperature.

But as the days of September ticked by and the water
temperature stayed in the eighties, the locals stopped talking about the weather. Bad luck. Despite their conspiracy
of silence, the atmosphere hissed with a new urgency. The
slow-moving townspeople walked a little faster. Their
Southern drawls sped up just a bit. Frequently they interrupted their conversations to stare for long moments at the
sea. Anyone keeping track of such things would have noticed that stores of canned goods and bottled water kept
disappearing from Newton's Grocery.

The remaining vacationers and weekend beachgoers patted themselves on the back—how wise they'd been, taking
their holiday after the summer crunch went back north to
the cities.

But the vacationers didn't notice that crisp electricity in
the air. Didn't pay attention to the weather reports of a
tropical depression in the Caribbean. The vacationers didn't
understand the signs: wide expanses of eighty-degree ocean

water, warm, humid air, and high winds blowing in the same direction as those near the surface.

The seafaring islanders understood all the signs. They could smell it in the air. They could feel it in their bones. Closer and closer came the oppressive feeling of doom.

A hurricane was on the way—and they were ensnared in its path.

Chapter One

Elisa Montoya scuffed her foot in the frothy white foam that tickled her toes through her sandals. The water was warm and satiny as it washed the fine grains of sand from her feet.

She glanced around, watching other tourists frolicking in the surf, or lazing on colorful beach towels. The scene was magical and serene, yet she stared at her surroundings with apathy. The charm of the tiny island off North Carolina's coast was lost on Elisa.

"A change of scenery will do you good," her mother had argued.

She hadn't understood that for Elisa, a change of environment wouldn't ease the confusion and nameless fear that clouded her days and plagued her nights. Nor would a different location blur the half memories that were too painful to remember.

The night Jay had killed himself.

The letter she'd received shortly after his death. She still couldn't bring herself to open it, because she knew Jay's suicide note would blame her. Remind her of her hurtful final words that must have shoved him over the brink.

In the short time they dated, she'd grown fond of Jay Morrow, but her brutal rehearsal and performance schedule had put a heavy strain on the budding relationship. Elisa closed her eyes, recalling their last date, when he'd unexpectedly asked her to marry him. Although she blamed the rigors of her career, they'd both known the truth. She simply hadn't loved him.

Elisa would never forget the hurt mirrored in his eyes when he'd slipped the ring box back into his pocket.

A beach ball skipped across the sand and nudged Elisa's sore foot. Suddenly she had to escape the blaring radios and children squealing with delight. There were too many memories, too many regrets, in their laughter. Yet, even when she was alone, she couldn't gain a moment's respite from the gaping hole in her memory.

If only she could have that time back. Those precious few hours before the accident. The damage was done, nothing would change that. But if she could just remember why it had happened, perhaps she could find a measure of peace.

She turned her face into the sharpening wind and gathered her towel and tote bag and limped farther up the beach—toward solitude. A quarter mile. Then a half mile. She trudged on, ignoring the sand's bite against her bare legs, until an enormous dune blocked her path. With a growl of determination, Elisa slipped off her thongs and slogged up the grainy slope.

When she reached the crest, she stopped and looked around. Fifteen feet beneath her was a narrow inlet, an inverted vee cut into the high bank. The incision left a small, perfect beach, populated only by a family of skittering sand crabs. A pile of rocks reposed almost in the center, as if delivered by the sea for Elisa's private use.

She closed her eyes and breathed in the tangy air. Surely here, for a short while, she could forget her problems.

Smiling for the first time in days, she hobbled down the dune. As her bare feet crunched across the hot sand, she noticed that the beach was below the high-tide mark. Right now the tide was out, but she would have to make sure to climb back over the dune before her private cove became submerged in seawater.

One of the boulders was relatively flat and sloped at an

angle toward the sea. Perfect. She spread her beach towel and stretched out. She was tired, so very tired. Her eyelids drooped, and Elisa blinked rapidly, willing herself to stay awake. Sleep was no longer a friend; these days, her dreams were like movies, filled with images of happier times. And nightmares about the single night that had ended them.

Switching on her portable radio, she scanned the dial for soothing classical music. Only a news broadcast pre-empted the static. Elisa listened for a few moments to a report of a tropical storm being upgraded to a hurricane. She looked out toward the horizon. Maybe the fringes of the storm would bring rain to the island. A respite from this hot, muggy wind.

Unable to find any music, she snapped off the radio and leaned back, hugging her knees to her chest. Music wouldn't soothe the savage beast snarling inside her, anyway.

Almost in spite of herself, she lowered her head, allowing her gaze to travel down her body, lingering on her torso before moving on to her long, slender legs. Then, as if she wanted to taunt herself, her eyes fastened on her right foot.

Except for a few bright red welts, the physical healing was almost complete. At least, as much as it ever would be. Even though she'd sustained a badly mangled ankle and a skull fracture, the hospital staff said she was lucky, very lucky, to have recovered with so little residual damage. Although her ankle still throbbed and burned, the headaches were easing with time. And for most people, a broken ankle and mild amnesia would be a small price to pay for the horrific automobile crash she had survived.

But for Elisa Montoya, prima ballerina, a weakened right foot meant the end of her career. The end of life as she knew it. At only twenty-six, she was faced with a forced retirement, and she didn't know what to do with the rest of her life.

Nor could she go on with her future until she could remember what had propelled her into the darkness on that fateful night. A night that had ended in tragedy.

Ignoring the darkening clouds rolling in on the horizon, she wound her long black hair into a knot and leaned back on the beach towel. Closing her eyes, she once again tried to recall those elusive hours before her little red sports car had plunged over the side of a steep ravine.

What chain of events had transpired on that rainy night on the Pennsylvania Turnpike? The police intimated she was fleeing the scene of a suspicious death, but, fortunately, they had only circumstantial evidence. They'd grilled her for hours in the hospital before mercifully leaving her in peace.

But she couldn't be so kind to herself. Where had she been going? Why had she been traveling alone? If only she could remember. A shudder rippled through her body as she slid into slumber. If only, if only, if...

F. STORM DELANEY III, M.D., held the binoculars to his eyes, scanning the deserted beach. Here and there a plastic wrapper skipped along the sand, propelled by the ever-increasing gusts of wind. The seagulls and pelicans had deserted their flight patterns and were huddled, hundreds of them, along the shoreline.

He looked back at the darkening horizon. Before going off to college and, ultimately, medical school, he had lived on the Outer Banks his entire life. His father, and his father before that, had been fishermen who spent their lives pitting their nautical skills against the treacherous sea. If anyone should have been able to gauge the intensity of the approaching tempest, it was he.

Two days ago, the initial forecast had called for Hurricane Jake to slam into shore down in Florida, but wily old Jake had changed his mind, looping back out to sea. Now he was headed north, currently spiraling off the coast of Georgia. No telling where the fickle bastard would actually touch land.

Storm's ruminations were interrupted by Deputy Sheriff Roger Guidry, who was stalking across the blustering sand, his hand atop his head, hanging on to his hat. "All clear!" Roger shouted, when he was close enough to be heard over the roaring wind.

Storm wasn't so sure. Something kept nagging at him. Something they'd overlooked.

But what? Heading up the volunteer unit in the North Beach area, Storm had personally supervised the evacuation of the beachfront. At the mere mention of Hurricane Jake's possible approach, the remaining sunbathers had practically raced over one another to get to their cars. By now, all the beachgoers were safely stowed on the last ferry back to the mainland. But something didn't feel right. What was he missing?

He looked at his watch. The ferryman was going to start for Cape Hatteras at four o'clock sharp. Anyone left on the island had only forty minutes to make that boat back to relative safety.

"I guess you're right," he finally conceded. "Why don't you head on to the ferry?"

"How about you? Aren't you coming with us?"

Storm cupped his hands around his mouth and shouted into the quickening wind. "I'm going to check out a few of those shacks off the main road! Most of them don't have electricity—let alone a radio!"

The deputy reached up to grab his hat as a gust of wind tried to steal it. "Most of them are staying out of pure cussedness. No sense you getting blown to kingdom come along with them."

"Maybe so." Storm's voice rose over the howling wind. "That's their right. Mine, too. And I'm staying."

Guidry stuffed his hat back onto his head. "Doggone it, Doc, you're one stubborn cuss. I ain't going to waste my breath arguing with you. If you want to commit suicide, I guess nobody's going to be able to stop you."

Suicide? Was that what the islanders thought was his

goal? Storm shrugged. That might have been a possibility a year ago, but now...now he just wanted to be left alone. Besides, he didn't think he was facing any immediate danger. Everyone knew this hurricane was a "loop-the-looper." Like the metal sphere in a pinball machine, a loop-the-looper headed for one spot, only to glance off sharply and aim in a different direction. Hurricane Jake *might* hit the Carolina coast, or it might come ashore much farther north.

He slapped Guidry on the shoulder. "Quit mothering me and head for the ferry. Otherwise you're going to be stranded with me."

"Your funeral, Doc." Throwing up his hands in resignation, Guidry loped down the path between the shifting dunes to the parking lot.

Turning back to the deserted beach, Storm raised his binoculars once again and scanned the shore. Why couldn't he shake this feeling that they'd missed something? Or someone?

With a growl of frustration, he spun on his heel and started back to his Jeep. A momentary shift of the clouds cast a stark beam of sunlight on the soft sand, reminding him that it was still the middle of the afternoon. In another hour, if the hurricane kept heading their way, the sky would be as black as a sea cave. He couldn't afford to waste what little daylight remained. He needed to get back to the village and help Danziger board up the hotel's windows. Then he should take a last walk through—

He stopped. Something flashed for an instant where an errant sunbeam touched the ground. At first Storm thought he had imagined the light, for the somber clouds smothered the frail sparkle almost immediately. He walked slowly, pushing aside waist-high blades of sea oats. There, behind that small dune, something silver...

He brushed aside the last sheaf of weeds. Half-hidden by the blowing sand was a shiny silver bicycle.

Just like the one he'd seen that dark, beautiful woman riding around town the past few days.

The same hauntingly beautiful woman he *hadn't* seen boarding the ferry.

The "mystery lady," as the villagers called her, had become a familiar sight lately. Although pleasant enough when spoken to, she kept to herself, seldom initiating conversation. But what a rare and lovely picture she was traversing the island on her bicycle—her long blue-black hair snapping in the breeze. Lean, supple legs pedaling effortlessly.

But where was she now? Storm knew without a doubt that she hadn't boarded the ferry.

Drawing in a deep breath, he sighed and stared back toward the beach. The cloud cover drifted again, and the sky darkened perceptibly. Was she down there? Alone? Possibly hurt?

With grim determination etched across his strong features, Storm stalked back to the beach.

IT HAD BEEN a good performance. Although Elisa's eyes were closed, the roar of the audience was proof enough. The offstage wind machine was hard at work, but the air it was blowing was hot and humid. She raised a hand to wipe a trickle of sweat from her brow. Funny, her heavy stage makeup felt unusually grimy. Too heavy for her face.

She tried to open her eyes but was momentarily blinded by stinging perspiration that dripped off her fine black eyebrows and clung to her thick lashes.

They hadn't turned up the houselights yet. The audience was still a dark, roaring blur in front of her. Someone had cranked up the wind machine, it was whirring the thick air around her in a steamy vortex.

She stretched her slender arms out, curtsying again for the appreciative audience. Their applause was a solid wall of sound.

Suddenly a gush of warm water slapped Elisa's face and

poured down her body. Her deep brown eyes flew open, immediately focusing on her bare foot. The ugly red scars.

She looked around in bewilderment.

Where in the... What... Where *was* she?

The answer flooded her like the dark sea surrounding the boulder on which she was resting. She wasn't onstage. The tide had come in, and was lapping against the rock beneath her.

Elisa stared around in horror. The sky had been blue when she fell asleep. Now it was black and ominous. The strap of her beach bag was tangled around her ankle, but the gusting winds had pitched the rest of her belongings into the angry sea. She saw her sandals drifting like flotsam ten feet away.

Another wave crashed against the rock and her fingers sought a tighter hold on the slippery surface. Although the seawater was warm, an icy chill crept over her flesh.

Realization hit her with a sharp, debilitating blow.

Dear God, she was going to be swept out to sea.

Chapter Two

Frozen with fear, Elisa barely felt the slap of water crashing higher and higher up the side of the boulder. How long had she slept? It had seemed like only moments.

Leaning on one elbow, she looked over the edge of the rock. There was no way to gauge the depth of the roiling water below. She lifted her gaze to the dune she'd climbed earlier. The sea had climbed more than halfway up the bank. Seven or eight feet. Was she a strong enough swimmer to reach that dune?

Or should she stay where she was and hope the tide receded soon?

A gust of wind almost lifted her off the rock, giving Elisa her answer. If she had any hope of survival, she'd have to move. Now!

Willing her wobbly legs to hold her up, she slowly rose to her feet, took a deep breath, and jumped off the boulder.

The ocean water was tepid, but tumbling and grabbing with a frenzy she'd never experienced. Within an instant, her entire body was sucked beneath the white-capped surface.

Choking saltwater filled her mouth, her nose. Coughing and retching, she treaded water while she cleared her lungs. Once she'd caught her breath, she dived beneath the surface and put every fiber of her strength into swimming toward the dune.

Two strokes. Three. The ocean was churning. Agitated. Gritty sand crept beneath her lashes. She clenched her eyelids tighter and fought against the angry sea.

Five strokes. Six. Her lungs burned, and her ankle throbbed.

Seven strokes. Ten. Elisa came to the surface for breath and assessed the distance to the dune. She'd advanced only a few feet.

A thunderous wave picked up her tired body and tossed her like a minnow against the rocks. She instinctively held out her forearm, shielding her head from injury. But the undertow pulled her away, only to dash her back against the stones a moment later.

Her head thumped against the boulder. Blackness swam before her eyes. The only sound was the roar of the ocean. She felt herself drifting from consciousness. She wasn't going to make it. She was going to die without ever really having lived. Without having loved. A lonely dancer meeting a solitary death.

No! She wouldn't give up. Gritting her teeth in determination, she reached out and levered herself away from the punishing rocks.

Swallowing a sob, she sucked in another life-sustaining breath and plunged under the water again. But her strength had deserted her. She was still too weak from the accident and the resultant surgery.

At that moment, something clamped around her injured ankle.

She screamed, drinking in another mouthful of salty water.

Kicking furiously, she tried to free herself from whatever was clutching her leg. Then something grabbed at her shoulder.

Her mind conjured visions of a sea monster, a giant octopus, gripping her with its huge tentacles. Then the creature moved its grasp to around her chest. Clutching. Summoning the remains of her fleeting strength, she tightened her arm at a right angle and lashed out. A small burst of satisfaction blossomed as her elbow made contact with something warm. And large.

THE MYSTERY LADY was kicking furiously, obviously trying to distance herself from the dangerous rock pile. He shouted at her to be still and let him tow her to safety, but if she heard him over the thundering surf, she gave no indication.

"Come on, now, take it easy." He made a grab for her as she thrashed the water around them.

Her foot caught Storm on the thigh, sending a shock wave down his leg. Ow! What was this woman—a damned black belt in karate? He grappled with her frenzied leg, finally securing a firm hold on a slender ankle.

With his other arm, he reached up and clamped his hand on her shoulder. If she would just stop thrashing around, he'd have a better chance of getting them safely out of the cove.

But his touch set off some kind of primal fury. She fought like a sackful of wet alley cats. Her strong limbs were everywhere. Kicking. Pummeling. Her fist swung back, thumping him in the chest. Another kick, this time to his shin. Even though the blow was tempered by the water, it stung. It never occurred to him to try to calm her with words. Storm was too busy fighting the feisty hellion for his life.

Finally he inched behind her and slipped his arm around her slender waist. His hand glided over her wet, sleek flesh. She wriggled. Squirmed. Evaded his every attempt. Until his hand slid around her upper torso and, at last, his fingers found purchase.

He gasped and almost released his precarious hold. His hand was firmly clasping a small, perfectly shaped breast. An odd, hungry clawing in his loins reminded him of a time when his libido had still been alive—rampant.

A sharp elbow in his rib cage reminded him of his purpose. Reluctantly releasing his hold on her breast, he snaked a powerful forearm around her upper chest. He pulled her closer, until he could feel the silky texture of her skin against his.

Then, abruptly, she stopped fighting. A second later, she was floating, limp. Praying she hadn't drowned in his arms, he angled her face out of the water and started towing the unconscious woman toward the shoreline. His strength was ebbing, and the shoreline looked miles away.

But now that he only had the Atlantic Ocean to contend with, Storm found the job relatively easy, and he reached safety in a few scant moments.

With a single deft movement, he plucked her from the sea's grip and into his arms. She didn't weigh much more than a foundling infant, he thought grimly. When he was in practice he'd treated a number of adolescents with eating disorders. Anorexia was a difficult enemy to defeat; this slender woman was so light, he couldn't help but wonder if she wasn't a victim of the disorder. Still, her muscle tone felt good. Extraordinary, in fact.

He shrugged. He wasn't in private practice any longer. In fact, he hadn't practiced in his chosen field of psychiatry in over two years. This woman's possible fixation with her weight was no concern of his. Storm no longer felt it was his destiny to save every injured psyche he encountered. Not after he'd failed to save the most important person in his world.

Turning so that the wind was against his back, he easily carried her up the slope.

He laid her gently on the sand, and dropped to his knees beside her. With tender fingers, he tilted back her head in preparation for starting CPR. She moaned softly and turned away from his touch.

"It's all right," he murmured, brushing strands of ebony hair from her face. "You're going to be just fine. Relax now."

He held her hand loosely in his while taking her pulse. Weak, but steady.

She sighed and lay quiet, allowing Storm to resume his cursory examination. Clad only in an exquisite black-and-gold bikini, she lay before him like a sumptuous offering from the sea. Gritting his teeth, he forced himself to remember that this mermaid wasn't meant for his pleasure. Whether he wanted the role or not, he was a physician, a healer, and right now this woman needed his help.

Keeping a tight rein on his libido, he ran his fingertips over her head, her torso, as well as her arms and her incredibly long legs. Other than a nasty goose egg forming on her left temple, there were no other obvious signs of trauma. Although, judging by the surgical scar on her ankle, she'd been operated on within the past month or so.

The mystery lady stirred softly beneath his touch, a ragged sigh escaping her lips. He looked down, taking in her lovely face for the first time. Her dusky tan skin had tawny undertones, as if it had been brushed with gold dust. Her eyebrows were straight, fine—a perfect frame for large eyes fringed with incredibly thick lashes. But it was her mouth that drew him. Soft and delicate, like the rest of her, yet her bottom lip pouted with a bold lushness.

She coughed, distracting him from his renegade thoughts. Could she still have fluid on her lungs? Without a stethoscope, he only knew one way to find out. Feeling slightly awkward, he lowered his head to her chest and forced himself to concentrate on her vital signs.

He closed his eyes, listening, until he could disassociate himself from the sounds of nature's fury. Finally he heard a steady *ta-thump, ta-thump*—the reassuring beat of her heart.

The woman wriggled softly beneath him, and he nestled his face closer against her bosom, in order to better hear the rhythmic aspirations of her lungs. Or at least that was what he assured himself. But the sweet firmness of her breast pressing against his cheek almost took his breath away.

He gritted his teeth, cursing the scant bikini top that only accentuated the alluring nearness of her flesh. He was a doctor, a professional, for crying out loud! Just because he was a little rusty, that was no excuse. Taking deep, calming breaths, Storm forced his thoroughly masculine urges aside long enough to concentrate on the rhythm of her breathing. Just as he made the determination that her lungs were clear and free of fluid, a sudden shriek from her brought him up to his knees with a start.

Realizing that she'd come to only to discover a stranger's head nestled against her breast, he leaned back, holding up his hands in the universal gesture of surrender. "I...I'm sorry," he sputtered, trying to think of some way to explain.

"Just get away from me!" She sat up and walloped his chest with her small but mighty fists. The mystery lady sprang to her feet. "Ohh," she moaned, clutching her head and swaying on her wobbly legs. "My head."

"Here, let me help you—"

"No. I'm fine." Yanking her arm from his grasp, she rubbed her temple, watching him with wary black eyes.

The rain was beating harder now. Storm knew he had to get them to shelter. From the rapid changes over the past couple of hours, he knew the hurricane must have picked up speed. He had to get back and board up his cabin before Jake touched land.

"Look, I'm sorry if I startled you, but I'm a doctor. Wanted to make sure you didn't have any water in your lungs." His green eyes widened earnestly.

Green eyes... A sudden memory flashed through her. When she was in the ocean, fighting for her life—what *had* she been fighting? Her mind conjured up a faint recollection of some kind of sea monster—a giant octopus—wrapping its tentacles around her throat.

Elisa's look of wary confusion dissolved into sudden

comprehension. This particular sea monster had stunning green eyes. "Ohh... You...you pulled me out of the water." She chewed her lower lip and crossed her arms over her bikini top. "I don't know what to say...except thank you."

Somehow, the simple words were more eloquent, and more meaningful, than a flowery speech would have been. He looked away in embarrassment and shrugged. "We've got to get out of here. Bad storm's headed right at us."

Her gaze darted around the deserted beach. She nodded once and wordlessly turned on her heel and started marching toward the road, barely slowed by her slight limp.

He had to admire her spirit. For a little thing, she sure was a spitfire. "Wait!" he shouted when she stepped out of sight behind a stand of sea grass. Grabbing his discarded shirt and sneakers, Storm raced after her.

She'd made it as far as the parking lot when he caught up with her. "My Jeep's over there." He pointed.

The rain was coming down in torrents, and the wind direction had shifted. Despite the approaching danger, a rare grin teased his lips. The mystery lady wasn't daunted in the slightest, either by the approaching hurricane or by her own near drowning.

But Storm knew that ignoring danger wouldn't make it go away, and they were facing great peril if they didn't get off the beach.

She was so slightly built, he worried that a strong gust would actually pick her up and hurl her through space. For every step she took forward, the wind knocked her sideways a half step. But she showed no sign of giving up. Hunching her shoulders, she burrowed into the gale and started forward again. Then she veered away from his Jeep and headed toward the dune.

He knew she'd taken a severe blow to the head. Her thinking and reactions could be skewed. Taking a few precious seconds to slip on his Reeboks, he raced after her. "This way!" he shouted. "Where are you going?"

"I'll take my bike back to my cabin. We're staying just down the road." She pointed to the windward side of the island.

"At one of those cabins on Windjammer Point?"

She nodded. "The Grebbing place. Sunny Haven."

"It's already been evacuated. That section of the island will take the brunt of the storm. You can't go back there."

"I have to get my stuff. And my roommate's still there!"

"No time!" he shouted, pointing toward the darkening sky. "And your roommate would have been evacuated with all the other residents."

"No." She stood her ground. "Heather wouldn't leave without me."

"She's gone, I'm telling you! Don't you understand what kind of damage a hurricane can do? Those cabins weren't built to withstand gale-force winds. The big hotel over by the harbor is the only place on the island that can withstand hundred-and-forty-mile winds. And that's what they're predicting for Hurricane Jake."

ELISA'S HEAD whipped around as she looked at the murky brownish green sea with a new awareness. Until this moment, she'd thought the gathering clouds were merely a strong summer storm. But a hurricane?

She had grown up in the Los Angeles barrio. The past several years had been divided among San Francisco, Chicago, Rome and, most recently, New York City, each of which had its own brand of danger. Dirty, gritty, poverty-stricken inner cities, with their escalating crime rates. Yet she'd survived those grinding environments pretty well unscathed. How ironic that she might face her greatest test of courage here on this tranquil island.

Though she'd never been exposed to the fury of a hurricane, she'd seen enough news broadcasts to know he was right. They had to find shelter.

Nodding her understanding of their grim situation, she stalked past him to the lone vehicle parked on the asphalt lot. By the time she was settled in the passenger seat, he'd already jumped behind the wheel and started the engine.

They pulled out of the parking lot and headed toward the village. Storm rummaged in the back seat, found a mostly dry blanket and draped it around her bare shoulders. Elisa was soon grateful for the protection the blanket offered against the biting rain pelting her through the open side.

She huddled against the door, feeling vulnerable and fearful in this battle against the elements.

"Hold on!" he shouted suddenly.

Reflexively she braced herself, palms against the dashboard, as he swerved to miss an enormous branch jutting into their lane.

The vehicle hydroplaned on the wet surface, but he held a firm grasp on the steering wheel. After they slid in a half circle, the Jeep miraculously righted its course and they continued down the narrow road.

He turned toward her, concern replacing his normal scowl. "Are you okay?"

"Mmm-hmm." Her teeth were chattering so hard she couldn't speak.

A few minutes later, they approached the Y-shaped intersection that divided the island. Elisa knew that the right branch led to the cabin she'd been sharing with Heather for the past three weeks. The left fork curved upward and eventually led to the inner, higher section of the island, where the small village was located. They were only about a mile from her cabin now.

Then, amazingly, he took the left turnoff—the one *away* from her cabin. She reached across the gearshift and grabbed his arm, her security blanket sliding off her shoulder. "Wh-where are you taking me? I live back that way!"

He nodded. "I know. But I have to get you to the hotel before I can go batten down my own place."

"But you said there wasn't time."

With a slight shrug, he gave her a half smile. "There

wasn't. Not to go to your cabin, then mine. Yours is rented, so that makes mine more important. Besides, I told you, Windjammer Point has already been evacuated."

Absolute bullfeathers! She'd been on the beach only two or three hours. Surely Hurricane Jake couldn't travel that fast. What was this guy up to? Suddenly aware that she knew nothing about him, not even his name, Elisa edged closer to the door.

Suddenly, the gray fog that was becoming so familiar, so frighteningly familiar, shrouded her in its confusing mists. For the briefest moment, she wasn't sure where she was, as jagged segments of lost memories whizzed through her mind in a confusing kaleidoscope of color and sensation.

Once again, she was held prisoner by shattered images of running, terrified, from Jay's office that night. Of someone close behind her, chasing her. Intent on killing her. Elisa's heart pounded and her pulse raced as she relived flashes of that awful flight through the empty office building. During these episodes, she could actually hear unrelenting footsteps dogging her pace.

In her mind, she stopped and turned, looking to see the face of her pursuer. But she couldn't will the elusive memory into focus. The concussion she'd suffered in the subsequent accident had left her with a condition known as selective amnesia. Some things she vividly recalled. Others teased at the edge of her consciousness, but never emerged.

But she'd never forget the blurred figure hovering in the shadows.

A figure who could be anyone. Even this man who'd seemingly saved her from drowning. Could his apparent kindness cover a hidden agenda?

But all that was over now; she had to go forward. But no matter how often she told herself she was safe, cleated footprints of fear continued to scale her spine. And she couldn't shake that ever-present sense of being followed. Watched. The horror of that night never retreated far from her consciousness. But was her unseen watcher real or imaginary? She couldn't risk finding out.

"I want you to take me to my cabin," she said slowly, hoping he wouldn't hear the edge of fear in her voice.

"I told you, it's all boarded up by now."

Elisa turned and gratefully saw her bike nestled in the rear. "Stop and let me out. I'll take my bicycle back."

"The wind would blow you halfway to Hatteras," he said with a dry laugh.

Her alarm rapidly building, she felt panic welling up inside her. "If you don't turn around right now, I'm going to jump out."

"Don't be ridiculous, you'll kill yourself."

Maybe so, she acknowledged, but it might be better than whatever he was planning for her. She put her hand on the door handle. "I mean it. My death will be on your hands. It's up to you, but on the count of three, I'm jumping. One…"

He set his jaw and continued driving.

"Two…"

Even in profile, Elisa could see his eyes narrowing in determination. She twisted the door handle, and the Jeep's door swung open—almost pulling her out with its wake. "Three—"

"All right! Close the damned door, I'll take you back to an empty cabin. Hell, for that matter, I'll take your skinny rear end back to the beach and you can go sit on that rock until you're swept into the Bermuda Triangle. If you're so determined to kill yourself, pick your own method. Why should I care?"

She slammed the door.

He slowed down, and executed a U-turn. Glowering ferociously, he continued his harangue. "I nearly drowned trying to save your scrawny hide, and what thanks do I get? None. Not that I need your undying gratitude, but… Ah, what's the use?"

Elisa clutched her blanket and turned away, staring out

the open side. The biting rain was easier to bear than the accusation in his eyes.

She leaned back against the seat, waiting for his tirade to end. And somehow she knew his anger would soon taper off. After a few moments, his grip on the wheel eased. The color returned to his white knuckles. His fury was finally spent.

Her dark gaze raked over his profile again, itemizing and detailing every plane, every line. She might need to identify him for the authorities, she rationalized. But even after she'd committed a crystalline imprint of his face to her memory, she couldn't seem to look away from him.

He certainly didn't fit her stereotypical image of a skulking criminal. Actually, with the wind tousling his nape-length chestnut hair, his two-day growth of beard and the crinkly sun lines at the edges of his eyes, he reminded her of a world-weary philosopher. A man who'd spent his life studying humanity and found it lacking.

He turned his head and caught her watching him. For just an instant, humor glimmered in his eyes, hiding the scowl he normally wore.

Chagrined at having been caught so blatantly staring at him, she whipped around and gazed out through the driving rain. Determined to forget the enigmatic man at her side, she concentrated on the weather. A hurricane was coming, he'd said. What did she know about them? The same scant basics that everyone who watched television knew. High winds. Rain. Floods.

Were they really in extreme danger, or had he been using the storm as a ruse to get her to accompany him?

But as the floating terror began to subside, and her usual common sense began to work its way to the forefront of her mind, Elisa found herself seriously doubting that this man could be her watcher. It wasn't logical; that incident had happened hundreds of miles away. Besides, why would he have pulled her from the ocean if he meant to kill her?

But something about him had awakened her mindless fears and dormant memories.

She twisted her head and studied him surreptitiously, as if she could find the answer in his profile. Once more she found herself focusing on his expressions, his emotions. Did he really think she was skinny? She looked down at her body. It was tuned like a machine, for peak performance. Everyone in the company was slender—what did he know?

She swiped the rain from her eyes and scrutinized him more closely. Grudgingly she admired the way his hand held the steering wheel with a firm, sure grip. The way his tanned chest heaved with exertion as he expertly guided them around fallen branches, downed power lines.

Studying his face was like looking into a mirror, she thought with a start. His outside looked the way she felt inside. Lost, confused, exhausted. Only in his eyes, those dazzling emerald eyes, was there still a glimmer of light and laughter.

She was jerked from her musing by the Jeep's brakes squealing on the wet pavement as they turned off the main road. Ahead was Windjammer Point. Out of the corner of her eye she could see their cabin, Sunny Haven, stolidly awaiting her return. Relief washed over her like a suddenly clear sky.

She was safe. Safe from the blinding rain and the shrieking wind. Safe from nerves that jangled like those downed power lines. Most of all, safe from this stranger—and her frightening response to him.

Quickly, before he even had time to set the parking brake, she jumped to the ground, still wrapped in the cocoon of his beach blanket.

"Oomph," she groaned when she landed on her bad ankle. She reached down and rubbed the angry scar. Would she never remember to be more careful?

Before she could straighten up, he was beside her. "Here, let me help you."

"No! I'm okay." She yanked away from his touch and took a step toward the front door. Fire raced through her ankle and shot up her leg. She stopped, tears forming in her eyes.

She didn't argue when he slipped an arm around her waist and draped her own forearm across his wide, bare shoulders. Leaning against him, she hopped up the walk.

"Why don't you let me carry you?" he shouted over the roaring wind.

Stubbornly she shook her head.

When they reached the six steps leading to the bungalow's wide front porch, she gripped the back of his neck, then hopped, one step at a time, until they reached the top.

Perspiration mixed with the sheets of rain sliding down her face. Her lower lip trembled with emotion. For so many years, ballet had been her entire life. It had been hard enough adjusting to the loss of her livelihood, and her continued nagging fear of something or someone unknown. But the most difficult change of all to accept was her weakened physical condition.

Elisa was a dancer. An athlete. She could run for miles without being winded. Stand for hours at the barre practicing intricate maneuvers. Fly across the stage in an elaborate *ronde de jambe relevé*. At least the person she used to be could do all those things. But she wouldn't dance again. Wouldn't see her name flashing on the marquee. Her life— her real life—was over.

Eager to escape her scattered memories, and the silent man at her side, she wiggled free and hobbled across the porch. She twisted the doorknob, which was pebbled with rust from the salt air, but the door wouldn't open.

On the peaceful little island, they'd never felt the need to lock the cabin. Probably the change in air pressure had warped the door.

She pounded on the wooden panel with her fist.

His hand touched her arm.

His voice, at once soothing and concerned, shouted at

her. "It's locked! Come on, we have to..." Whatever suggestion he was going to offer was drowned by the storm's fury.

She knocked again. And again. When there was no response, she moved around to the window. It was covered with a plywood panel. Moving back to the door, she hammered once more.

Only the howling wind answered.

Chapter Three

"Come on, let's try the back!" Storm tugged at her hand until she relinquished her death grip on the doorknob.

Nodding mutely, she allowed him to half lead, half carry her around the rambling wooden structure. Fighting the ferocious wind, they hugged the building, holding up their hands as shields against the biting rain. Suddenly a strong gust of wind forced Elisa off the flagstone path. "Damn!"

Storm turned at the sound of her voice. Glancing down, he immediately saw her dilemma. She was ankle-deep in thick, oozing mud. Wrapped in his ratty old blanket, moisture glimmering in her ink-dark hair and a stricken expression on her face, she looked tiny, yielding, and heartbreakingly fragile.

Kneeling in the mud in front of her, he tossed her over his shoulder in a fireman's-carry stance and eased her feet from the thick muck. He ignored her indignant cries and flailing fists, trotting around the building until they reached the relative calmness of the rear of the cabin.

Fortunately, the back door wasn't locked. He propped the screen open with his foot while he carried her into the deserted kitchen.

"Put me down! I'm not a child, I can walk!"

"If you say so." With an unceremonious plop, Storm deposited his unruly burden on a kitchen chair.

"Ouch! Don't be so rough," she grumbled, surreptitiously rubbing her backside.

"I'm so sorry, Your Highness. Next time I'll just leave you sitting on your keister in the mud."

"Sorry." The glower on her face gave the lie to the apology.

"Yeah."

"Look, Mr.— Good grief! I don't even know your name."

Storm rolled his eyes. "And after all we've meant to each other."

"I *said* I was sorry. Get over it, will you?"

He grabbed a dishtowel from a rack next to the stove and stalked over to the sink. He'd had about all he wanted of the mystery woman. When he watched her riding her bike around the village, he'd dreamed up a number of romantic fantasies about her: She was hiding from the mob, or running from a broken love affair, or even wasting away from consumption. In all his daydreams, she'd been sweet, gentle, and unfailingly kind to animals and small children.

Reality, however, gave him a new perspective on the mystery woman. Based on what he'd seen so far, she was abrasive, touchy and oversensitive. And she ticked him off with every third word she uttered.

He paused while the water heated and reflected on how easily she pushed his buttons. Now that *was* surprising. For over two years, Storm hadn't felt much of anything. Not anger, fear, love, kindness, or even lust. He'd been a shell of nonemotion, and he liked it that way.

But when he saw this sea nymph bobbing helplessly in the water, some peculiar emotion he'd thought long dead had resurfaced. He didn't want to examine that errant emotion, but he did wonder why he was so irritated by her every word.

That was a crock.

He knew perfectly well why this woman annoyed him beyond reason. Obviously, she was unstable to a certain degree. She was also frightened—that much was painfully clear. Though he still possessed a medical licence, it didn't take one to determine that she was confused, tormented and in desperate need of psychological help. And Storm needed to be needed.

He slapped his palm on the Formica counter. He was retired, dammit. Permanently. And he resented being hauled back into the profession he'd so gladly abandoned.

Now that the water was steaming, he doused the towel beneath the faucet. After wringing out the excess, he returned to the table and began wiping the mud from her bare legs and feet.

She pulled away. "You don't have to do that."

"Yes, I do. With my luck, you'll slip and break the other leg. I don't want to even imagine what *that* would do to your sunny disposition."

"Oh." Elisa kept quiet as he gently wiped the muck from her bare feet. Then he carefully palpated the bones in her injured ankle.

She looked up, pinning him with her curious gaze. "What are you, a doctor or something?"

"Retired," was his offhand reply. Satisfied that her ankle had suffered no further injury, he returned to the double stainless-steel sink and washed out the dirty dishtowel.

As if caught off guard by his ministrations, Elisa asked meekly, "So what *is* your name?"

"Storm. Storm Delaney."

"Storm? Odd, but I like it."

"I'm glad to know Your Highness is pleased. And you?"

"Elisa. Elisa Montoya."

His eyes widened. "The ballet star?"

She blinked in obvious surprise. "You mean you've heard of me? I didn't think you were the type. I mean..."

He shot her a sideways glance. "You mean you didn't think us good ol' boys could be interested in anything that didn't take place in a sports arena?"

She laughed in good-natured chagrin. "Either that or it would have to involve hunting, fishing, wrestling grizzlies, that kind of thing."

"I'm surprised at you, Princess. Perpetuating a stereotype." He wiped his hands on the pockets of his tight-fitting, damp jeans.

Their repartee was interrupted when the outside door opened and a tall, leggy redhead almost fell into the room. She pushed the door closed and leaned against it. "Whew! That's one hell of a storm out there. And where have you been, Elisa? I've been up and down the beach looking for you."

"I'm sorry if you were worried, Heather, but I—"

"You didn't have another...episode, did you? I mean, you were gone so long I was afraid you might've freaked out again."

Storm cocked an appraising eyebrow at Heather's rather crude words. Elisa didn't seem bothered by her friend's insensitivity, however. She smiled wanly and apologized again. "I really didn't mean to worry you. I fell asleep and kind of got washed to sea."

"What!"

Elisa nodded toward Storm. "Where I was handily rescued by Dr. Storm Delaney. Storm, my roomie, Heather Gellis."

She pushed away from the door and sauntered across the room to cradle his extended hand in both of hers. "I guess we owe you a debt of gratitude, Dr. Delaney." She continued to hold on to his hand, slowly rubbing her fingertip along the edge of his thumb.

He was trying to think of a way to delicately extricate his hand when Heather leaned forward until her full mouth was only inches from his. "There must be *something* I can do to repay you?"

Her blatant sexual innuendo was so unexpected, Storm felt a hot blush climb up his neck. He hadn't blushed since he was twelve and Suzie Walters caught him staring down her blouse during science lab and doinked him with her workbook. Suzie hadn't liked being sexual prey, and now Storm discovered he didn't much care for the feeling, either.

He managed to free himself and walked around the table until he was standing behind Elisa's chair. "No repayment necessary, Ms. Gellis. Right now, though, we need to get over to the hotel. It's the safest building on the island—even has a fully stocked storm cellar, if the hurricane comes ashore."

Heather clasped her hands against her impressive bosom. "A hurricane—how exciting! So the sheriff was right?"

Storm nodded. "Most of the island's already been evacuated to the mainland. I'm surprised the sheriff didn't put you on the last ferry."

Shoving her mass of red hair away from her face, Heather smiled coyly. "He did try to convince me to go."

Elisa looked up, surprise evident in her dark eyes. "For heaven's sake, why didn't you?"

"Leave without knowing what had happened to you? Don't be silly." She patted Elisa's blanket-wrapped shoulder. "What kind of friend would that be?"

Elisa turned and smiled up at Storm. "See why I couldn't go to the hotel without Heather? She's been like a…sister to me since…"

Her lower lip trembled, and Storm realized that her scant reserve of strength was about to melt away. He glanced again at her ankle, and the angry red welt of recent surgery. Although he wasn't an osteopath, he recognized the telltale surgical markings of a compound fracture. Probably a stainless-steel pin or two held her slender ankle together.

It was obvious that whatever trauma she'd recently sustained had taken its toll on her emotional equilibrium. Which might explain her lapse in character judgment, he thought with a covert glance at Heather. The two women seemed oddly discordant to have formed such a close bond. He shrugged. Who understood women, anyway? Even after years of psychiatric training and experience, he felt he had only a nominal perception of the female psyche.

He did understand hurricanes, though. And this one was racing toward them, if the gusts of screaming wind were any indication. It was time to head for safety.

"Okay, ladies, listen up." He glanced at his watch. "You've got exactly ten minutes to gather up whatever essentials you'll need for the next three or four days."

"Four days! Surely we won't be stranded that long." Heather tossed her wild red hair.

"Probably not," he concurred. "But it's always best to prepare for the worst scenario."

"But—"

"Heather, don't argue," Elisa said, interrupting her, as she rose to her feet. "Dr. Delaney has kindly offered to take us to the hotel, and I know he still needs to secure his own place. So let's get a move on and stop wasting his time."

She drew the blanket closer around her shoulders and hurried out of the kitchen. Storm blinked at Elisa's sudden surge of spirit. The forlorn waif was gone, replaced by a no-nonsense leader. Hmm. Seemed he'd underestimated the mystery woman. A mistake he wasn't likely to make a second time.

TEN MINUTES LATER, Storm had just shut off the gas and was unplugging the remaining electrical appliances when the women returned to the kitchen. Elisa had exchanged her bikini for a well-worn sweat suit and a pair of Reeboks. She was certainly better outfitted for the weather, but he had grown kind of attached to that skimpy swimsuit.

Surprisingly, each woman had stuffed her "essentials" into a single duffel bag apiece. He'd fully expected Heather to show up with an eight-piece set of matching luggage.

"All ready?" he asked as he hefted Elisa's duffel bag onto his shoulder and reached for Heather's.

"I guess," Elisa murmured, taking a searching look

around the kitchen. "I feel like I'm forgetting something, though. Something important."

"I saw you pack your purse and jewel case," Heather said. "What else do you have of value?"

Elisa shrugged. "Nothing I guess. Still..."

At that moment, the kitchen door burst open as if a bomb had exploded behind it. A large man wearing a bright yellow slicker stepped through the doorway. Since he offered no apology for entering without knocking, Storm could only assume that the newcomer was well-known to the occupants.

He pulled off his rain cap, exposing a wiry mop of gingery red hair, then wiped his face with the sleeve of his raincoat. "The radio said old Jake is moving straight at us," he announced. "I'm not sure this cabin can withstand gale-force winds, ladies, so maybe you'd better—" He broke off when he spotted Storm. "Who are you?"

Storm hoisted the two duffel bags higher on his shoulders and took a step toward the kitchen door. With a brief nod at the stranger, he muttered his name and said he was taking the women to the hotel.

The stranger reached for one of the bags, but Storm waved him away. "I'm balanced. They're not that heavy."

Heather moved to the stranger and took his arm. "Brian, meet Dr. Storm Delaney. Storm, this is our neighbor, Brian McPherson. He's been so much help to us this summer. Are you coming to the hotel, Bri?"

"Nah," the ruddy-faced man replied. "My place should be fine. It's fortified with extra hurricane straps and bracing. It'll hold its own with winds up to a hundred and forty miles per hour."

Storm's eyes narrowed at the man's naiveté. "You'll still be cut off from any help, should a power line come down or something."

"Maybe so. But I've got a shortwave radio and plenty of provisions. I'm kind of looking forward to meeting old Jake."

Storm shook his head, but didn't say anything. These barrier islands had claimed the lives of dozens of people who thought they could match wits with a force-four or -five hurricane. He hoped their neighbor didn't add to those morbid statistics. "Well, I certainly wish you luck, McPherson, but if you change your mind, the Danzigers have plenty of room at the hotel."

The red-haired man grinned. "Don't worry about me, buddy boy. I'll be over and help you folks dig out after old Jake wears himself out trying to blow my cabin off the beach. But you'd better get these ladies to safety. I'll finish securing this place after you leave."

Heather kissed him on his weathered cheek. "You're wonderful, Bri. I'd stay with you, but I don't want to abandon Elisa. Being a West Coast girl, she's never been in a hurricane before."

Storm grimaced. Heather's insinuation, of course, was that Elisa wasn't capable of bringing herself in out of the weather if Heather wasn't around to direct her. He wondered anew at their "friendship."

Elisa, once again, took the initiative and led the way out of the cabin. The squalls had increased in intensity, and Storm was worried that she would be tossed aside by the powerful tempest. He hurried to follow and ran directly into her as she rushed back into the kitchen.

"What's wrong?" Storm and Heather asked in unison.

Elisa lightly slapped her forehead. "I just remembered what I forgot! It won't take me a minute."

She ran out of the room and, true to her word, returned in less than a minute. A pink terry-cloth robe was folded over her arm.

Heather tapped her toe in irritation. "You held us up for a bathrobe?"

Elisa folded the garment into a small parcel and held it against her body. "Not the robe, but something in the pocket." She reached inside the robe and held up a folded manila envelope.

"What's that?" Heather asked, half reaching for the envelope.

Elisa quickly shoved it back into the terry-cloth folds. "It's a letter. From Jay." As if embarrassed by the admission, she headed for the door again.

Her progress was halted when Heather grabbed her arm. "What kind of letter?"

"I, uh, haven't read it yet. It arrived a few days after…the, uh, accident. I've been trying to get the courage to read it."

Brian McPherson pulled his rain hat over his head and started ushering them toward the door. "Hate to break this up, but ol' Jake ain't going to wait while we jabber about an old letter. You folks better get a move on."

Although he was intrigued by the sudden heavy atmosphere that followed Elisa's producing her letter, Storm knew McPherson was right. There was no way of gauging how close the hurricane was, or the speed at which it was traveling. He reached over and pulled Elisa close to him and wrapped a protective arm around her waist. "McPherson, you want to help Heather?"

"Be my pleasure," he replied, opening his rubber raincoat to envelop her.

"Then let's make a run for it." Storm kept a firm arm around Elisa's waist as they made a dash for the relative dryness of his Jeep.

CONVERSATION was minimal as they made the twenty-minute drive to the Double Dare Hotel. The angry storm buffeting the Jeep made verbal communication a worthless skill. Elisa saw Storm's lips move as he dodged a fallen tree limb, but she couldn't hear the dark epithet he muttered.

A half mile up the road, a downed power line sparked and hissed across the blacktop like an angry snake.

Thankful for his driving skills, and the Jeep's four-wheel drive, Elisa held her breath as Storm nudged the vehicle down a small ravine and up onto a windswept plateau of sandy soil. She exhaled in relief as he gave the flapping power line a wide berth and reentered the paved road some distance past it.

Finally, they reached the relative quiet of the leeward village, and he pulled into the guest parking lot in the rear of the ancient hotel.

Wordlessly the threesome made an awkward dash for the rear door. The wind had changed course. The women were blown backward time and again, their clothing pressed against their skin as if it were being absorbed into their bodies.

News reports had always given Elisa the notion that a hurricane brought cold weather, but she'd been wrong. The heavy atmosphere was as hot and moist as a sauna, and the wind smacked her face like hot air emerging from a heated oven.

Finally, they made the shelter of a roofed porch. Storm held open the door, and they thankfully stepped into a gleaming white kitchen.

A sturdy silver-haired woman wearing a starched white blouse and a no-nonsense navy skirt was standing at the stove, stirring a pot of something that emitted a heavenly aroma. When she spoke, her soft Southern drawl clashed with her storm-trooper demeanor. "I swan! Look what the wind blew in. I expected you some time ago, Storm. And who have you brought with you?"

"Hey, Miriam." He set the bags on the floor and leaned over the older woman's shoulder, sniffing the redolent steam over the cook pot. "Got room for a few stranded souls?"

She laughed, not disturbing a single lacquered gray hair. "I reckon we can find a spare bed or two." She wiped her hands on a spotless apron. "Are you going to introduce me to your friends or not?"

Storm made the introductions, and Elisa learned that Miriam Danziger and her husband, Hank, were the owners of the Double Dare Hotel.

"Y'all are soaking wet, bless your souls. Stay right here while I get some towels from the laundry room." She stepped through a small door off the kitchen, and returned a few seconds later with an armful of fluffy white towels.

As soon as she handed them out, they wiped the moisture from their faces and rubbed their hair.

"Where *is* Hank?" Storm asked as he filched a carrot from under Miriam's watchful eye. "Figured you two might have headed for the mainland."

Miriam dismissed that idea with a wave of her hand. "That ornery old coot? He's too afraid somebody would get stranded and he wouldn't be here to rent 'em a room. Seems he was right, too." She cocked her head toward the front of the hotel. "We've already had a few folks turn up. Hank's in hog heaven—us being the only folks foolish enough to be open for business in the middle of a hurricane!"

Storm's hand flew to his mouth as he faked a cough to stifle a sudden chuckle.

Miriam stepped forward, elbowing him out of her way. She wrapped a pudgy arm around Elisa's shoulders. "Say, you wouldn't be that ballet dancer, would you?"

Amazed by the cultural awareness that seemed to prevail on this tiny island, Elisa quickly recovered from her surprise. "Why, yes, I am. Are you an aficionado, Mrs. Danziger?"

"Call me Miriam. No, can't say that I'm a big fan of the ballet, although I used to take my girl Elizabeth up to Norfolk every winter to see *The Nutcracker*. Does that count?"

Elisa smiled. "Of course. *The Nutcracker* is a wonderful production. I hope you enjoyed it."

"After I got over there not being any dialogue, I reckon I liked it well enough."

Elisa frowned in confusion. If Miriam's entire ballet experience was an occasional performance of *The Nutcracker,* how had she known that Elisa was a dancer?

As if picking up on the question echoed in Elisa's eyes, Miriam laughed. "Oh, you were wondering how I knew about you."

"Well, yes, I—"

Miriam hooked a thumb toward the open doorway leading from the kitchen to the main portion of the hotel. "Fella was asking about you earlier."

Heather edged closer and leaned over Elisa's shoulder. "Someone was asking about Elisa? Here?"

Miriam nodded. "Real smartly dressed fella. I reckon he's in the parlor with Hank. Got hisself stranded here with the rest of us. Said he was a lawyer—from New York."

A cold chill of apprehension washed down Elisa's back. Why would a New York lawyer be this far south, looking for her? As far as she knew, she'd signed all the necessary papers terminating her affiliation with the dance company before she left. If there was more paperwork, why hadn't the director simply mailed it to her?

Why had an attorney come looking for her?

A shudder rippled through her body as the truth dawned on her. Somehow, this lawyer had to be connected with…Jay's death. Could she be held legally, as well as morally, responsible for his suicide? What was the penalty for causing another to end his life?

Her head began to throb in the familiar rhythm as a fragmented memory fought to bring itself to her conscious mind. Another flash of the shadowy person, and subtle movement as the figure stepped toward her. And then…then it was gone. Once again, the elusive recollection darted away.

She was still trembling with the repressed fear that always accompanied these "visions" when Miriam Danziger took her chin between her fingers. "I swan, honey, you look plumb tuckered out. And a little scared. You'll be fine here, honey." She gave her a hearty squeeze.

"Storm, why don't you take these gals into the front parlor while I see what rooms are clean enough to give them. The entire staff hightailed it to the mainland."

"Where should I put their bags?"

"Just leave them right where they are till we get the room situation sorted out. Now go on into the parlor and dry off." She glanced at the clock on the wall. "It's after four. I imagine Hank's pouring libations right about now."

"I think I could use a libation right about now," Storm said as he ushered the women into the parlor.

The owner, Hank Danziger, was pouring wine from crystal decanters while several people lounged on the overstuffed furniture. He raised an arm in greeting, but Elisa barely noted the gesture. Her gaze was pinned on the man sitting alone in the corner, his dark eyes watching her every move.

Although she'd met him only on three occasions, Elisa immediately recognized him. David Allen Welton. A third-generation Harvard attorney. A junior partner in the family firm and, from what she'd heard, particularly adept at keeping his wealthy clients out of the grasp of the IRS.

He'd also been Jay's attorney. Elisa had met him once socially when she and Jay first started dating. Then, he'd come to the hospital twice, after her accident, asking interminable questions for which she had no answers.

And now he was here. Far from Manhattan, where he normally plied his trade. Why? What could he possibly want with her?

Forcing what she hoped was a self-assured smile, she crossed the room to greet him. David rose to his feet and took her chilled hand in his.

"Elisa! Do you think we'll ever run into each other when there's no crisis to contend with?"

She shook her head in a rueful disavowal of his remark. They hadn't "run into" each other. David Welton had come several hundred miles south with the express intent of seeking her out. Why was he now pretending their meeting was mere happenstance?

Across the room, Storm kept a watchful eye on Elisa while he spoke to Hank Danziger about conditions on the island. She didn't look particularly happy to see her friend from New York. Rather, she looked disconcerted and...frightened.

In fact, unless he was badly mistaken, Elisa Montoya wasn't at all pleased about waiting out Hurricane Jake with her old acquaintance. Still, she put on a good show. From a distance, he heard her laugh as she chatted with the expensively dressed lawyer. But there was brittle tension in her too-hearty laughter. He could see her jaw tighten and her shoulders stiffen with anxiety. Strain made a deep groove across her forehead.

Not that any of this was his business, he reminded himself, no matter how much the sexy dancer fired up his testosterone. To put more distance between himself and Elisa, he moseyed over to speak to the few people he knew. Mark and Betty Bowman were local restaurateurs who'd missed the last ferry when their car wouldn't start.

Standing alone in the corner was Carey Howard. A relative newcomer to the island, Carey owned a small fleet of sport-fishing boats. He raised a beer glass in acknowledgment of Storm's greeting, but didn't move to join the others.

Although the Bowmans were pleasant, and even entertaining, with their tales of unusual customers they'd encountered, Storm's attention kept wandering to Elisa and her companion. While her chatter continued to be punctuated with bursts of hollow laughter, she kept looking expectantly at the lawyer, as if waiting for some cue. Since attorneys were generally talkative, in Storm's experience, he couldn't help wondering what had the young lawyer so preoccupied. Elisa seemed to be doing most of the talking.

"So how long have you lived on the island, Dr. Delaney?"

"What? Oh, sorry." Storm reluctantly pulled his attention from Elisa. He was startled to find Heather hovering at his elbow. The Bowmans had drifted away to chat with Hank. "I've lived here about two years, I guess. What brings you down here?"

"Oh, we'd vacationed here several times, so when Elisa had her…accident, it seemed like the ideal place to help her recover." She glanced across the room, her gaze intent on Elisa and the lawyer. "So, here we are."

Storm wondered if he was getting cynical. Even Heather sounded uptight and distracted as she watched the attorney out of the corner of her eye. He looked up, and Heather turned away abruptly.

Despite himself, Storm found his interest piqued by the interplay between these people. Although the attorney hadn't yet acknowledged Heather's presence, Storm couldn't help but wonder if there wasn't some history between them. Maybe Elisa had replaced Heather in a romantic relationship with the lawyer. He found the idea strangely discomfiting.

"What do you people do for fun around here?" Heather suddenly asked. "I mean, it's so isolated." She hugged her lush torso and shivered eloquently. Without waiting for his response, she cast another quick glance at Elisa and the lawyer.

There was a definite undercurrent of tension flowing between the three of them. Granted, Storm was a virtual stranger, but he could almost feel the sizzle of apprehension burning through the air. With each passing moment, the anxiety level increased, like the gale-force winds that were hurling branches against the hotel. He had a strong sense that everyone was waiting. But for what?

His speculations were cut short when Miriam Danziger swept in and announced that their rooms were ready. The Bowmans quickly followed her into the hallway.

Turning back to Heather, Storm nodded toward the attorney. "Don't you want to say hello to your friend?"

Heather shrugged. "He's no friend of mine. But hang on to your wallet, the lawyer approacheth."

Sure enough, Elisa and her companion were moving in their direction. Now that they were closer, Storm could hear the man speaking in a cultured Boston accent. "Isn't it cocktail hour yet? Wine is nice, but I really need a drink. This storm is getting on my nerves."

Elisa stopped beside them and made the introductions, a hint of stress apparent in the white spots high on her cheekbones. "I'd like you to meet David Welton, the attorney Mrs. Danziger mentioned. And this is Storm Delaney. Of course, you know Heather."

"David," Heather murmured as she extended her hand. "Nice to see you again."

Welton frowned. "Where do I know you from? The country club? Or do you play bridge with my wife?"

Heather's shoulders stiffened. "Nothing so exalted, I'm afraid. I was Jay Morrow's secretary."

"Of course! Sorry I didn't recognize you. Out of context, so to speak. But...whatever are you doing down here?"

"Even secretaries are allowed the occasional vacation," she snapped. "But then, I could ask you the same question."

"Yes, of course. I didn't mean..." Welton rubbed his forehead and turned his attention to Storm. "You live on this godforsaken island? How long *will* we have to stay here, do you think?"

Storm shrugged. "Until this hurricane passes. A day, a week, no way of telling right now."

David sighed, a loud expression of disgust. "Wonderful. Trapped in Dogpatch. Exactly how I've always wanted to spend my free time."

Heather reached over and snagged a glass of wine from a tray Hank Danziger was passing around. "You could always swim back to the mainland. I'm sure you know how to dog-paddle, don't you?"

In a transparent effort to forestall further biting comment,

Elisa moved toward the doorway. "Let's postpone the argument while Mrs. Danziger shows us to our rooms, otherwise dinner won't be ready on time. And I'm starved."

Storm couldn't help admiring Elisa's pluck. Her weariness was painted on her face, in the dark circles ringing her even darker eyes. She stood off kilter. Obviously, her injured ankle was tormenting her. What had happened to the lovely ballerina? Would she ever dance again? It would be a tragedy indeed if the world had lost the talents of such a gifted performer.

Yet, despite her pain and weariness, she kept smiling and nodding in an effort to ease the obvious friction between her friends. Recognizing her attempt to defuse the increasingly volatile atmosphere, Storm followed her into the foyer. "Which room did you put me in, Miriam?"

Heather and David gave up their squabbling and fell into line at the bottom of the staircase, where the Bowmans were waiting with Miriam. Even Carey Howard had given up his solitary post and was waiting with the others for room assignments.

All the luggage was in a jumbled pile at the foot of the stairs. One by one, the morose group picked up their gear and waited for further direction.

Miriam climbed three stairs in order to be seen and heard by everyone. Consulting a scrap of paper, she read off the numbers of the rooms that she'd assigned to each of them.

"Now listen up," she said loudly. "That's a hurricane outside—not just a summer squall. Before the night's over, we'll be lucky if the only thing we lose is the electricity. Which also means the pump on the well won't work. Water's at a premium. We've filled all the tubs, for sponge baths and quick washups only. Until we tell you different, I'm afraid there'll be no baths or showers. Everybody understand that?"

Instead of the complaints Storm expected to follow Miriam's announcement, there was only a shocked silence from the small group. One look at their faces told him they finally understood the seriousness of their situation.

Until this moment, Heather and David had been behaving like spoiled children at a birthday party. Expecting to be thrilled and entertained by the approaching storm, much as those spoiled youngsters would anticipate a magician "sawing" one of them in half.

But Hurricane Jake wasn't a show or an illusion. It was real life, harsh and relentless. Storm only hoped Elisa's friends were up to the challenge.

Miriam gave the newcomers to the island a reassuring smile and beckoned to everyone to follow her up the stairs. Moving in a tight bunch, the docile group quietly ascended the wide staircase.

They were just approaching the second-floor landing when the overhead light flickered.

"Don't worry," Miriam hastened to reassure them. "There are kerosene lanterns and candles in every room. We also have our own backup generator that can be used sparingly."

Storm glanced at Elisa, who was huddled against the rail, her dark eyes intent on the oscillating fixture. As if she had somehow willed it to happen, the lights flickered once more. Then they were abruptly plunged into darkness.

The small troop broke into collective nervous chatter, and Storm sensed a sudden movement on his left.

The next sound was a frightened scream, right beside him. Elisa!

Chapter Four

"What is it? What's happened?" Heather's voice climbed above the others.

"Elisa's fallen," Storm snapped. "Who has a flashlight? Quick!"

"Here." Miriam's voice was clear as she switched on a penlight and handed it down to him.

He swept the funnel of light down the staircase until it stopped on the crumpled body at the bottom. "Elisa! Are you all right?"

The only response was an ominous silence.

Pushing past the Bowmans and Carey Howard, Storm hurried down the steps and knelt beside her. Holding the small flashlight between his teeth, he quickly felt for her pulse.

She was still alive. Her pulse was strong and steady, though she'd lost consciousness.

As he flicked the light over her, he noticed that she'd landed with her duffel bag beneath her head. Somehow she'd managed to hang on to it while tumbling down the staircase. The canvas bag filled with clothing must have broken her fall, protecting her from serious injury. At least he hoped so. As long as they were stuck on this island, he was the only avenue of medical treatment. And his skills were rusty—very rusty. Not to mention the fact that he had no equipment and no access to medication.

Dredging up fragments of memory from his rotation in the ER, he carefully ran his hands down her limbs, checking for obvious fractures. Finding none, he refocused the penlight and raised each eyelid with his fingertip. Her pupils were equal, and reactive to the light. Relief poured through him. It was unlikely she'd suffered brain damage. But there was no way to tell if she'd sustained a neck or spinal injury without moving her, and any movement could exacerbate her injuries.

While he was trying to think of what else he could do, she moaned and stirred slightly.

He leaned over and touched her soft face. "Elisa? Can you hear me?"

"Mmm. Wh-what happened?" she mumbled as her eyes fluttered open. She blinked rapidly, and he moved the beam from her face.

"You fell down the stairs."

"N-no. No, I didn't fall." She lifted her head and struggled to rise.

Mental confusion and disorientation were often symptomatic of concussion, and Storm made a mental note to watch for further signs. Right now, he needed to keep her still until the extent of her injuries could be determined.

"Here, lie back down. Just rest for a few minutes."

"I don't want to rest on the floor. How about if I just go upstairs and lie down?"

He tossed his head. "Not yet. I don't want you to move until we can be sure everything's okay."

She rubbed her temple. "I must've conked my head on something. It hurts like the devil."

Storm gently palpated the knot forming at her hairline. "Whoo..." He whistled. "That's another fine trophy you've collected. Do you hurt anyplace else?"

As if mentally checking her body for injury, she hesitated for a moment. "No. My ankle throbs, but it does most of the time anyway. But my head feels like I downed an entire bottle of Jose Cuervo by myself."

Relieved that her injuries appeared minor, and that her mental confusion seemed to be clearing, Storm chuckled in relief. "So how much experience have you had? Drinking entire bottles of tequila, I mean."

She raised up on her right elbow. "None. But I have a good imagination and a rotten headache."

Since it appeared she'd escaped serious injury, Storm relaxed enough to sense the others descending the staircase. He raised a hand, forgetting for a moment that no one could see it. "Stay back. She needs air."

Only Heather ignored him to inch forward. "Elisa? Honey, are you okay? Did you have another episode and get dizzy again?"

Storm felt like throttling her for exposing Elisa's medical disorder to the others. Didn't Heather have a spark of concern for her friend's feelings? And exactly what were these "episodes" she kept referring to? He wondered if Elisa suffered from epilepsy; that would explain a lot.

As if she, too, were irritated by the tone of Heather's query, Elisa didn't answer, but grabbed Storm's hand in an effort to sit up.

"Are you sure you feel up to it?" he asked.

"No. But I can't lie on the floor forever."

She tugged on his hand again. Realizing that further arguing would be futile, he helped her to a sitting position. "Any more dizziness?" he asked. "You took a heck of a blow to the head."

She laughed grimly. "My poor head's getting used to being battered. First the car wreck, then my dip in the ocean, and now an unplanned leap down the stairs." She looked up sharply. "I'm beginning to wonder if someone's trying to kill me."

Storm was still considering the serious tone of her last remark when Miriam pushed her way through the crowd and bent over his shoulder.

She patted Elisa's cheek. "Honey, you just stay still and

I'll get you some water. Or would you rather have brandy?''

"No, water will be fine. Thanks."

Miriam's ample frame nudged Storm aside as she hurried past. No sooner had she disappeared than the lights flickered again as the distant hum of the generator motor whined into action. Hank must have found his way to the basement, Storm reflected. A few seconds later, the hall and staircase were flooded with light, revealing a semicircle of pale, concerned faces looking over their shoulders.

Betty Bowman was the first to speak. "Is she okay, Storm? Is there anything we can do to help?"

Reassured by the alert expression on Elisa's face, he shook his head. "Everything's under control. Why don't you all go on to your rooms? Ms. Montoya will be fine by dinner, although she might welcome an aspirin or two, if anybody has some."

"I do." Heather raised her hand like a schoolgirl and raced back up the stairs. A moment later, she returned and shook two tablets into Elisa's outstretched hand. Miriam appeared with a glass of water, and Elisa gratefully swallowed the pills.

"Okay." She nodded to Storm. "Guess I'm as ready as I'll ever be. Heave-ho!"

As gently as possible, he helped her up, then draped a securing arm around her waist when she wobbled a bit. "Take your time, don't rush it," he cautioned. Once again showing that fierce determination that had so intrigued him, Elisa ignored his warning and stepped away from his steadying grasp.

"I'm fine," she whispered. Then, as if gathering strength, she repeated herself in a stronger voice. "I'm fine, everybody. Thanks for your concern."

Everyone except Heather murmured their sympathies and headed upstairs, to the second-floor bedrooms.

Heather marched beside Elisa and replaced Storm's grasp with her own. "Well, I, for one, *am* concerned. I think we need to get you upstairs right away. I'll have Mrs. Danziger prepare a tray for your dinner.''

"Heather, I'm not an invalid, you know," Elisa gently chided. "Sometimes I think you'd be happier if I was in a full body cast, locked up in a glass case.''

Heather's hands flew to her own waist as she thrust out a hip in an indignant stance. "Well, blame a friend for trying! Elisa, sometimes you're just too independent for your own good. You can keep ignoring this whole string of 'accidents' that you've been having, but I can't. You haven't given yourself time to recover from your surgery.''

Storm frowned. Once again, with just a few well-chosen words, Heather had managed to dump the entire responsibility for Elisa's problems right back in her lap. As if, by not allowing herself time to properly recuperate, Elisa had somehow brought on these other incidents.

On the other hand, were Heather's crude accusations the truth? Was Elisa suffering from some psychosis that caused her to injure herself?

And why did he keep sticking his nose into Elisa Montoya's problems? She had nothing to do with him. He was emotionally shut off from everything and everyone—remember?

Ignoring Elisa's attempt to shrug off his helping hand, Storm took her arm, while Heather continued to hold on to her waist. Together, they made their way upstairs, to the room Mrs. Danziger had assigned Elisa.

Heather pulled back the coverlet on the bed, and they eased the former dancer between the crisp white sheets.

"I wish you two mother hens would stop hovering over me," she grumbled as Storm slipped off her Reeboks.

"No problem," he muttered. "I'd be glad to leave you alone, Princess, if you'd stop hurling yourself into the sea or down the stairs.''

"I already told you—I didn't fall!''

He tucked the coverlet under her chin and feathered a

silky strand of ebony hair from her eyes. "Okay, you didn't fall. Now lay back, I want to check you over."

"Are you *sure* you're a doctor?" she asked, her eyelids slitted suspiciously.

"No. I'm really a pervert who hangs around deserted beaches looking for drowning women to molest."

"I thought so," she muttered as she fell against the pillow and closed her eyes, clearly fighting her headache.

When she opened them a moment later, she focused on Heather, who was standing behind Storm, her blue eyes wide and anxious. "I'm sorry, Heather. I didn't mean to bite your head off. I just feel...kind of vulnerable right now."

"No problem, 'Leese. Why don't you get some rest like the good doctor ordered?"

"I will. Promise. But would you be a dear and go get my duffel? I want to change out of these damp clothes."

"Oh, that's right. All your stuff is still downstairs. I'll be right back." Heather grinned and bolted for the door, as if relieved to have some minor chore to attend to.

As soon as the door closed behind her, Elisa grabbed his wrist. "I don't want to worry Heather, but I was serious, Storm. I *didn't* fall."

A gut-wrenching tightness constricted his gut. Not wanting to hear her response, he nevertheless found himself asking, "Then what did happen?"

Dropping her voice even more, she whispered, "Someone pushed me."

"What!"

She tightened her grip on his wrist, as if she could force him to believe her. "I'm not mistaken or joking. At first I thought it was Heather hovering over me like she does. But then...those hands pressed against my back. Hard. Then..." She paused and sucked in a lungful of breath. "Then whoever it was pushed me and I lost my balance."

The clenched feeling in his stomach tightened like a vise. Despite all the evidence to the contrary, he couldn't believe that Elisa was imagining this. Her face was too earnest, her voice filled with fear and pleading. The woman was frightened, possibly with good cause.

But they were a small group, and she was a virtual stranger to the island. Who would want to kill her?

Did they have a homicidal maniac running amok in the hotel?

As if in answer, the wind suddenly picked up its tempo, shrieking like a tortured banshee.

TWO HOURS LATER, after changing into dry clothing and wolfing down a bowl of Miriam's savory corn chowder, accompanied by a chunk of homemade bread smeared with butter, Elisa felt well enough to go downstairs and join the others.

She emptied her duffel, stowing the few pieces of clothing she'd brought in the huge mahogany wardrobe adjacent to the ornately carved bed. Carrying her toothbrush and cosmetics into the adjoining bathroom, she came back in the bedroom and frowned at the rumpled bedcovers.

A vision of her mother's disapproving gaze prompted her to action. Hurriedly she yanked up the coverlet and headed for the door. Pausing to see if she'd forgotten anything, she giggled at the haphazard way she'd made the bed. She'd forgotten about the extra pillow she'd propped under her leg. With the thin blanket pulled over it, the lumpy form resembled a sleeping body.

Oh, well, she'd straighten it later. Mom wasn't here to see it anyway.

When she reached the staircase, she paused, recalling her earlier tumble. Her headache had faded to a dull throb and, thankfully, her ankle hadn't been reinjured. All things considered, Elisa decided, she'd come through the accident pretty much unscathed. Still, she couldn't forget the feel of those hands against her back. Pressing. Pushing. Then, finally, shoving.

Why would someone want to hurt her? It couldn't have

been an accident. Could it? Had she somehow misinterpreted the incident? Perhaps she had stepped away from those hands and, in the darkness, moved too close to the edge of the step, causing her own fall.

Earlier, when she was talking to Storm, everything had seemed so clear. So certain. But now…now she was filled with self-doubt. After all, as Heather often pointed out, Elisa had been under a terrible strain, both emotional and physical, these past few weeks.

It wouldn't be unusual for someone in her condition to experience confusion, even misunderstand certain events.

Placing her right hand firmly on the railing, she slowly began descending the stairs. As much as she hated to admit to any sort of mental weakness, that explanation made far more sense than believing someone was trying to harm her. After all, she'd been alone on the beach. As for the car crash…well, no amount of effort could bring back all the pieces of that night. She simply couldn't remember anything after walking into Jay's office shortly after 5:00 p.m.

When she reached the first-floor landing, Elisa followed the sound of festive voices into the parlor. When she stepped into the inviting room, with its flickering light and comfy furniture, she saw that the others were playing charades. Storm was the first to notice her arrival, and he jumped to his feet.

"Elisa! You must be feeling better—I didn't expect to see you again tonight. Here, sit down."

He pointed to the corner of the sofa where he'd been sitting.

"Thanks," she murmured, gratefully accepting his offer. It was amazing how wobbly she felt after merely walking downstairs. "What's all the laughing about?" she asked as Storm lowered himself to the floor beside her feet.

"We're having a hurricane party," Miriam offered.

"Local custom," Hank added.

Elisa realized that was the first time she'd actually heard

him speak. Though apparently a man of few words, he surprised her by continuing, "Get you a drink?"

"No, thanks. I'm just fine. You all go ahead with whatever you were doing."

Betty Bowman shook her short blond curls. "Oh, honey, we're just playing a silly game. Trying to drown out that horrid noise."

Elisa cocked her head and listened. Sure enough, the intensity of the storm had increased. Heavy branches and metal debris buffeted the building. Clanging and crashing under the force of nature's fury. Jake was moving closer.

Miriam reached over and plucked at the sleeve of Elisa's blouse. "Are you *sure* you're okay, sweetie? Me and Hank feel just terrible about your slipping on those stairs. I just don't understand it. We had the carpeting replaced just a few months ago, so I'm sure it's tacked down all over."

Realizing the genial hotel owners were probably concerned about her pressing a lawsuit, Elisa hurriedly reassured them that the accident had been entirely her fault, and that she'd only suffered a few bruises.

After expressing their relief that she hadn't been seriously injured, the others returned to their game. Elisa glanced around the room. That niggling doubt in the back of her mind kept her wondering which one of them could have pushed her.

Not one of the local restaurateurs, Betty and Mark Bowman. She'd never seen either of them before today, so surely they couldn't harbor any animosity toward her.

The same thing was true of Hank and Miriam Danziger.

Her gaze flicked to the far corner by the bar, where Heather and Carey Howard, who owned a fleet of sportfishing boats, were cozily sharing a love seat. They were chatting so animatedly, a casual observer would think they were old friends. Yet Heather had never mentioned him. If they'd just met, they'd certainly hit it off well.

Still, Carey was a virtual stranger, with no reason to wish Elisa any harm.

That left only Storm and David Welton.

She glanced down, to where Storm was leaning against her leg, his tumbled chestnut hair tickling her slightly through her cotton slacks. As if completely unaware of her presence, he twisted his head, his unshaven cheek nuzzling her thigh. A slight tickle unfurled in the pit of her stomach, sending sweetly exhilarating shock waves through the lower half of her body.

Elisa breathed shallowly, not wanting to disrupt the unexpected soft pleasure of his nearness. It wasn't really him she was responding to, she reasoned. It was the artificial closeness people sometimes felt when they'd been through a crisis together. In the space of a single afternoon, she and Storm had weathered two frightening crises. No wonder she felt drawn to him. It was mere gratitude for his saving her life. When Hurricane Jake ran his course, she'd go back to the mainland and Storm would go on with his quiet life here on the island.

Their paths wouldn't cross again, but once in a while they'd think of each other and smile at having survived a dangerous experience together.

Still, she couldn't, wouldn't, believe he had pushed her. Even if he hadn't already saved her life, she couldn't have believed him capable of such ruthlessness. But David Welton?

She flicked her gaze to where he was standing alone, by the fireplace, taking no part in the party game. His coal-black hair and razor-sharp profile were book-cover perfect. And yet…there was something aloof, cold, that made him unappealing.

Of course, to make it in the lawyer-eat-lawyer world of Wall Street, David Welton *had* to be ruthless. In fact, Jay had once said that was his best character trait.

Nor had David fully explained why he'd made the trek from Manhattan to North Carolina. He'd only remarked that he had some documents he needed to go over with her. When she asked what sort of documents, he'd put her off with a vague response, promising they'd get together alone in the morning to discuss it.

She rubbed her temple; all this fretting and wondering was bringing back her headache. She had to let it go, at least for now.

Determined not to give in to the anxiety welling up inside her, she forced herself to pay attention to the game.

Betty Bowman was standing in front of them now, and she drew a slip of paper from a bowl on the coffee table. After studying it for a moment, she nodded. Moving her hand as if she were cranking an old movie camera, she conveyed that her charade was the title of a film.

She held up two fingers.

"Two words!" Heather shouted.

Betty held up her forefinger. She was going to act out the first word. She reached into her pocket and extracted an imagined object, then held it in front of her and gave it a turn.

"A key," Elisa blurted, surprised at herself for taking part. She'd never played games before. Exercising and rehearsing had been her recreation.

Betty touched the tip of her nose and pointed to Elisa, indicating that her answer had been correct. Then she held up two fingers again, to announce that she was going to act out the second word.

Holding her arms wide, as if to encompass the room, Betty invited their guesses.

"Room," Heather guessed, incorrectly.

"Large," Storm said, and Betty nodded, then made a stretching motion with her hands, the clue that his answer was close but not exact. "Large key. Key large," Storm said thoughtfully. "Oh, of course, *Key Largo!*"

The small gathering broke into mild applause.

"I don't get it," Heather said, her lips puckered in a small pout. "What kind of movie is that?"

"Oh, sweetie—" Miriam clucked "—you *are* a young

thing. I can't believe you never heard of *Key Largo*. Bogie and Bacall?''

David pushed his long, lean body from the fireplace wall and addressed Heather in an authoritative courtroom voice. ''My dear, you've been watching too much 'Beavis and Butt-head.' *Key Largo* is a classic, and a highly appropriate choice for our situation.''

Her color high with embarrassment, Heather puffed up her chest. ''Since you seem to be the fountain from which all knowledge flows, David, why don't you enlighten me?''

Smiling archly, the attorney replied, ''I'd be delighted. *Key Largo* takes place on an island, where the remaining inhabitants are trapped in an inn during a tropical storm. Sound familiar? There are also some unsavory characters lurking about, making trouble for our hero, Humphrey Bogart.''

Heather jumped up. ''Exactly who are you calling an unsavory character?''

David raised his hands and shrugged, as if bewildered by her attitude. ''Why, Heather, darling, I wasn't referring to anyone. Did I strike a nerve?''

Heather's mouth worked furiously for a few seconds, but she couldn't seem to verbalize her anger. Flapping her arms at her sides, she stormed out of the room.

Carey Howard, who'd been quiet during the exchange, jumped to his feet. His face was a brilliant scarlet, and the muscles along his cheeks clenched furiously, as if his pent-up rage was fighting for release. Thrusting his chin at David, he muttered between tightly clamped teeth, ''You're a jerk, Welton. A rude, obnoxious jerk. But I'm sure you already knew that, Counselor, since you have such a vast store of knowledge. Must make you feel big to belittle someone else. But you know what? You're just about the smallest person I've ever met.''

Turning on his heel, he stalked out behind Heather.

A stunned silence flooded the room, but Elisa felt like applauding Carey Howard. She was glad he'd jumped to

Heather's defense, and she couldn't help wondering why David was impelled to snap at Heather at every opportunity. It was almost as if they shared some disturbing history. What else could explain their overt hostility?

Not appearing even slightly embarrassed, David stepped forward and gave a mock bow to the silent onlookers. "Heather and her friend seemed to take my joking comments to heart. Sorry if I've offended anyone else."

With that, he lazily strolled out of the room.

No one spoke for several long moments. Then Betty cast a quick glance at her husband, and they stood up. "Guess it's time to call it a night," Mark Bowman said. "See everyone in the morning."

Their departure left the Danzigers alone with Storm and Elisa.

Miriam also heaved to her feet. "My word, that was peculiar, wasn't it?"

Hank reached up and patted her ample backside. "Now, hon, you know these storms bring out the worst in folks. They're just worried and a little afraid, that's all. Had to release all that steam somewhere."

"Well, in my day, people didn't air their grievances in public. If you ask me, there's more going on between those two than meets the eye." Miriam turned to Elisa. "You know, I think him askin' for you was just a cover-up. I think it was that other girl he really came to see."

Elisa had been thinking along those same lines, but, feeling disloyal to her friend, she merely said, "I think Hank's right. Just a little pressure boiling over."

"Maybe so," Miriam agreed in a grudging tone. "But I've got more to do than worry about a couple of silly fools. Hank, you've still got to get the plywood nailed up on those top-floor windows, and I need to get things ready for breakfast."

"Okay, you nagging old woman," Hank muttered as he rose to stand beside his wife. His adoring grin gave the lie to his less-than-complimentary words.

Elisa reached down and tapped Storm's shoulder. "Oh, my gosh! I completely forgot—you were going to secure your own house and never got the chance. Can we still get over there? Or do you think the roads are already washed out? I'd be glad to help."

Silent until now, Storm lazily unfurled his long legs and stood up. He swiped an errant strand of hair from his forehead and gave her a lopsided grin. "Hank and I went over and boarded up my place while you were snoring away, Sleeping Beauty. Since it looks like we'll be stuck here a day or so, thought you all might appreciate it if I picked up some clean clothes."

Elisa laughed, then stopped suddenly when he continued in a more serious vein. "Needed my medical supplies, anyway."

Her breath caught. "You sound like you're expecting more...accidents."

He cocked his head, and gave her an oddly assessing glance. "No, I certainly hope not. But with debris flying all around us, it's better to be prepared."

"Makes sense," Elisa replied, embarrassed that she'd automatically thought he agreed with Heather in thinking she was accident-prone. Lately it seemed she looked for hidden meanings in everything. Paranoid? Or laudably wary?

Storm stood up. "Right now, I'm going to return the favor and give Hank a hand boarding his upstairs windows. Why don't you go on to bed? The rest will do you good."

She shook her head, then stopped abruptly when the sudden movement caused a furious pounding in her temple. "If I go to bed now, I'll be up all night. Miriam, can I help you in the kitchen?"

The older woman patted her shoulder. "Why, that's just sweet of you, honey, but like this old man I'm married to will tell you—Miriam Danziger doesn't allow anyone to mess around in her kitchen. Besides, I just need to slice some melons and take a sack of muffins out of the freezer. Won't take me a minute.''

Feeling like a small child who's been told to stay out of the way, Elisa was thankful when Hank made a suggestion. "You know what you can do, Miz Montoya? You could monitor that shortwave radio over there for a hurricane update. Sure would like to know if ol' Jake is going to hit us during the night."

Elisa crossed the room to where an ancient radio, about the size of a packing crate, rested on a scarred oak table. "Can you show me how to work it?"

Hank fiddled with a few knobs and, as if by magic, the static was replaced by a flurry of voices. "Stay on this band. This is where the Coast Guard and weather bureau will post their updates."

Glad to have something, anything, to do to pass the time, Elisa settled in the worn rocker. At first it was hard to pick out individual voices from the muddle, but after a few minutes of careful listening, she was finally able to follow the chaotic dialogue.

When she looked up, she was surprised to find that the others had already left to attend to their chores.

While she waited for the updated weather report, she thought back over the disturbing events of the evening. Miriam and Hank were doing their best to make their guests comfortable, and keep their minds off the danger of their situation. But despite the outwardly jovial atmosphere, Elisa felt weighted down by a sense of impending doom.

Was it the rapidly approaching hurricane that had her nerves on edge? Or was it something else, something...sinister, emanating from her fellow guests?

Chapter Five

The constant drone of voices, intermingled with long periods of white noise, was like a sedative, luring Elisa toward slumber. Time and again her eyes drifted closed and she almost fell asleep, but her deeply ingrained sense of duty kept forcing her awake. Finally, the radio chatter ceased as the peremptory voice of the Coast Guard announcer broke in. Adjusting the dial slightly, she waited breathlessly.

"This just in from the National Weather Service. Hurricane Jake, with winds reported in the hundred-mile-per-hour range, has taken another detour. Jake appears to be stalled approximately six hundred miles off the North Carolina coast. Repeat—Hurricane Jake is currently stalled six hundred miles from Cape Hatteras, North Carolina. Should the hurricane continue its expected westward route, it should be hitting the barrier islands sometime late tomorrow. Stay tuned to this radio band for updates every half hour. The hurricane warning is still in effect. U.S. Coast Guard, over and out."

She sat for a few moments, trying to make sense of the report. He'd said Jake was stalled. That meant not moving, didn't it? At least temporarily, the storm was no longer headed their way!

Jumping to her feet, she skipped up the stairs to tell Storm and Hank the good news. When she reached the rarely used third floor, she noticed that the noise generated by the hurricane was much louder than below. She checked each door as she passed, but Hank and Storm had been busy; the windows in each were covered with plywood sheets.

When she opened the last door at the end of the corridor, the tempest's full fury was all too evident. Broken tree branches slammed against the partly boarded window, the sound punctuated by the metallic clang of some object that was never meant to fly smashing into the brick building. Elisa had to remind herself that they were three floors off the ground and this was an old structure with lofty ceilings. Metallic objects weren't supposed to leap more than three stories in the air. Surely the laws of gravity had taken the night off.

They were at the window, Storm holding the heavy plywood panel in place while Hank hammered it into the frame. But because the protective board wasn't fully secure, the ferocious wind was howling its outrage around the edges of the oversize window.

Until this moment, Elisa had harbored no real fear of the hurricane. While they were buffeted by the gusts and driving rain on their way to the hotel, she'd somehow held on to her belief that the epicenter would never reach them. Now she shivered with fear, understanding at last the potential violence of a force-four hurricane.

Newsreel images of Jake's ancestors flashed through her mind: Hurricane Andrew stampeding through Florida, and Iniki all but destroying the island of Kauai. Entire roofs flying through the air like toy planes. Houses crushed beneath the tremendous pressure. Even hotels and immense government structures leveled by the raging bursts of energy.

This was no little rainstorm, to be celebrated by a "hurricane party" or simple games. Their lives were in mortal danger. Suddenly the overwhelming loss she'd felt when her ballet career ended no longer felt so tragic. She'd find another way to make a living. And her mother would always be proud of her, no matter what path she took. How foolish she'd been to think Elisa Montoya was only important when she donned a tutu and whirled across the stage.

Elisa Montoya, prima ballerina, had missed out on a lot of things others took for granted: home, family, husband, children. Stability.

Now that she'd been given this new awareness of the value of life, she wasn't ever again going to define herself by her work. *If* she survived to have a second chance at her life.

Feeling renewed and empowered by her realization, she hurried to help the men. It took only a few more minutes for them to finish covering the large window. When the fever pitch of the raging storm was muffled by the board, it would be easy to allow herself to be lulled into a false sense of security. But she knew better. They wouldn't be safe until Jake either changed direction or spent his fury.

Completely exhausted by their efforts, Hank dropped to the floor, while Storm leaned against the wall to catch his breath. Even in the near darkness, she could see the sheen of exertion glistening on his forehead. His thick golden-brown hair was damp, and his glorious green eyes were rimmed with red, the only evidence of his fatigue.

Elisa leaned against him, resting her head on his shoulder as if he were an old and trusted friend. Somehow, tonight, he was. "Are you guys up to hearing some news?"

"Only if it's good news," Storm muttered.

"Amen to that," Hank added.

Happy to ease their worries, if only temporarily, she repeated the last weather report.

"Now that *is* good news!" Hank pushed himself upright. "I hope that durned old Jake spins in a circle till he plumb wears hisself out."

Storm chuckled. "I'll second that motion, Hank. Elisa, I always knew you were an angel. Thanks for the good tidings."

She ducked her eyes, unaccountably embarrassed by the teasing praise.

Hank gently poked her with his elbow. "Did you tell that worrisome wife of mine what the radio said?"

"No, I ran straight upstairs."

Hank strolled across the room, pausing in the doorway. "Reckon I'd better go on and tell her before she worries herself into a tizzy." He paused and tossed Storm his flashlight. "You'd better hang on to this—I'm fixing to shut off the generator. See you folks in the morning. Thanks for the help, Storm."

"Don't mention it. Good night."

When they heard Hank's slow tread on the stairs, Storm and Elisa looked at each other. The very idea of the staunch, unflappable Miriam Danziger worrying herself into a "tizzy" was so outlandish that they broke into laughter. Storm was the first to recover. "Yeah, Miriam needs to be calmed down. Like Newt Gingrich needs to be more outspoken."

"I think it's sweet," Elisa murmured. "He still thinks his wife is a fragile little thing who couldn't get by without his broad shoulders to lean on."

Storm wheeled around and placed his hands flat on either side of Elisa's body. Leaning forward until he was only a breath away, he murmured, "And what about you, fair ballerina? Are you a fragile little thing who needs a pair of strong arms to protect you from the storm?"

Her heart thumping like a runaway train, Elisa drew shallow breaths, then licked her lips to dispel the sudden dryness in her mouth. When she found her voice, she was chagrined to hear a croaking whisper. "There's at least one Storm that I might need protection from."

The generator whined and fizzled out, and once more they were plunged into the blackness of midnight. In the dark, Storm seemed much closer. Too close for comfort. Everything had changed, and the expectant tension was palpable. She reached out and poked his chest, meaning the gesture to be playful and diverting. But her hand lingered on his chambray shirt, and she felt the strong beat of his heart pulsing against her palm.

He moved one hand, tangling his fingers in a length of her midnight-black hair. "You have the sexiest hair in the world. It's like...raw silk, soft, but still strong and healthy."

Elisa felt that same tingling in her lower abdomen, that delicious sensation of butterflies tickling her insides and fluttering up to encircle her heart. "And you, *señor*, are a sweet-talking Southern gigolo."

A husky chuckle rasped from his throat. "Oh, no, sweet ballerina, I'm not a gigolo. I'd *never* charge you. My shoulders are yours to do with as you please."

Elisa turned her head away, embarrassed by having chosen the wrong word and given him more ammunition for this...seductive game he'd started. This was insane, completely irresponsible. She barely knew this man, and she wasn't given to casual affairs. Drawing a deep breath, she tried so very hard to push him away. To tell him she wasn't interested.

But his very nearness was too compelling, too coercive, and she knew in her heart she would be lying. Elisa was definitely interested. Foolishly. Devastatingly.

Her entire life had been devoted to dance. Every moment had been controlled, scheduled and regimented. For once, she wanted to give up her control, to live for this moment. To let this madness consume her.

Unable to do otherwise, she twisted her head to face him again. Instantly impaled by the hypnotic spell of his jewel-green eyes, she gave up any pretense of indifference.

She waited breathlessly for his next provocative gambit, but apparently Storm had no further desire to talk. Slowly, a scant fraction of an inch at a time, he lowered his head, until his lips were all but touching hers.

The butterflies in her midsection soared and flitted madly, as if to escape from an encroaching net. But she had no such desire for escape. In fact, she was no longer aware of conscious thought; her every instinct was taken up with his tantalizing nearness. Finally, a breathless lifetime later, his dark lashes fluttered closed as his mouth pressed against hers.

Her blood racing through her body like the maelstrom whirling outdoors, Elisa's lips parted gently to receive his probing tongue.

Then, a tremendous crash reverberated through the quiet building. A sound so great it dwarfed the hurricane's yowling shriek.

"What the hell was that?" Storm swore as he whirled toward the thunderous noise.

"It sounded like it came from downstairs."

He grabbed her hand. "We'd better check it out. If a tree limb or utility pole came through a window, someone could be hurt."

Her breath still coming in hard gasps, as if she'd just completed a vigorous solo performance, Elisa willed her rubbery legs to hold her upright as they raced down the staircase. When they reached the second-floor landing, the other guests were already milling in the hallway. Several of them carried candles, as if they were part of a ghostly funeral procession in the night.

While Storm shone his torch around the small assemblage, Elisa mentally called the roll. Heather and Carey were huddled by Elisa's door. David Welton was, as usual, off by himself, looking bored. The Bowmans were by the staircase, obviously roused from their sleep, both appearing dazed and confused.

As she expected, Storm quickly took control of the situation. "Was anyone hurt?"

Getting no one response, he turned to Carey Howard. "What happened?"

Carey moved slightly away from Heather and shrugged. "Don't know. Just heard a crash. On this floor, I think."

Storm directed the beam around the small area. "Anyone

else have any problem in their room, or know what happened?''

Betty Bowman nervously stepped forward. ''I—I'm not sure, but I *think* the noise might have come from Elisa's room. We're right next door, and it sounded like the wall between us was going to cave in.''

Elisa's heart skipped a beat. *Her room?* But...she was upstairs with Storm; her room should have been empty. An ugly foreboding rippled her body with gooseflesh. Whatever they found inside her bedroom, Elisa was sure she wasn't going to be pleased.

Heather padded forward in her fuzzy slippers and wrapped an arm around Elisa's shoulders. ''Honey, what's happened now? Were you walking in your sleep?''

For the first time in their brief friendship, Elisa felt her temper flare. She was rapidly tiring of Heather's constant insinuations that she had brought all her troubles on herself. Just as she opened her mouth to rebut Heather's comment, Hank's querulous voice carried up the staircase.

''What the devil's going on up there?'' A moment later, he thumped into view, looking slightly incongruous in his bathrobe and brogans.

''We're just getting ready to check it out,'' Storm replied. ''Doesn't look like anyone was hurt, though.''

''Well, thank the good Lord for small favors,'' Hank muttered.

After Storm explained the situation, Hank sent the others back to bed, and led the way into Elisa's room. She hung back, grateful for Storm's firm hand holding hers.

Before her accident, she'd never been such a coward. But all these unexplained incidents, and the feeling of being watched and followed, combined with the gaping holes in her memory, left her feeling alone and vulnerable. She couldn't protect herself if she didn't even know what she was up against.

Inside the door, they paused while Hank directed his high-powered flashlight into all the nooks and crannies.

When the window area was illuminated, she was gratified and yet surprised to find the plywood covering still intact. If the thunderous noise had indeed come from her room, then the hurricane wasn't the culprit.

"Looks like everything's fine in here," Hank said, the relief evident in his voice.

"Wait!" Storm said. "Look at the bed."

A startled gasp escaped Elisa's lips as Hank's spotlight swept the king-size bed. *"Dios mio,"* she whispered, as she reverted to her childhood habit of making the sign of the cross.

Releasing her hand, Storm stalked toward the bed. Following him with her eyes, she stood in stunned silence. The ornately carved walnut bed frame was smashed into a hundred useless pieces. The mattress and box spring straddled the splintered wood, all but resting on the floor. The heavy mahogany wardrobe that used to stand against the wall was now lying, kitty-corner, across the top of her pillow. Right where her head should have been.

Elisa's hands grew cold and her body trembled as she began to grasp the implication; if she'd been asleep, that armoire could have killed her. *Would* have killed her.

She sagged against the door frame. This was too much, the odds were too astronomical, for her to dismiss the incident as another unfortunate mishap. Even discounting her near drowning, she'd had *two* near-fatal accidents in a single day. Unbelievable. And truly horrifying.

In the background, she barely noted Storm and Hank quietly discussing the situation. Her mind exploded with shattered images, emotions and fears; it was as if every childhood nightmare were descending upon her at once. What was happening to her?

A single tear escaped and trailed down her cheek. She was afraid, yes, but more than that, she was hurt and bewildered. This was no accident. Storm and Hank could make excuses all night, but they all knew that wardrobe hadn't toppled over of its own volition. The only window was boarded up, so no burst of wind had dislodged the immense cabinet.

Someone had stolen into her room, believing her asleep in her bed. That same unseen intruder had willfully, maliciously, levered that massive wardrobe onto her bed. Where the would-be killer had thought she was sleeping.

Elisa's head ached from the effort as she went over every event, every conversation, every encounter she'd had, since she came to this island. Had she upset or angered anyone? Or did she possess some arcane knowledge that threatened another person? Why, oh, why, would anyone hate her so much?

She barely sensed Storm taking her into her arms before she broke down and sobbed at the painful truth. Someone in this hotel, one of eight people she'd conversed with, laughed with, was trying to murder her.

STORM STOOD in a darkness that was penetrated only by a small, flickering candle on the dresser. Although she was still fretful, tossing and murmuring, Elisa had finally dozed off. The long, silken strands of her pitch-colored hair spread across his pillow like a puddle of shiny black ink on a clean sheet of paper. But her hair was only part of the allure that captivated him. She was a mystery, a puzzle waiting to be solved. She'd piqued his interest—and he hadn't been interested in anything, even living, for a very long time.

He remembered when he'd first seen Elisa. Three years ago. Performing at Lincoln Center. She'd been flawlessly graceful, enchanting and serene. Meeting her in person, he'd found her no less enchanting or graceful. But the former ballerina was no longer serene. Something or someone had shattered her spirit, and Storm felt an incomprehensible need to help her regain it.

She stirred and moaned softly before turning over.

How long had he been watching her sleep? An hour? Two. He found it incredible that the woman could extract even a moment's peace from her slumber, after all the emotional upheaval she'd encountered in this single day.

But what in hell was he doing involving himself in her problems? Okay, she was sexy, with her smoldering dark eyes and exotic bone structure. She was demure, with an intriguing dash of fiery temper. But he'd met lots of sexy women, and he no longer wanted to be intrigued.

For the past two years, he had found it no hardship to keep himself emotionally insulated. He no longer believed in love, compassion, tenderness or himself. All the facets that made him a complete man had died with Karen.

Storm had gladly given up his home, his car, his prestigious position at the University Hospital, in his quest for solitude. Ben, his colleague and best friend, had warned that he was punishing himself, donning sackcloth and ashes in his efforts to atone. But Storm knew better. There was no punishment severe enough for his transgression. He *wanted* isolation from meaningful human contact.

At least that was what he'd thought until he saw Elisa floundering in the surf. For that split second, he hadn't thought about the ramifications of involvement, of meddling in another person's life. He'd only known that she was in danger and he could help her. But it didn't mean he was becoming involved with her. Cared about her. Hauling her out of the ocean had only been a simple act of kindness. He would do no less for a drowning puppy.

So why couldn't he now let go?

Why did he feel so protective? So dazzled by her snapping black eyes? What was it about Elisa Montoya that made him want her? Not need; he understood physical need. During the past two years, he'd occasionally succumbed to the basic animal instinct for release. But this was the first time he'd *wanted,* and the intensity of his desire scared the hell out of him.

He sat on the edge of the bed and ran a fingertip down the smooth plane of her cheek. She was truly beautiful, but the world was full of beautiful women. This deluge of forsaken emotions surging in his chest was more primal than male predation. More exciting than the challenge of the sexual hunt. He desperately wanted to protect her from the evil that seemed to surround her.

But in order to help, he needed to know more about her. Somehow he had to get her to open up and talk about the trauma of her past that had followed her to the island. But if he did convince her to confide in him, could he bear the responsibility again?

Storm pulled out his wallet and stared at the stained and frayed business card. He'd abandoned his practice, vowing never again to try to penetrate the treacherous path of the human psyche. It hurt too much when he failed.

He sighed and shoved his fingers through his unruly hair. This time he couldn't fail. Couldn't afford to divert his attention for a single moment. Elisa's life might well depend on him.

In any event, there was nothing more he could do tonight. He needed to snag a few hours' sleep, or he wouldn't be much help to her in the morning. Carefully lifting the coverlet on the far side of the bed, he slipped off his loafers and eased in beside her. Although he feared sleep would never come, the soft, steady rhythm of her breathing was like a soothing lullaby, and in a matter of minutes, he drifted into a dreamless slumber.

IT SEEMED only moments later when his respite was shattered by a loud, furious pounding on his door. Opening his eyes, he automatically glanced at the bedside clock and was amazed to discover that it was almost eight in the morning.

Raising on one elbow, he was further surprised to find Elisa's side of the bed empty. The hammering on his door continued, even louder than before.

"Dr. Delaney, can you hear me? Someone needs your help. Dr. Delaney!" Storm could hear the hysteria in Hank's voice. And even took groggy notice that the older man, who always called him by his first name, had suddenly started addressing him by his title.

He jumped out of bed and thrust his feet into his loafers. "Just a second, Hank! I'm up."

"Well, hurry! We got us another emergency. There's blood spurtin' everywhere!"

Elisa! Stricken by a blinding assault of sick fear, Storm hurriedly grabbed the medical bag he'd retrieved from his cabin the day before and raced to the door.

He yanked at Hank's arm and growled, "What's happened? Is it Elisa?"

Hank shook his nearly bald head. "No, son. She's fine. But there's a fella bleeding all over Miriam's kitchen."

As they hurried downstairs, Storm continued to question the older man. "Is he conscious? Where is he hurt? How'd it happen?"

"Barely. Looks like his arm. Don't know. Miriam thought she heard something by the back door, and sure enough, this fella was hardly able to stand, what with the wind and all. Anyways, he had a bath towel wrapped around his arm, but the blood was just a-drippin'. Miriam sent me after you, and now you know as much as I do, Doc."

Almost running in his haste to reach the injured man, Storm slipped on the hardwood floor as they raced through the dining room. Quickly recovering his balance, he slapped open the swinging door. All four women were gathered around the table, hiding the injured man from view.

"Step aside," Storm muttered, as he elbowed his way between Betty and a very pale Heather.

The ruddy-faced man holding a sopping towel looked vaguely familiar, but Storm's immediate concern was his injury. "Could you ladies give me some room here? If any of you are queasy, now's a good time to make your escape."

No one moved.

As Storm began unwrapping the makeshift bandage, the man started trembling. "C-cold. Really cold."

Storm looked up and saw that his patient was going into shock. Glad to have the women to help, he barked out his immediate needs. "Miriam, do you have any sterile bandages? I used most of my gauze patching up that boy's foot the other day."

"Should be plenty in our first aid kit."

Storm nodded. "Good. Bring everything you've got. But first, get a shot of brandy or whiskey—whatever you can find."

He turned to Heather. "Go gather up some more towels. Betty, fetch a blanket. No! Make that two. And Elisa, would you boil some water?"

Wordlessly the women scurried away to their tasks as he finished unwinding the bloodied white towel. The man had lost so much blood, Storm could barely discern the distinctive blue Double Dare Hotel crest embroidered on the towel. An ugly gash ran almost three inches from his wrist up his inner forearm. Sweat popped on his forehead. God, don't let it be an artery, he breathed. His specialty was psychiatry; he hadn't practiced physical medicine since his internship. He didn't have the surgical experience to mend a severed artery.

Since old Doc Otis passed away in the spring, Storm had been called upon to treat a few mild emergencies. Twisted ankles from surfboard and skateboard injuries, mostly. In all those cases, he'd only had to wrap the injury and send the patient to the mainland for X rays.

Miriam hurried back, a tumbler of amber liquid sloshing as she ran. "It's only whiskey, Doc, but I brought the good stuff."

"Great." Storm reached for the glass and held it to the man's lips. *Where* had he seen him before?

He swabbed away as much blood as he could with the soiled towel, and bent over to examine the injury more closely. The heat in the confined hotel was so stifling, he could barely see for the drizzle of perspiration leaking into his eyes. Grimacing at the unsanitary conditions, he swiped at his face with his forearm and looked again.

The artery was intact. He'd only nicked a vein. The blood was already coagulating. Storm sighed with relief. He wouldn't lose another patient, at least not today.

"I have the water on high. It should be boiling soon," Elisa called from the stove.

Storm glanced up to thank her and caught a glimpse of Heather still standing motionless behind him. She looked almost as shocky as the injured man. "Heather! Where are the clean towels?"

She only stared back, her normally tanned face scoured white with bewilderment and fear.

"I'll go for the towels," Elisa said, quickly saving the situation. "How many do you need?"

"Three or four. And take her with you before she faints."

"No!" Heather suddenly broke out of her stupor. "No, I want to stay here. At least until we know if Brian's going to be all right."

Ah, Brian McPherson, Heather and Elisa's next-door neighbor. No wonder he looked so familiar.

Nodding slightly, he placed his free hand on Heather's shoulder. It was surprising to him that she should be this upset over a neighbor. In fact, as self-centered as she appeared, he couldn't believe she had this much compassion for anyone other than herself. Still, crisis situations often brought out the best in people, and he was pleased to find that he'd been at least partially wrong about her.

Although his thoughts were still locked on the need to stitch up McPherson, he forced himself to speak slowly and gently. "Mr. McPherson's wound looks much worse than it is, Heather. He's going to be fine. Why don't you go with Elisa to fetch those towels, so we can get him patched up?"

"You promise he'll be okay?" Her normally grating, attention-grabbing voice was muted and tremulous.

"I promise," he intoned solemnly.

Though still hesitant, she nevertheless allowed Elisa to wrap an arm around her shoulder and lead her from the room.

While waiting for the water to boil so that he could properly cleanse the wound, Storm extracted a minute fragment of glass that was lightly embedded an inch away from the deep cut. "Nasty cut, Brian, but fortunately not serious. I'll have to probe the wound for more glass fragments before I sew you up."

"Thought I'd got most of them."

Storm held up the tiny sliver. "Might be more. So how did you manage to cut yourself so deeply?"

Brian cleared his throat. "I, uh, broke a window. Say, Doc, could I have a glass of water?"

"Sure." Storm prowled through the cupboards for a glass and found a gallon jug of purified water in the fridge. He handed the glass to McPherson, who clutched it with both hands, as if too weak to hold it securely.

Elisa dashed back into the kitchen, panting heavily, her arms burdened with a stack of clean white towels. Storm hooked his foot around a chair leg. "Thanks. Here, sit down. I don't want you to faint from exertion."

Her lips tightened, but she took the seat. "I hardly think going up and down a single flight of stairs would compare with dancing the lead in a full-scale performance of *Giselle*."

"No, I wouldn't think so. But then, you didn't dance the lead a few weeks after surgery, did you? And you damn sure didn't dance on that barely healed ankle."

"How did you know—"

"Give me a little credit, huh?" He gave her right foot a sharp glance as he went to the stove and poured some of the steaming water into a stainless-steel bowl. "A third-grader could see that ankle was recently operated on."

Elisa opened her mouth to retort, but apparently decided it wasn't worth the effort.

After adding enough of the distilled water from the refrigerator to lower the hot water to a comfortable temperature, Storm came back to the table. He dipped the corner of a clean towel into the water and started wiping the dried blood from McPherson's arm.

Betty rushed in with a couple of blankets. With Elisa's help, they swaddled Brian in a blanket cocoon, while Storm finished cleaning his arm.

"Do you need me anymore, Dr. Delaney?" Betty asked timidly. "I'd like to go see about that other girl. She doesn't look very well."

"That would be great, Betty. I appreciate all your help."

She giggled like a schoolgirl at the small compliment, then tittered again and fled the room, freeing Storm to return his attention to his patient. "Feeling any better, Brian?"

"A little. Is this gonna hurt?"

Storm smiled. Adults were consistently more skittish than kids about medical procedures. "Ever had stitches before?"

Brian shook his head. "Not that I can recall. Am I gonna have to be awake?"

Storm's smile widened to a grin. He cocked his head and winked at Elisa, who was struggling to contain a laugh. "Don't worry, you won't feel a thing. And if you don't want to look, why don't you turn around and talk to Elisa?"

McPherson was having none of that. "So what kind of needle do you use? Like a sewing needle?"

"Sort of. Maybe I'd better explain the procedure. While my instruments are sterilizing in that boiling water, I'm going to give you an anesthetic. An injection of lidocaine."

"In my cut?" Brian sat bolt upright.

"No, but close to it. Hasn't your dentist ever given you a shot of novocaine?"

"Yeah, but that hurts like hell," Brian grumbled.

No wonder he'd chosen psychiatry, Storm thought. Drawing on his scant training in bedside manners, he patiently explained the full procedure of swabbing the injured area with Betadine and applying a topical anesthetic before administering the injection. After Storm's reassurance that he wouldn't feel anything except a slight needle prick, McPherson finally relaxed enough to let him continue.

Crossing to the stove, Storm dumped the instruments he would be using into the boiling water, just as the swinging door opened wide and Miriam bustled into the room carrying a flat tray of neatly rolled strips if cloth.

"Sorry I took so long. I couldn't find our first aid kit with all the sterile bandages—that danged Hank probably took it out on the fishing boat. Anyhow, I had a brand-new sheet still wrapped in plastic, so I cut that into strips for you, Storm. Hope that's okay."

While he would have preferred to use sterile gauze, he'd have to make do with the sheeting. "That's fine, Miriam, why don't you set it on the table?"

She carried it over and smiled at McPherson. "We'll have you patched up in a flash. Storm, do you need me to help?"

He glanced at Elisa, who didn't appear the slightest bit squeamish as she continued to dab blood off McPherson's arm. "I think we can manage without you."

"Oh, good. The wind is picking up again, so I want to catch the weather update. Hank's in the basement trying to nail some plywood over one of the windows he must have missed. Then he has to clean up the broken glass that flew all over the floor."

"I'll give him a hand when I finish up here," Storm said as he plucked a glass shard from the wound with a pair of tweezers.

Miriam waved aside his offer. "Shouldn't take him much longer. Mark Bowman and that lawyer fella are helping. I'll let you all know as soon as I get the hurricane update," she said, turning to include Elisa and Brian McPherson.

"Thanks, Miriam." Storm looked up and smiled, as he and Elisa responded in unison. Like a pair of bookends, he thought, then tempered the romantic idea. Yeah, like a pair of *broken* bookends.

As the heavy door whooshed closed behind her, he retrieved his instruments from the boiling water and laid them out on a soft, clean towel. While he waited for them to cool enough to handle, he listened to Elisa chatting animatedly with McPherson in an obvious attempt to distract him.

"How did this happen?" she asked, unwittingly repeating Storm's earlier query.

"Glass," he muttered.

"Oh, goodness, did you wreck your truck on the way over here?"

He shot her a scornful glance. "No, I didn't wreck my truck. I cut my damn arm on a window at my cabin, and when it wouldn't stop bleeding, I remembered your pal was a doctor and drove over here to have him fix it."

He clamped his lips shut and stared at the wall behind the stove, giving rapt attention to the clock, which was shaped like a black cat and waved its plastic tail in time with the second hand.

Storm paused in his stitching to scan McPherson's face. Why was he so short with Elisa? Yesterday, he'd given the appearance of being a hale and hearty good-neighbor type.

Yesterday, in fact, McPherson had seemed so macho he was almost unbearable. The way he'd slammed his ham-size fists on his hips and declared his scorn for the oncoming tempest. Today, even though he was dressed in black from head to toe, like an oversize cat burglar, Brian's mood was darker than his clothing.

Giving him the benefit of the doubt, Storm decided the man was just embarrassed because he'd whined so much. And in front of the women, no less.

He snipped the last thread and applied a gel antiseptic. "That must have been some ride. It's a wonder you could hold on to the wheel with only one good arm."

McPherson straightened in his chair, his chest slightly puffed. "I spent some time driving on the stock-car circuit. Guess I'm as good a driver as any."

"Still, the roads must be a mess. They were half-filled with debris when I went to secure my place last evening."

"Like I said, Doc, I'm a good driver."

Storm said nothing as he secured the last bandage. Something about McPherson's story didn't ring true. He couldn't put his finger on it at the moment, but he knew it would come later.

Chapter Six

"Think that lady would mind if I used her washroom before I head back home?" Brian McPherson picked up a
black windbreaker that had fallen unnoticed to the floor.

Storm broke off the end of the needle and tossed the
used syringe into the trash. Going to the stove, he plunged
his hands into the remaining bit of sterilized water before
he responded. "I don't imagine she would. But I can't believe you intend to try and cross this island again. Especially in your condition."

"Hey, Doc, you telling me you botched the surgery? I'd
hate to have to sue you for bad needlework." For the first
time, a hint of Brian's jocular personality emerged in his
wide grin. Although, to Elisa's eyes, the gesture seemed
forced.

Storm wiped his hands on a dishtowel and crossed the
large kitchen, coming to a halt in front of McPherson. "A
reasonable man would stay right here. You run into trouble
out there, you could break open your stitches and reinjure
yourself. Next time, you might not be so lucky."

McPherson gingerly slipped on the windbreaker. "I'm
always lucky." He pointed to his injured arm. "You being
stuck on this island when I needed some patching up is
proof enough. And I thank you. Truly appreciate it, Doc.
But I'm going to be fine—you said so." With the tip of an

imaginary hat, he left the kitchen, treading as silently on the linoleum as a sassy, overfed house cat.

When she and Storm were once more alone, he raised a thoughtful eyebrow. "Interesting man. Known him long?"

She tossed her head. "Just since we arrived. Heather's known him a lot longer. They became friends the first time she vacationed here."

"What's he do for a living?"

Elisa shrugged. "I think he's retired. He might have been an accountant. Heather says he's sharp with money."

Storm cocked his head. "Odd sort, isn't he? I mean, I've been on the island for two years and I've never run across him. That's strange, in a small community like this. He must live like a hermit."

"A lot of people hide out, Doc, you ought to know that," she murmured thoughtfully.

Ignoring her barb, he asked, "Do you like him?"

Elisa shrugged. "Heather really does. Like I said, she's known him for quite a while."

"Did she also know Carey Howard from before?"

Knowing that he was referring to Heather's obvious flirtation the night before, she bristled to her friend's defense. "Men like Heather—they always have. It's not her fault they're always coming on to her."

Storm's quick laugh was devoid of humor. "Looks to me like Heather likes men just as well."

"Is that a problem for you?"

He ran his fingers through his always ruffled hair and shrugged. "Might be a problem for you."

Stunned breathless by the implication of his words, she blurted, "No problem for me. None at all. But if you want to try your luck with Heather, you'll just have to take a number and wait in line."

Her response was more biting than she'd intended, but his remark couldn't be misconstrued. The only way Heather's seductive way with men would be a problem for Elisa was if Storm was the seducee. After last night, he had to know that.

Elisa's felt her face flame with humiliation and pure, unadulterated rage. Last night he'd started to kiss *her,* but this morning he'd lost no time pointing out that his real attraction was to Heather.

She forced herself to gaze directly into Storm's duplicitous green eyes, while her ferocious scowl flashed an unspoken warning. She'd almost made a fool of herself last night. It wouldn't happen again.

Turning on her heels, she started to stalk away, but he grabbed her arm and spun her back around. "You think I want Heather? Is that what you think?"

"That's what you implied."

"No. That's what you *assumed.* And you know what they say about people who make assumptions, don't you, Princess?"

Elisa couldn't help but recall the little ditty she'd learned in seventh-grade English: To assume is to make an *ass* out of *u* and *me.* Filled with embarrassed fury at how easily he'd beguiled her, then toyed with her until he was tired of the game, she lifted her chin defiantly. "I hardly think I'm the one making an ass out of herself, Dr. Delaney. A more appropriate maxim might be 'Physician, heal thyself.'"

She jerked her arm away just as Miriam pushed open the door.

Seemingly oblivious to the dense, thunderous atmosphere of the room, she calmly started pulling sandwich fixings out of the refrigerator. "May as well eat everything before it spoils."

His voice still tight and raspy, Storm asked, "Did you hear the update yet?"

Miriam swung around. "Oh, kids, I'm sorry! I forgot to tell you two. Jake's still hovering out in the Bermuda Triangle. Maybe whatever's out there will pick him up and toss him into outer space."

Not wanting to face Storm again—ever—Elisa marched over to Miriam. "What can I do to help?"

"Not a thing, sweetie. But listen…"

"Hmm?"

"When you folks came in yesterday, you were all drenched from the storm. And you were carrying some pink thing. It was all soggy."

"My robe! I forgot all about it."

"Well, I went to hang it up in the laundry room, so's it could dry faster, and when I shook it out, an envelope fell on the floor. Did you lose something?"

Elisa's hands flew to her face. She'd forgotten Jay's letter. That must be why David Welton had come down from New York! Something to do with that letter.

Despite the painful memories Jay's final words were sure to evoke, she made a mental vow to read it as soon as she reached the privacy of her room. Forcing a smile, she reached for the envelope. "Yes, I did have a letter wrapped up in my bathrobe. I must be losing my mind."

Storm muttered from behind her, "I think you already have."

She whirled around and pointed a finger at him. "And I thought we had finished our conversation."

"Sweetheart, we haven't even started it."

Miriam watched the exchange with wide eyes. "Hey, kids, this is no time to be at each other's throats." She stepped between them and looped a fleshy arm through theirs. "It's all this waiting. Gets on everybody's nerves. Waiting to see if you're going to live through a hurricane is enough to drive a senior citizen to listen to rap music."

Elisa giggled and caught the half smile on Storm's face before she quickly averted her eyes. Miriam's attempt at humor had worked. And she was right; Elisa's nerves *were* frayed. But Storm was dead wrong if he thought she was going to make the same mistake twice.

Patting Miriam's arm, she said, "I agree. We've all got

to watch our tempers. So, to get a grip on mine, I think I'll go take a quick nap before lunch.''

Miriam stopped her just as she reached the door. "You forgot that envelope, honey. I laid it on the top of the refrigerator. Under that glass bowl."

Elisa stood on tiptoe and stretched until her fingertips dusted the top edge of the refrigerator, but she couldn't reach the bowl without using a chair. That should give Storm a laugh, she thought, just as he reached over her shoulder and slid the padded envelope out from under the cut-glass bowl. Wordlessly, he handed it over.

"Thanks," she muttered, feeling Miriam's blue eyes intently watching their every move.

"No problem," he replied tersely.

Backing away from his stifling closeness, she held Jay's letter protectively close to her chest, a bulletproof vest against Storm's disconcerting ability to confuse her. Taking advantage of Miriam's presence, she turned to flee to her room. She'd almost made it to the door when his voice stopped her.

"Can we make an appointment to continue our discussion?"

Turning slowly, she drew a deep breath as the blood coursed hotly through her veins. He was right in front of her. Only inches away. Too close. Despite her hurt, Elisa knew she was still vulnerable to the compelling male pheromones that leaped like fleas from his skin to nibble on hers.

"I—I don't want to talk anymore."

"But I still have plenty to say," he countered.

"I don't want to hear it." She listened to the words as they escaped her lips, knowing they were false. She wanted to listen to his every word. Wanted him to convince her that she was wrong about his interest in Heather. But she'd been so deceived by the events of the past few weeks, even deceived by her own traitorous memory, that she couldn't stand another betrayal. She simply couldn't take any more chances.

EN ROUTE TO HER ROOM, Elisa stopped outside the arched opening to the hotel sitting room. David Welton was alone there, standing pensively by the bookcase, scanning the diverse titles. He was wearing white jeans, and a thin white sweater with navy blue stripes above the cuffs, and he was resplendent in the expensive resort wear. But like the male models of designer clothing in upscale magazines, David struck her as one-dimensional. Oh, he presented a dashing facade, but his charm was only skin-deep, never revealing a glimpse of the personality beneath the showy exterior.

Glancing at the padded envelope she was absently hefting in her right hand, she decided this might be her best opportunity to have a private conversation with the attorney.

"Good morning, David." She flashed him a bright smile as she approached.

"Elisa! I've been wondering where you were. What was all that ruckus in your room last night?"

"A large wardrobe toppled over."

"I thought all the windows were battened down for just that reason—to prevent wind damage?" His frown and quick response exhibited the facile adversarial mind so prized by his wealthy clients.

A little judicious discretion might be a good idea until he'd revealed his motive for following her to the island, she thought. Wouldn't hurt to fudge the truth just a smidgen. "Guess the plywood on my window worked loose. Anyway, no big deal."

"Oh?" David arched a thin dark eyebrow. "If it wasn't 'a big deal,' as you called it, why didn't you stay in your own room last night?"

A red warning beacon flashed inside her head. How did he know where she'd spent the night? And what concern was it of his? She chose her words with care. "Hank wasn't able to straighten things up until daylight. Remember? He turned the generator off shortly before the mishap.''

''I see. So rather than simply give you another room, he decided it was...more convenient...to have you bunk with Delaney?''

Elisa opened her mouth to fabricate another lie, to say there were no other rooms ready. But David seemed to be having too much fun grilling her. She'd come in here seeking answers from *him,* instead she was doing all the talking. Time to change the rules.

Cocking her head to the side, she said thoughtfully, ''David, I'm afraid I don't understand. You'd already returned to your room before my sleeping arrangements were decided. Were you watching me from behind your door?''

A dark flush stole up his cheeks as, for once, the razor-sharp attorney was caught off guard.

Leaping on her small gain, she charged ahead. ''So you *were* peeking from behind your door?''

''No! I wasn't peeking. Exactly. I, uh, wanted to get you alone for a few minutes. We hadn't had a chance to talk privately since my arrival in this godforsaken place.'' He straightened his shoulders and tugged at his sleeves, obviously stalling to recover his aplomb.

She started to ask him why he hadn't made his presence known, but knew he would just manufacture another smooth response that she couldn't dispute. Deciding to get on with her own concerns, she gave him a wry smile. ''Well, we're both here now. So why don't we sit down and be comfortable while you tell me why you came down here in the first place?''

He followed her to the sofa, then sat in the more authoritative wing chair across from her. Leaning forward, he clasped his hands between his knees. ''I'm really sorry that I've apparently upset you by my unscheduled arrival.''

She briefly thought of denying his charge, but didn't want to interrupt him. Now that he was finally willing to talk. She gave him a faint smile, encouraging him to continue.

After a small hesitation, he did. "Do you remember my coming to see you in the hospital?"

"Of course." That was when he'd brought Jay's letter. Some instinct caused her to slip the padded envelope between the sofa cushions. Out of sight.

"I don't know if you realize this," he said, picking up the thread of his recital, "but the police were never completely happy with your story."

"My *story!* I didn't have a *story.* I simply told the truth. At least as much as I could remember."

David inched closer. "How about now? Do you recall more details of that night?"

She tossed her head in frustration. "I feel like I've answered this question for a thousand different people. No. My memory still has more holes than a crocheted doily. Oh, bits and pieces of broken images flash in my mind from time to time, but no lucid memories. Why? What does it matter now?"

Slowing his words to a solemn, courtroom cadence, he intoned, "Because a new element has come to light. An element that will surely cause the authorities to take another look at your involvement in Jay's death."

Elisa's heart raced like a frightened gazelle. What on earth could have been uncovered after all this time that might implicate her in Jay's suicide? She felt like running full tilt and pounding her head into the wall until she forced out those hidden memories.

Until *she* knew what had really happened that night, how could she possibly hope to defend herself against a charge of...of what? Assisting a suicide? Conspiracy?

"Wh-what kind of element could possibly implicate me?" Her voice was a dry, rusty croak, as if she were losing her ability to speak. She wondered if he could see the guilt she carried around her neck as if it were a millstone.

David stood up and reached behind his back, extracting a thin sheaf of papers, folded in half lengthwise. He tossed the stapled sheets on the coffee table between them.

Sitting back down he nodded toward the papers. "While going through Jay's correspondence in my capacity as executor of his estate, I discovered he had a second safe-deposit box. After requesting and receiving court approval to have the box forced open, I found a single envelope inside."

He paused dramatically.

Elisa's nerves jangled like a jailer's key ring. Just when she thought she might have to leap across the table and shake the words out of him, David cleared his throat.

"Jay had apparently made out a new will, superseding the one I prepared for him last April."

This was his big pronouncement? Her heart slowed to a near-normal pace. But she was still bewildered as to how this information could possibly affect her. "A new will?"

"Yes. One naming you as sole heir to his estate."

Her heartbeat took off again, stampeding through her chest. "Me? But we'd only been dating a couple of months."

"Precisely."

Dumbfounded by this turn of events, she reached for the papers. "May I?"

"By all means," he replied. "That copy is for you. The original, of course, has been filed with the probate court. We are currently trying to authenticate it before we proceed with disposing of the estate."

Slipping her hand beneath the sofa cushions, Elisa extracted the manila envelope she'd hidden there. How silly that action now seemed, in light of this new, and damning, evidence.

Surely she hadn't misled Jay? Hadn't she broken off with him the first time he mentioned commitment?

Rising to her feet, she held both documents in a vise grip against her chest. "I don't understand anything that's going on, David. But what puzzles me the most is why this would interest the police?''

He also stood and hesitated for a ten-count before speaking, his voice grave. "Elisa, I know this is all a shock to you, but you must try to understand. By whatever means you can utilize, you must make every effort to regain your memory. To reconstruct a lucid account of the events of that night. Your life may well depend upon it."

More confused than ever, she breathed, "My life?"

He pushed up the sleeves of his white sweater. "There has never been a formal ruling on the cause of Jay's death. Perhaps it *was* suicide. We found reason enough when we started going through his books."

"Reason? What reason? Please, David, you have to tell me why Jay killed himself!" *Please, God, don't let it be because of me.*

As if oblivious to her anguish, he continued, in his maddeningly calm voice. "I'll be happy to share what information I have—in the event suicide is ultimately determined to be the cause of death."

He paused and drew a deep breath while Elisa moved from one foot to the other, waiting, and praying that her pounding heart wouldn't explode.

David tapped his upper lip with a manicured fingertip. "Although the investigating officers won't give me any details, they found some piece of evidence that leads them to suspect foul play. You had means and opportunity, Elisa. Jay's new will now gives you ample motive. I'd suggest you find a good criminal attorney.

"You could be charged with murder."

Chapter Seven

It wasn't that Storm was eavesdropping. Not really.

Elisa's irrational behavior in the kitchen had irked him so much he actually started to kick the oven to relieve some of his frustration.

Miriam stopped him with a gentle touch. "Wouldn't take it out on the stove if I were you, Storm. That thing's made of cast iron. You'd be getting off lucky if your ankle was the only bone you broke."

Heeding her advice, he lowered his leg.

Stomping over to the refrigerator, he grabbed a lukewarm can of Bud Light. He pulled the metal tab and waited until the foam stopped fizzing to take a long, satisfying swallow. He counted to ten and drank again, half emptying the aluminum can. Damn, she'd ticked him off!

One minute she was smiling like a sloe-eyed Mexican angel; the next she was hotter than a mouthful of habañero chilies. What could have lit her extremely short fuse?

"There's no rhyme or reason to it," Miriam murmured from the kitchen table, where she was chopping veggies.

He glared at her over the lip of the can. "No rhyme or reason to what?"

"To love."

Storm snorted. "Love? You think this is about love?"

Miriam cut the greenery off another carrot and smiled knowingly.

"I do not love her," Storm declared, stalking across the room. "I hardly know the woman. And what little I *do* know, I don't much like." He pulled out a chair, whirled it around and straddled it, all the while glowering at Miriam. "You women think everything is about love."

"Isn't it?"

"No. This is about that prima ballerina. As in prima donna. You should see the way she twisted everything I said. Unbelievable."

"You must've said something to upset her."

"Humph! I can't imagine what it was. All I said…"

Miriam listened quietly until he finished unloading. Putting down the paring knife, she smiled at him. Storm kind of reminded her of Hank—about forty years ago. "She thinks you're interested in her friend. That Heather."

Storm closed his eyes and slowly shook his head. He was completely baffled. "Why in heaven's name would she think a thing like that?"

"Because that's what you told her. Although maybe not in those actual words."

His head jerked up. "Is every woman in this hotel suffering from some…hormonal thing?"

Miriam winked and tossed him a grin. "Honey, my hormonals have been retired for longer than I care to remember."

"Maybe so," he said, deciding he'd opened a subject he'd rather not pursue. "But I *never* said I was interested in Heather. I lost interest in boy-crazy girls when I was still in high school."

Pushing her bowl of vegetables aside, Miriam reached across the table and took his hand. "I normally don't get involved in other folks' squabbles, but…what the heck? I'm bored."

Kneading Storm's fingers with hers, she slowly explained where his and Elisa's conversation had taken a wrong turn. When she finished, his first thought was to argue with her, explain his side. Then he realized he was talking to the wrong woman. He should be having this conversation with Elisa.

Rising to his feet, he shoved the chair back into place. Walking around the table, he gave the older woman a soft kiss on her weathered cheek. "Think I need to go straighten out a misunderstanding."

Miriam smiled up at him and patted his hand, showing a momentary flash of what must have been youthful beauty before it had been ravaged by time. Instead of feeling sorry about her lost girlhood, Storm suddenly realized just how fleeting and brief a lifetime could be. Whistling softly, he went in search of Elisa.

He had just rounded the hall corner and was heading for the central staircase when he heard the murmur of voices in the front room. Hesitating, he tilted his head toward the arched doorway in an effort to hear whether Elisa might be one of the speakers.

After his hearing adjusted to the muted conversation, he was able to pick out a female voice, but she was talking so softly, he couldn't identify her. Not wanting to intrude if a private conversation were taking place, he slipped off his loafers and tiptoed in his bare feet toward the archway.

The voices were slightly louder now, and he recognized Elisa, talking to that lawyer from New York. Judging from their tones, Welton was calmly professional. At his ease and in complete control. Elisa, however, was clearly distraught. She was shouting about someone named Jay, who'd apparently killed himself.

An uneasy knot started forming in the pit of his stomach. He intuitively knew that this death they were discussing was somehow connected to Elisa's recent "accidents."

The counselor's next words were muffled, as if the two of them had moved out of hearing range again. Cursing himself for getting lost in his own thoughts, Storm inched closer to the archway, determined to stay focused on their interchange. He hated spying on her but rationalized that he had to hear the rest of this conversation in order to help her. Closing his mind to everything but her welfare, he eased around the archway until he could see the entire room.

They were standing on either side of the coffee table. Elisa was huddled into herself, with her arms crossed over her chest in a classic body-language expression of self-protection. The lawyer clearly had the upper hand. He stood upright, staring down at her, his body rigid, his tone judgmental. They were obviously engaged in a serious battle, their arsenals stocked with hurtful words.

For a brief moment, Storm wondered if he'd misjudged the situation the previous evening. Because of Welton's hostility to Heather, he'd been fairly certain that they had been in a past relationship. But now, watching the way he seemed to relish browbeating Elisa, Storm was forced to reconsider the possibility that *she* had been Welton's lover.

Before he could reach a clear understanding of what they meant to each other, Welton pointed an accusing finger at her. Then announced that she could be charged with murder.

NOTING A SLIGHT MOVEMENT out of her peripheral vision, Elisa swung around and discovered Storm standing in the doorway. Watching them. A red haze of emotion whirled around her, blinding her, choking her. Fury, disbelief, embarrassment and fear blended into a raging river, flooding through her body and drowning her senses.

She was so stunned by the ferocity of the warring sensations, she couldn't tell which emotion was jolting her the hardest.

Summoning the few remaining segments of her pride, she raised her chin with what she hoped passed for righteous indignation. "Thank you for the information, David. I shall take what you've said under advisement."

She turned, hoping for a dignified departure, but the heat of Storm's gaze, centering on her khaki shorts and skimpy T-shirt, robbed her of even that small victory. A hot core of sensation formed in her stomach, and melted downward like a lava flow.

Gritting her teeth, she fought to hold on to her anger. Even her humiliation. Anything was preferable to this traitorous desire that welled inside her whenever Storm entered the area.

He was still standing in the archway when she approached. By sheer willpower, she managed to ignore her quaking insides, and glared into his eyes. Praying that her voice wouldn't quake, she tilted her chin up another imperious notch. "Did your eyes *and* ears get their fill?"

Without giving him time to respond, she swept past him. She'd almost made it to the staircase when he caught up with her. "Elisa! Stop. Wait a minute. Please."

To her utter dismay, she felt her footsteps faltering.

That was all the encouragement he needed. Reaching around her rigid back, he pried her fingers off the banister, gently urging her to face him.

Although her traitorous body turned at his silent command, she couldn't meet his eyes. Nor would she give him the satisfaction of seeing the depth of her pain. Drawing a deep, cleansing breath, she slowly exhaled her undiluted contempt. "Could you be brief? I'd like to go to my room."

"Elisa, it's not what you think. I wasn't spying on you or...or trying to meddle into your affairs—"

"Oh?" Still holding on to Jay's will and letter with her free hand, she gestured toward his shoes, which were lying on the hardwood floor, several inches from his bare feet.

His emerald eyes darkened to a deep, murky hue, the color she imagined the ocean floor would be—at midnight. His voice was calm, deadly calm, but the muscle tic at his temple gave the lie to his outward detachment. Slowly, distinctly, he enunciated each word. "For the record, I was *not* trying to horn in on your private conversation."

She refused to believe him. She wanted—needed—to hang on to this rage. If it diminished, the empty space inside her would instantly fill with thoughts of Jay, his unexplained death and his inexplicable will.

Elisa allowed the venom to flow from her anger into her words; to do otherwise would cost her last shred of dignity. "Is that why you took your shoes off? So you wouldn't disturb us? Or was it so we wouldn't hear you sneaking up?"

Storm kicked with his bare foot and sent his footwear flying across the hall. "Damn my shoes! I came looking for you to apologize for...for whatever the hell I did to tick you off in the first place. But when I overheard what that lawyer said to you—"

Heather's high, loud voice froze them in place. "Elisa, what's happened? What did David tell you?"

Storm uttered a vile epithet and released Elisa's hand. It tingled oddly for a moment, as if his residual energy still radiated through her palm.

Elisa hadn't noticed Heather's approach; she must have been cleaning the basement with the others and come up the back steps. Her latest obsession, Carey Howard, was firmly in tow.

Despite Storm's obvious annoyance, Heather's timing couldn't have been better. She'd probably saved Elisa from swallowing Storm's excuse and making a fool of herself. Again.

Edging past Storm's tense and unyielding body, Elisa made her way across the foyer where Heather and Carey were standing shoulder-to-shoulder. "Where have you two been all morning?"

Heather's gaze dipped down to where Elisa's hand rested against her thigh. When she looked up, her eyes were wide and shone with excitement. "You found Jay's letter!"

Elisa raised her hand and frowned at the documents. For a few moments, she'd managed to forget all about Jay and his damnable will. Dragging her weary mind back to Heather's question, she responded absentmindedly, "Yes, I did."

"Just out of curiosity, where was it?"

Forcing a weak grin, she shrugged. "Would you believe I left it wrapped up in my bathrobe? Miriam found it when she hung it up in the laundry room."

Heather's copper curls rippled as she tilted her head. "So, uh, what did he have to say?"

"Jay? Nothing. I mean, I haven't read it yet. That's what I'm going to do now."

Heather's brow furrowed. "Do you think that's a good idea?"

Elisa took a step back and stared quizzically at her friend. "Why on earth not? The worst has already happened."

Although her words were spoken to Heather, Elisa realized she was truly speaking to herself. Why on earth not? Jay's missive couldn't possibly hurt any more than the jagged guilt that already tormented her day and night. Why not read the damned letter and put the past behind her at last?

Reaching for Carey's hand, Heather tugged him to the staircase. "I don't know, except this whole thing has been very...traumatic for you." Her mouth curved down in a sympathetic frown as she patted Elisa's shoulder. "Maybe you shouldn't open up old wounds. It could only hurt you more."

Carey nodded sagely. "If you ask me, Heather's right."

Elisa refrained from reminding him that she hadn't asked.

Stroking his chin like a scholar contemplating the meaning of life, he continued, "Maybe you should let the past stay buried. All you could dig up are smelly old bones."

Storm shouldered his way between them and glared at the smaller man. "And maybe you should stay out of things that don't concern you."

"That's not fair!" Heather exploded. "You've only known us two days, and I've known Carey for...a lot longer!"

At that moment, David meandered out of the parlor, where he had been since Elisa's departure. Stepping into the fray, he poked Heather's shoulder with his forefinger. "Sorry, I couldn't help overhearing. Heather, in my capacity as Jay Morrow's attorney, I have to tell you that you're completely out of line insinuating yourself into his private concerns. If my client had wanted you to be privy to his affairs, he would have made the appropriate provisions to keep you informed."

Heather slapped aside David's hand. "I *was* privy to his affairs. I was his secretary. And since he died, I'm the one who's held everything together—including his girlfriend here. You think Jay trusted you? Think again. He went over every single document you drafted with a microscope. So—"

"All of you, please stop shouting." Elisa knew they couldn't hear her over their own raucous voices, but she had to try. Her head was splitting.

One cool, low-pitched voice resonated over the others. "I'll leave you to your friends." Storm picked up his shoes and, giving Elisa a last, searching gaze, ambled back toward the kitchen.

Her first thought was that she'd lost her only ally. Then she remembered Storm wasn't her ally; he was…was what? That was the problem, she thought sighing inwardly, he was really nothing to her. Nothing but a willing transitory lover.

The fury of mingled voices erupted anew, drawing her attention from the distracting problem of Storm Delaney. The trio gathered around her were all shouting at once, their opinions falling on a closed-minded audience.

A jagged spear of light pierced her temple, and she knew another of her "episodes" as Heather called them, was rapidly approaching. The pounding in her head, combined with the cacophony of their voices, was nearly unbearable. She felt dizzy, and a bolt of nausea sliced through her stomach.

Dreading the kaleidoscopic frenzy of memory fragments she knew would shortly follow, she held up her hand. "Stop! All of you. Just stop." When she saw she had their grudging attention, she tried to defuse the situation. "As much as I appreciate your concern, I'm perfectly capable of deciding whether or not to read my own mail. Believe me, if Jay's death didn't destroy me, then reading his suicide note isn't going to do it either."

Heather was the first to respond. Even through the throbbing in her temples, Elisa noted that her tone was disbelieving, suspicious. "A suicide note? You mean that's all he sent you?"

Stunned by the younger woman's coldness, Elisa stared at her friend through narrowed eyes, wondering if she'd ever really known Heather at all. "That's all?" she repeated. "I should think a man's last words would be enough."

"That's not the way I meant it," Heather protested. "I only meant that—"

Elisa held up her hand, precluding further clarification. "It's okay. Truly. Just forget it, please?"

Heather's fisted hands wedged against her hipbones. "What's the matter with you these last couple days?"

"I'm just tired. And this hurricane has me on edge."

Giving a sagacious nod, Carey concurred. "Of course it does. All of us are restless and jittery."

But Heather wouldn't be sidetracked. "I think it's more than some howling wind that has you upset. You haven't been the same since you brought Dr. Doolittle home with you."

Refusing to be drawn into another argument, Elisa silently turned away and plodded up the stairs. Her ankle burned on the third step, and she wondered if there was any part of her that *was* still functional. Certainly not her mind.

Going to her own room, instead of Storm's, where she'd spent her most peaceful night in weeks, she was heartened to discover that Hank had accomplished miracles. The armoire was upright, and in its rightful place against the wall. Only an extremely critical eye could have spotted the tiny nicks and mars on the mahogany finish. He must have used a whole bottle of scratch cover.

The demolished bedstead had been replaced by a homey brass headboard. Decades of gentle polishing had left a lustrous patina on the antique that couldn't be duplicated by modern reproductions.

Plumping up her pillow, Elisa stretched out to see if the new bed was as comfy as it looked. "Mmm..." She closed her eyes and yawned. Soft as an old-fashioned feather bed, but with enough firmness to prevent backaches. Perfect.

She lay with her eyes closed for a few moments, but the sanctuary of sleep wouldn't come. She knew why; Jay's letter was weighing on her mind like a curtain ballast. There would be no rest until she read it.

One problem at a time. That was all she had to do. Examine the first one, resolve it, and then worry about the next. Jay's letter was certainly her most long-standing burden.

She scrunched upright and poked another fluffy pillow behind her back. Lifting the chimney off the kerosene lantern, she struck a match and lit the wick. In a moment, the room's dimness was brightened by a warm, flickering glow that somehow reminded her of childhood, and the secure feeling of her mother's fleshy arms wrapped around her. When this was over, maybe she'd go back to the barrio after all.

Since she couldn't think of anything else to delay the unwelcome task, she slid a fingernail under the flap and ripped open the edge of the padded envelope. She blew softly into the opening and shook the envelope to dislodge its contents. A small blue plastic computer disk fell to the bed, followed by a folded sheet of paper.

She wrinkled her brow, unable to grasp Jay's intention. Why would he put his suicide note on a computer disk? He'd known she was a computer-illiterate. Setting the disk on the night table, she opened the single sheet of paper.

It was Jay's letterhead, all right. Creamy bond paper with

a stylized blue jay in the upper corner, followed by the clean, uncluttered block heading he favored. The body of the letter had been typed, and it ended with Jay's precise signature.

It was dated the day he had died. She retrieved the envelope; it was postmarked that same awful day. Taking a deep breath against the guilt that always engulfed her when she thought about him, Elisa lowered her head and began reading Jay Morrow's final words.

Dear Elisa,
It seems silly writing a letter to you at lunchtime when you're coming by the office tonight. I hope you're coming to tell me that you realize you've made a mistake, and you want to marry me after all. That's what I hope. You're the only one who can make that happen. In case something unexpected happens and we don't see each other tonight, I want to make sure you get this disk. Please don't tell anyone that I sent it to you. Not anyone. It could be dangerous. Just put it in a safe place until I ask for it. And trust me. I'm entrusting my life to you. Please don't let me down.

Jay

The short note fluttered from Elisa's numb fingers. What could it mean? What was on this small piece of plastic that had been so important to Jay?

Something in that missive had hit a discordant note. She thought about his curious, almost sinister words. One section, and she couldn't pinpoint it, wasn't logical. And Jay Morrow had been a logical man.

She picked up the note and read it again. And again. After the third time, she carefully folded it, stuffed everything back into the envelope and wedged it between her mattress and box springs.

She didn't know what the disk contained or why Jay had

asked her to hold it for him. But one thing was painfully, alarmingly, clear. The police were right; his death *hadn't* been a suicide. He had not opened his fourteenth-floor window and pitched himself to the ground. Not on purpose.

Because if Jay Morrow was contemplating suicide, he would have had no reason to slip out of the office and mail this package. No reason to ask her to hold on to the disk until he wanted it back.

If Jay had known he was going to be dead before nightfall, he had also known that he wouldn't have further need of this disk. He wouldn't need anything ever again.

Chapter Eight

Giving up on any thought of a nap, Elisa took a soothing sponge bath and changed into her favorite summer outfit, a blue-and-white striped cotton skirt and white scoop-neck T-shirt. She wrapped a wide jute belt around her slender waist and slipped on a pair of leather sandals. Running a brush through her long, straight hair, she dabbed a bit of gloss on her lips.

She stepped in front of the mirror and whirled around, enjoying the play of fabric as her full skirt ballooned out, exposing her dancer's legs. If she closed her eyes and flexed her imagination, she could almost believe her skirt was an organdy tutu and she was doing her warm-ups before a performance.

She sank onto the bed and dropped her chin into her hands. No point reliving dead dreams, she thought, with a surge of uncharacteristic self-pity. That wonderful-horrible period when she'd been the star, heralded on marquees and wined and dined by every wealthy man in New York, was over.

One night.

That was all it had taken to bring the curtain down forever. A single night. And the worst part was that she couldn't even remember how it had happened. Oh, she'd picked up enough from news stories and police reports to have a pretty clear picture of that fateful—and fatal—night.

She and Jay had been dating for a few months. At first they'd been strictly friends, casual partners for sporadic dinners and the occasional show. Elisa had enjoyed his company and thought she had the best of all worlds; a demanding yet absorbing career, and a no-pressure relationship. Jay, however, hadn't been content with the status quo.

As time passed and he pressed for more and more emotional involvement, Elisa could no longer ignore one glaring truth: She didn't love him.

The evening before he died, they'd gone out to dinner and she'd gently told him she was breaking off the relationship. Jay had taken it badly. He'd even broken into tears and begged her to reconsider. When she rejected that possibility, his professed love had turned to raging hate.

He'd screamed at her, calling her a cold, selfish bitch who always wanted everything her way. One role suited her, he said, that of the snow queen. Ice-cold Elisa, the beautiful shell with no heart.

His words had burned like salt pellets hurled into open wounds. Unable to fathom his sudden personality change, she had run from the restaurant. And that had been the last time she saw Jay Morrow alive.

He'd phoned her at the rehearsal hall the next morning, sheepish and remorseful. Saying he'd been under tremendous stress the past few weeks, he'd begged her to see him once more. Just one more dinner, so that they could end their relationship as friends—the way it had begun. He'd also said he needed her advice on something he couldn't discuss on the phone.

She sat bolt upright. Why hadn't he told her over the telephone? Had he been afraid of being overheard? What had been so important it could be conveyed only in person?

She reached beneath the mattress and grabbed the envelope. Walking around the bed, she hid Jay's letter and will inside an old pair of sneakers. Then she dropped the bright blue disk into her skirt pocket and dashed out the door.

Heather had been Jay's private secretary for over a year. If anyone would know what had been on his mind, it was surely her. Elisa glanced at her watch. Lunchtime. Right after their meal, she'd get Heather alone and ask the questions she should have posed weeks ago.

After all these weeks of racking her brain with no progress, wouldn't it be ironic if Heather possessed the scrap of information Elisa needed to open up those repressed memories?

STORM WAS SITTING in the empty parlor, staring at the landscape painting on the far wall by the boarded-up window. He'd been focused on it for nearly fifteen minutes, but even under threat of death, he couldn't have said what the painting portrayed. Sunset? Seascape? A mountain village? He had no inkling, because his mind was locked on Elisa.

Boy, he'd really screwed up. Yeah, Mr. Big Shot psychiatrist, going to fix the helpless little dancer. The fact that she hadn't *asked* for any help hadn't distracted him in the least. What a jerk.

What had he been thinking? That she wouldn't mind if he eavesdropped, because he was "trying to help"? He'd been smart enough to earn a medical license—why hadn't he been smart enough to mind his own business?

Hearing the dainty tap of footsteps coming down the staircase, he cocked his head and listened. Elisa was finally leaving the sanctuary of her room. He stood up and shifted his weight from one foot to the other. He wouldn't blame her if she never spoke to him again. But if he could just get her to listen...

Drawing a deep, prayerful breath, he went to the doorway, just as she strode into view. That same deep breath whooshed out of his lungs as if he'd been struck in the chest with an eight-pound sledgehammer.

For the first time since he'd met her, Elisa's stride was

strong, invigorated. There was purpose in the set of her shoulders and confidence in the tilt of her chin. Her long hair fell in a glistening ebony waterfall to the middle of her back. He leaned against the door frame, enjoying the way she moved.

Compared to the others staying at the dark, dreary hotel, Elisa stood out like an illuminated angel atop an undecorated Christmas tree.

Just as she drew abreast, he stepped into the foyer. "Hi, Princess. Can I talk to you?"

She hesitated, glancing around as if searching for an escape route.

"It'll just take a minute. Promise."

Staring deep into his eyes for a long, probing moment, she finally nodded and preceded him into the parlor. Storm noticed she deliberately sought out the wing chair in the far corner; she didn't want him too close.

Grabbing the ottoman from in front of Hank's easy chair, Storm dropped it at her feet and hunkered down. "I don't know which thing I should apologize for first, but—"

"An apology truly isn't necessary." She made as if to rise, but after locking gazes with him, dropped back into the chair.

Ignoring her comment, he continued, "Let's start with my first blunder. I don't know how our conversation in the kitchen got so twisted up. But in the immortal words of a former president, read my lips—I am not now, nor have I ever been, interested in Heather Gellis."

Elisa gave him an appraising look. "Interesting analogy. If I recall correctly, that former president lived to eat those words."

"Yeah, well, I'm not much on metaphors or similes. But I excel in honesty."

"That remains to be seen."

Whew… Despite the sweltering heat, the lovely Ms. Montoya was ice-cold. And she wasn't going to melt easily. But at least she was still here, still listening. He cleared his throat. "Okeydokey. Going on to my second apology. This one, I know what I did wrong—and it was unforgivable. But there *were* mitigating circumstances."

She raised a perfectly arched dark brow. "Oh? That's an interesting defense. Yes, Your Honor, I did take off my shoes so I could sneak over to the door without being heard. And, yes, I did actually listen to a private conversation to which I was not a party. But, Your Honor, my motives were really pure."

"And they were!" Rising to his feet, Storm's hands flew to his temple, then buried themselves in his hair as he paced to the fireplace and back. "If you'd drop the sarcasm for one minute and listen—"

"You've certainly exceeded a minute. I presume you need more time to fabricate—I mean elaborate—your story?"

For the first time since his fifth birthday, Storm felt like stomping his foot in anger. Elisa had imprisoned herself in a fortress of bland indifference. She wouldn't allow anything or anyone to scale that wall and pierce her hidden emotions. And he knew she had strong feelings; he'd had just an inkling last night. Just before that ill-timed kiss. The fire in her firm body had been close to blazing.

Well, if something worked once…

He gripped her by both shoulders and drew her to her feet. Before she had time to protest, he dropped his hands and cupped her face, drawing her mouth to his.

She froze, and her hands rose to his chest, pushing him away. But he was incapable of withdrawal. After a moment, he felt her body soften in his arms, as her lips melded into his in a perfect mating. Her mouth was an echo of her enigmatic personality. She was Mexican candy, sweet, tangy, but with the slightest hint of fiery jalapeño peppers.

Storm kissed her as if they were the last two people on earth. Desperately, frantically, and thoroughly. It was a kiss that couldn't end, because if it did, the world would surely die with it.

His hands slid down to her hips, and found the firm flesh of her bottom and pulled her close against him, until she moaned at the feel of his arousal. Her fingers tangled in his hair, and the wellspring of desire in his groin bubbled and burned like an active lava pool.

Somehow, a noise penetrated the haze of passion that enveloped him. Voices. Coming closer. Slowly, with great reluctance, he pulled his lips from hers and held her head against his chest until they both recovered from the paralyzing burst of passion that had held them captive.

The murmur of voices drew closer, and he stepped away just as Betty and Mark Bowman came into the room.

"Hey, guys," Betty said, her wide grin a dead giveaway that she'd taken in the entire situation at a glance. "Miriam sent us to tell you to come eat. She left a plate of sandwiches for you in the fridge. Hank's turned the power off again, so they probably won't stay cold long."

Mark absently tossed a grape into his mouth. "We've already eaten, but we're going downstairs with the others to play Trivial Pursuit. You two should come join us."

His wife nudged him sharply with her elbow. "I think they have another game in mind, hon."

He rubbed his side. "What are you talking about? And why'd you hit me?"

Betty hooked her arm through his and winked at the other couple. "You'll probably have the upstairs to yourselves for, oh, at least an hour." With that, she tugged on Mark's arm and pulled him out of the room.

Storm frowned at the departing pair and shook his head. "Women never cease to amaze me."

"In what way?" Elisa spoke from behind him, her breath warmly perceptible on the back of his neck.

Facing her, he ran the edge of his thumb down her cheek. "Because you're so smart, so intuitive. Poor old Mark didn't have a clue, but Betty was wise to us the minute she stepped into the room. How do women do that?"

Elisa chuckled and reached for his shoulders. Turning

him around, she marched him toward the mirror over the mantel. Glancing at his image, he finally laughed, too. His hair stood on end in jagged spikes, as if he'd joined a rock band. His face was flushed and his mouth was smeared with the faint pink tinge of Elisa's lipstick.

He glanced at her reflection. Her hair didn't look much better. Her lustrous dark tresses were in wild disarray, and her lips were bright and slightly swollen. She looked like a wild, wanton gypsy. And Storm had always had this fantasy about gypsies and all those bright scarves they wore....

He reached to pull her close again, but she did a half pirouette and whirled out of reach. Laughing, she shook her forefinger. "Oh, no, you don't. You never finished explaining your mitigating circumstances."

Taking her by the hand, he led her to the sofa, where they sat close in the corner. "Okay, you want mitigating circumstances?"

"Umm-hmmm."

He scratched his head as if conjuring up the recollection, then explained how he'd come looking for her so that he could apologize. Then he'd heard the voices in the drawing room. From their tone, he'd realized a serious discussion was going on, and he hadn't wanted to interrupt.

"But I didn't know if it was you."

"I see." Her smile faded, as if the mere remembrance of her conversation with David had instantly spoiled her mood.

Determined to get this over with, he doggedly continued, telling her everything, except that he'd overheard David's last remark. When he'd warned Elisa that she could be charged with murder.

Storm wanted her to confide in him. To tell him in her own words about her mountainous problems. With all his training in counseling, he had no doubt he could manipulate her into sharing with him. But for some unaccountable reason, he wanted, no, *needed* her to trust him.

When he'd finished, the atmosphere was no longer sensual or playful. A somber climate of dangerous secrets and lost memories had stolen into the room, robbing them of the few moments of closeness they had shared.

It would be hard for someone like Elisa to open up. She was obviously accustomed to keeping her own counsel, and putting her trust in no one but herself.

To help break the ice, he took her hands in his and gently kneaded her delicate fingers. Without looking into her eyes, he tentatively mentioned that she seemed worried.

"Worried? What on earth would give you that idea?" But she continued avoiding his eyes.

Ignoring her obvious nervous attempt to deflect his curiosity, he continued. "I'm concerned about you. I feel that you might be in danger, but unless you talk to me, I'm helpless."

She pulled her hands from his grasp under the pretense of smoothing her hair. "So you agree with Heather? You think I'm a danger to myself?"

He looked up, startled. "Of course not! That never entered my mind. Oh, I think you're in danger, all right, but why am I trying to convince *you?* You told me yourself that someone pushed you down the stairs."

"It might have been my imagination." She touched her temple. "Things have been kind of…hazy for me lately. Heather tells me all the time that I'm confused."

Reaching up, he took her chin between his thumb and forefinger and lifted gently until her eyes were locked with his. "That wardrobe falling across your pillow wasn't your imagination. That was real, and you can't explain it away as another accident."

She lowered her gaze, and he saw her bottom lip quiver. "Elisa, you can't hide from this any longer. You know, or at least have some idea, what's going on. And harboring secrets may end up getting you killed."

"I don't have any secrets," she whispered. "At least, I can't remember any."

He leaned against the cushions and pulled her beside

him. Tilting her head onto his shoulder, he lightly massaged her temple with his fingertips. "Why don't you tell me what you *do* recall, and we'll figure out where to go from there?"

After a long hesitation, as if considering her options, she began to tell her story. She started by talking about her relationship with Jay Morrow, a successful securities broker, and how their last dinner had ended on a sour note.

"Anyway," she continued, "I agreed to go to dinner one last time so we could part company as friends. We moved in the same social circles and knew so many of the same people, it would have been sad if our friendship deteriorated to the point that we couldn't risk seeing each other in public."

"Mature decision," Storm murmured, not wanting to interrupt the flow of her dialogue. "So you had dinner together the next night?"

"Not exactly. Jay didn't know what time he'd be able to leave the office, some big crisis was going on. So I said I'd meet him there after rehearsal. This is where it starts getting fuzzy."

"Go ahead, you're doing fine."

Drawing another hesitant breath, she closed her eyes, as if by concentrating she could pull the memory from her subconscious. Storm could tell that whatever was coming next had been incredibly traumatic for her.

"I remember arriving at Jay's office shortly after seven. I was surprised Heather was still there. The rest of the building, in fact the entire business area, was almost deserted. But Heather was still working—she was so devoted to her job. Anyway, she was coming out of his office just as I reached the reception area. I asked how much longer he'd be tied up, and she pointed to her telephone console. One red light was blinking. Like a warning beacon. But I didn't heed the warning."

"Take it easy," he intoned, trying to infuse her with the confidence to complete the story. He knew that once she forced herself to talk it out, her share of the burden would be considerably lighter.

"Heather left right away. I sat in the chair and glanced through some of those dull financial magazines. I hate financial stuff—that's why I have an accountant."

Storm knew her subconscious was trying to lure her away from a painful experience, so he gently pushed her back on track. "How long did you have to wait?"

Elisa's voice grew weaker. "After forty minutes, I decided to interrupt.

"Funny," she said after a brief pause. "It's like being in a movie and seeing it at the same time. I mean, I can actually hear the whisper of my feet on the thick carpet. I can see my hand reaching for the shiny brass doorknob. I was surprised, because the door was partially open. Anyway, I'm almost sure I actually went into his office, and then...and then..."

She sat bolt upright and turned to face him. The lightly-toasted color of her skin had an ashy undertone, as if she hadn't been outdoors in a very long time. Her breathing was shallow, and her pulse raced wildly in her throat.

"Shh. Don't force it, Princess, let it come."

She tossed her head, her long tresses snapping through the air like whips. "But that's it! That's all I remember. I don't remember any more. If I try too hard, my mind falls into a black hole, like a deep well that's embedded with jagged shards of glass. Once in a while a piece of that glass will pierce the darkness and I'll get an image—a cracked and distorted one—but that's all. I don't recall another moment about that night."

"And you haven't learned any more about what happened? From others, maybe?"

She shrugged and chewed on her bottom lip. "I woke up in the hospital three days later. In Pennsylvania. I'd wrecked my car. Almost totaled myself in the bargain. Thank God no one else was involved. Just me and that ditch."

"That's when you injured your ankle?"

"Yeah. A compound fracture. Two shiny little screws now hold my foot on to my leg. Goodbye, career, goodbye, life."

Storm wanted to gather her into his arms, but he knew instinctively that now wasn't the time for comfort. She needed to purge the facts of that night. At least as much as she could recall. Forcing a detached, clinical tone into his voice, he asked, "Were the police able to help you reconstruct the events?"

She laughed—a harsh, mirthless sound that clearly told what kind of help she'd received from the authorities. "I could hardly think, my head hurt so bad, but they grilled me for days. Finally, David showed up at the hospital and told me what had happened. Then he told the police not to question me again without my attorney present. They pretty much left me alone after that."

"So what did David tell you?"

"According to the police reconstruction, which David shared with me, I must have walked into Jay's office shortly after he'd thrown himself out the window. His office was on the fourteenth floor. Guess it was pretty grisly."

Her bland, almost robotic recitation of the facts surrounding her former boyfriend's suicide was enough to tell Storm that she knew more than she'd admitted. But he was concerned that she'd hidden the tormenting secrets so deep in her psyche that she might never retrieve them.

Repressed memories were powerful psychological defense mechanisms. When a person was so shattered he couldn't bear to face an experience, the human brain was so complex that it would lock those memories away in self-protection.

Obviously, Elisa had seen *something* that night. Something frightening enough to cause her to run out and drive for hours. Whatever she'd seen, whatever she knew, kept her in constant danger.

Storm had strong doubts about whether or not the securities broker had committed suicide. And if Elisa had seen what happened, or could somehow pinpoint the killer, her own life was in jeopardy until the murderer was apprehended. But unless she recovered her memory and could give sworn testimony, that wasn't likely to happen.

Chapter Nine

By the time she'd finished telling Storm about that night, Elisa's stomach was quivering and shaking as if a giant jellyfish had taken up residence in her abdomen.

"I think I'm going to be sick."

He laughed and wrapped an arm around her shoulder. "Nah. That's a good sign. It's called relief."

"I don't feel relieved."

"Not yet, but you will soon. It's like you've swallowed poison and it's burning and clenching in your gut, slowly killing you. Then you go to the ER and get your stomach pumped. Afterward, you feel queasy, dizzy, shaky, kind of like you caught the flu. But the poison's gone. And now your body's natural healing resources kick into motion. A few minutes later, you're on your feet and raring to go."

The corners of her lips tipped upward. Finally she gave in and laughed. "And you said analogies weren't your strong suit. Why, Doctor, I've never heard such a lousy conglomeration of metaphoric hogwash since I gave up creative writing in the tenth grade. Although I'm ashamed to admit, it did make sense. I think."

He jumped up, winked and extended his hand. "Just call me Dr. Feelgood. Now let's eat before I start nibbling on your leg."

Actually, that was a rather enticing idea, Elisa thought as they strolled to the kitchen. But then again, she was famished, so the tempting thought of his lips trailing up her leg would have to be postponed until later. She could wallow in that delicious fantasy tonight, as if it were an adult bedtime story.

Storm pushed open the swinging door to the kitchen. The cheery hotelkeeper was at her usual post in front of the sink; otherwise, the room was deserted. "Hey, Miriam," he called, "looks like everybody abandoned ship when it was time to do the dishes."

She turned around and swatted at him with her dishtowel. "Speaking of deserters, where have you two been hiding? Or maybe I shouldn't ask."

Apparently she'd enjoyed a little tête-à-tête with Betty Bowman. Even with the phone lines down and all means of communication severed, a juicy tidbit of gossip still found its mark. Still, there was no sense denying it. And, strangely enough, he didn't really care. For the past two years, the island's matchmakers had plotted to match him up with several local sweet young things. Until now, he'd resisted every attempt.

Once they heard of his "involvement" with Elisa, maybe the well-intentioned old hens would give him a break now. Reaching over to peck Miriam's neck, he backed against the counter and grinned. "This *is* the No-Tell Motel, isn't it? Aren't your room rates by the hour?"

Her mouth opened wide, in feigned shock, and she flicked him again with the dishtowel. "Well, I swan! Never heard such talk in all my days. Storm Delaney, you're a pure devil, that's what you are. Now go on and get your sandwiches before I have to turn you over my knee."

"Now, Miriam, I know that would be a pure delight, I'm sure, but Hank's a good friend of mine." Ducking away from her flapping dishtowel, he pulled a plastic-wrapped plate of sandwiches out of the fridge.

"What on earth put you in such a good mood? Never mind, I don't think I want to know." Miriam clucked a few times, and wiped her hands on her apron. Going to the kitchen table, she wrapped an arm around Elisa's shoulders. "Now don't you look pretty this afternoon? Storm, she's too thin. Hurry up with that food."

"Yes, ma'am."

Miriam's voice melted to honey when she spoke to Elisa again. "What would you like to drink, sugar? You need you some flesh on these little bones."

Elisa laughed and patted the older woman's hand. "You sound just like my mother. Always trying to fatten me up. When I go home she piles plates of food in front of me—tamales, chilaquiles, tortillas, beans, rice and even more beans."

"Sounds good to me," Storm said from over her shoulder. "How about if *I* go visit your mother?"

He dropped the platter on the kitchen table and started rummaging through the cupboards for sandwich plates.

"There's paper plates in the that cabinet to your right," Miriam called. "I don't want to waste water washing dishes."

Storm gathered the paper plates and napkins, and drew up a chair. While he and Elisa munched on egg-salad sandwiches, Miriam filled them in on the latest news from the weather bureau.

"Jake's been hovering within the same hundred-mile radius for almost twenty-four hours now."

Elisa looked up. "That's good news, isn't it? Maybe the hurricane will just dissipate."

"Not necessarily." Storm wiped a bit of egg from his mouth. "When stalled like this, most times they're gathering up more energy. Jake has the potential for being one of the most severe hurricanes of this century."

Her slightly almond-shaped eyes widened. "Oh, my God. What can we do?"

Miriam hauled herself up from the table and returned to her chores at the sink. "Not much we can do but stay battened down until Mother Nature gets over her temper fit."

They finished their light meal, and Elisa cleared the table while he grabbed a couple of cans of soda from a cooler beside the refrigerator. Storm realized that their hosts were preparing for a full-fledged hit from the hurricane.

Veterans of many tropical storms and hurricanes, the Danzigers had the situation well in hand. With the canned drinks in the cooler, people wouldn't constantly open the refrigerator, preserving the perishables a little longer. Before Hank turned off the generator and auxiliary pumps that morning, they'd filled every available container with drinking water.

Then all the men had joined forces to tote canned goods, blankets, kerosene lanterns, flashlights, drinking water and a hundred other minor necessities to the cellar. If the hurricane began closing in, they could haul mattresses and personal belongings downstairs in a matter of minutes. They'd done as much as any mere mortals could accomplish while in the direct path of a deadly natural disaster.

"If you don't need us, Miriam, think we'll go downstairs and see what the others are up to." Storm eased Elisa's chair out.

"Are you sure we can't help?" she asked.

Swiveling her head, Miriam called over her shoulder. "Told you I don't like anybody messing around in my kitchen. Now go on downstairs and visit with the others."

When they reached the cellar, the Bowmans, Hank, Carey and Heather were gathered around a large card table, engaged in a boisterous game of Trivial Pursuit. As usual, David Welton was off to himself, sitting on a camp chair in the corner, flipping through a magazine.

"That's not fair." Heather yelled. "He always gets the easy questions."

"Whine, whine…" Carey grinned as he stuck a colored wedge in his game piece.

Storm and Elisa hung around the table, watching their progress, until Carey answered the last question correctly and won the game with a loud victory whoop.

Mark Bowman flexed his arms above his head. "I don't know about you guys, but I'm ready for a break."

"Quitter," Betty teased, but rose to her feet when he did. "Think I'll find a quiet corner and read for a while. I've only got twenty pages left, and I'm *dying* to know who the villain is."

"So am I," Storm muttered under his breath. Heather glanced up sharply, and he realized she must have heard him. He had to be more careful, or he'd alert the would-be killer.

Carey Howard looked around the room, a triumphant grin on his face. "Okay, who's next? Who among you care to challenge the master?"

Hank stood up and lifted his hands in a gesture of defeat. "Not me. A man doesn't need to have his shortcomings exposed twice in a row. I'm going up and tune in the short-wave. Sure wish ol' Jake would either come on or go away. This danged waiting is getting me down."

"How about you, Dave? Care to join us?" Despite their words of the evening before, Carey Howard, at least, seemed content to let bygones be bygones.

The lawyer tossed aside his magazine. "No. But thank you. I think I'll join our host at the radio. Maybe get an idea of how many more eons I'm going to be stuck in this hellhole."

Storm's backbone tensed. David Welton must be the token attorney who kept the stereotype alive; he was rude, obnoxious, condescending and pompous beyond belief. Waiting out a hurricane was hard on everybody. But this group had every convenience, pleasant company to share the tension, enough food and water and a very sturdy shelter. Storm was glad Hank had already gone upstairs; he wouldn't take kindly to hearing his beloved hotel referred to as a hellhole.

Heather chimed in. "So how about you two?"

"Sure, I'm game," Storm replied, happy for a chance to keep Elisa in sight.

When she continued to hesitate, Heather waggled her eyebrows in an exaggerated leer. "I realize you probably have other things you'd rather be doing, but you have to rest sometime."

"Give it a break," Elisa snapped. "I'm getting weary of the innuendo."

Heather threw the die onto the game board, and glared at her friend. "What is *eating* you? For the past two days you've been snapping and snarling like a dog tied just out of reach of the neighborhood cat. Now tell me what's up!"

Elisa's chewed on her lower lip. Instead of offering the apology Heather seemed to expect, she said, "Actually, I would like to talk to you for a few minutes before we start the next game. Alone, if that's okay."

Carey leaped up like an obedient servant. "I need to visit the, uh, little boys' room. If you ladies will excuse me?"

"Anybody need something to drink?" Storm asked. "I'm going to see if Miriam has any of her homemade cookies hidden away."

The two women shook their heads as the men disappeared up the staircase.

When they were alone, Elisa sat across from Heather. "I wanted to talk to you about Jay."

"Jay! I knew that damned David Welton was going to stir up trouble."

Elisa's hand slipped into her pocket, and she fingered the computer disk. "This has nothing to do with David. It's about the letter Jay mailed to me."

Leaning back in her chair, Heather cast an appraising gaze across the table. "What did he say? You know he was under a great deal of stress those last weeks, so I wouldn't pay much attention if he said anything, er, strange."

"What do you mean 'strange'?" Elisa frowned.

"I don't know, just strange. He was like a different person before he died, shouting, accusing, all sorts of odd behavior. To tell you the truth, I was looking for another job."

Elisa didn't doubt her claim. The night before his death, Jay had shouted accusations at her. But this was the first time Heather had hinted of problems in the office.

"Why haven't you told me all this before?" Elisa wanted to believe her friend, but to do so she would have to accept harsh truths about a man she'd once cared for.

Heather tucked a strand of copper hair behind her ear. "I don't know. At first you were so banged up, it never occurred to me to discuss anything serious. Then, when you started healing and couldn't remember stuff, I figured the less you had to worry about, the better off you'd be. Besides, with Jay gone, there didn't seem much point."

A spear of guilt shot through Elisa; she should be ashamed of having doubted her friend's motives. Even momentarily. Trust Heather to always have a logical explanation. Since the moment Elisa awakened in the hospital, the younger woman had been her constant companion. As punctual as a precisely tuned Swiss clock, Heather had skipped into the hospital at two sharp, every afternoon. She'd brought flowers, candy, balloons, raunchy get-well cards, and always a funny story to cheer her friend.

So how could Elisa question her veracity now?

"Anyway," Heather said, breaking into her troubled thoughts. "You never said what was in the letter."

Elisa shook her head. "Nothing. Literally. At least, nothing I could understand."

"Maybe I can help."

"I hope so. That's why I wanted to talk to you. Was Jay having...business or money troubles?"

Heather's blue gaze darted away and settled on a spot behind Elisa's shoulder. "I don't know for sure. But...but I was suspicious. He seemed awfully worried about something. I didn't have access to the clients' accounts, of course, but I knew if a securities broker went under and lost his clients' money, that the feds would take over and indict the whole staff, including the janitor. That's why I thought I should get out of there."

Elisa nodded. "It all seems to fall together, then. The day he died, Jay mailed me a computer disk, with a brief note asking me to hold on to it until he wanted it again. Why do you think he'd do something like that?"

Heather sucked in a deep breath and seemed to consider the question. "You know, I don't want to speak ill of the dead, but the only thing I can think of is a second set of books. I'm not into math or computers or anything, but what if he had set up some dummy accounts and was siphoning funds from his clients? Maybe he knew an audit was coming. He would have been disgraced, probably sent to jail, and his license would have been permanently revoked. Under that kind of threat, his suicide is understandable."

Elisa lifted her hand to her mouth, as if she could physically hold back the tears that were scalding her throat. Could Heather's conjecture possibly be true? If it was, it would explain so much. But what did it say about her? Was she such a poor judge of character that she could have dated a con man, a swindler, and never had a clue?

That was something she'd have to figure out later. But one thing was certain—she was going to be far more careful in the future. This wasn't the first time she'd been involved with a deceitful man, but it was an error she didn't intend to repeat.

The scuffle of footsteps and the murmur of male voices on the staircase heralded Storm and Carey's return. She took Heather's hand. "Thanks for sharing with me. This must have been very distressing for you. I...I really appreciate all you've done for me this summer."

Heather brushed her hand away and dismissed Elisa's words with a toss of her head. "Don't be silly. That's what friends are for. Hi, guys!" She waved as the men thundered down the wooden steps into the cellar. Before they crossed the cavernous room, she leaned over and whispered, "So what are you going to do about the disk?"

Lowering her voice, as well, Elisa said, "If he *was* bilking his clients, this might help recover their money. As soon as I can get back to the mainland, I'm turning it over to the federal accountants who are closing up Jay's office. If any of the other brokers were involved, I hope this puts them away for life.''

STORM'S JOVIAL MOOD lasted until about the middle of their second game. Heather's high, whiny voice was getting on his nerves, and Carey's instant obedience to her every command reminded him of an indulgent parent kowtowing to a rebellious two-year-old.

And since her private talk with Heather, Elisa had withdrawn into herself. She acted depressed. Morose. Scarcely seeming to recognize his existence.

When Heather finally squealed, "I won! I finally won!" Storm sighed with undiluted relief.

"I don't know about anybody else, but I've had enough. Think I'll try to find out what the latest weather report had to say. Elisa, are you coming or staying down here?"

"What?" She glanced up, her eyebrows raised as if she'd been startled. "I'm sorry, I wasn't listening."

When he patiently repeated his question, she rose to her feet. He took that as an indication that she was going with him. As she silently climbed the narrow staircase ahead of him, Storm could almost see the yoke of anxiety on her slumped shoulders. What could Heather have said or done to pile on this additional burden?

"Anything you want to talk about?" he asked as they passed through the kitchen.

"No. I need to think something through."

"Sometimes it helps to share."

He pushed open the dining room door and stepped aside, holding the heavy door for her.

Taking a few steps across the hardwood floor, she paused and spun to face him. "I don't understand this compulsion to hear all my problems. I thought you were a doctor, not a priest."

Taken aback by her bluntness, he led the way to a small table in the corner. Gathering his thoughts, he glanced around the old-fashioned room. All the tables were set with snowy white linens. Pale lavender candles in small glass pots served as centerpieces, and the napkins wore matching lavender rings. The room was perfect. Pristine. Waiting for the dinner crowd that wasn't coming. He wondered if this was how the dining room on the *Titanic* looked just before the ship went down.

He had the grim feeling that whatever progress he'd made with Elisa had just sunk to the bottom of the ocean floor.

She finally took the chair beside him and watched him with a wary eye.

Storm reached into his pocket and tossed his old business card on the table.

After a brief hesitation, she picked it up.

F. Storm Delaney, M.D.
Head of Pediatric Psychiatry

Confusion darkened her eyes to the color of charcoal. "You're a psychiatrist? I thought you were a regular doctor. I mean, you put stitches in Brian's arm. Is a shrink supposed to do that kind of thing?"

"For the record, I *am* a medical doctor. I went through the same grueling eight years as an internist. Then, when it came time to choose my specialty, I had another four years of intensive training in psychiatry. Granted, until these past few months I haven't had much occasion to practice physical medicine, but I've managed to stay qualified and am licensed to do so. Any more questions about my qualifications?"

He watched her expressive face as she processed the information and came to a conclusion that sent a flush of anger to her cheeks. "You should have told me! Instead of letting me pour out all my problems like I was talking to a friend, when the whole time you were—"

"An experienced professional who might be able to offer real help, instead of well-meaning but useless advice?"

She leaned back and folded her arms across her chest. "When you say it like that, it sounds so...so reasonable. I suppose you learned how to manipulate patients in Freudian Mumbo jumbo 101?"

He laughed. "Ah, a skeptic."

"I don't know," she grudgingly admitted. "I've never been to a shrink, never even met one that I can recall."

"Good for you. Your life must have been very stable and relatively untroubled. Until now."

"What do you know about 'now'?"

He leaned back and propped his feet on an adjacent chair. "I know what you told me this morning. And a couple more things I've guessed. I'm hoping you'll share the rest with me now."

When she didn't reply, he leaned across the table, taking care to keep his tone steady, relaxed and nonthreatening. "Look, Elisa, even without my training, I can still relate to your situation. I understand the guilt that sometimes goes along with being the survivor of a suicide victim. Your days and nights are haunted. Why hadn't you foreseen this? What could I have done to save her? You feel guilty about everything, including still being alive. I know. Believe me."

"That's exactly how I feel," she breathed. "But tell me, Doctor, does your empathy come from personal or professional experience?"

"Both," he said shortly.

In a rapid shift of subject, he said, "Look, I have two choices here—either I dismiss these apparent attempts on your life as a combination of your imagination and sheer coincidence, or I believe you. And you said someone is trying to kill you. Which option should I work from? *Are* you neurotic, paranoiac and mentally disturbed, as Heather implies, or do you truly believe your life is in jeopardy?''

She hesitated so long he feared she wasn't going to answer at all. Finally, in a voice so soft he had to lean even closer in order to hear it, she murmured, "When those things happened, I wasn't hallucinating, or under a paranoid delusion, if that's the proper term. I *felt* those hands on my back. And there was no way I could have engineered that wardrobe crashing onto my bed. But in the light of day, although we haven't actually had much light, it all seems so incredible. Unbelievable. So how would you diagnose that, Sigmund?''

"I don't think we have a choice. We have to operate on the assumption that you were in full possession of your faculties when you fell down those stairs. To proceed otherwise would be foolhardy, and could cost you your life. The question now is, where do we start?''

She scrunched up her mouth and nibbled on her lower lip. Sadly shaking her head, she admitted, "That's my problem in a nutshell, Storm. I've told you everything I know. This traumatic amnesia they say I have is keeping everything else locked in my brain. And no matter how hard I try, I can't remember. I just can't remember!''

Recognizing that she was pushing herself to the edge of her ability to cope, Storm decided to back off for now. She'd already opened up a great deal more than he had expected; maybe tomorrow they would make more inroads into her repressed memory bank.

Right now, he just hoped the killer was content to bide his or her time another day. When the generator was shut off tonight, and Elisa was alone in her room, she would be particularly vulnerable to another attempt on her life.

Chapter Ten

"Good night," Elisa called down the corridor to the others who'd decided to continue the hurricane watch from the comfort of their own rooms.

She closed the door, and lit the lantern wick. Darkness scared her right now. Rotating her shoulders to relieve the kinks, she dropped, fully clothed, onto her bed, deeply thankful for the coming hours of repose and relative tranquillity. Shutting her eyes, she waited for the vivid images of the day's events to fade. She was so weary. So confused.

But all Storm's talk of a killer in the hotel had turned her mind into a frenzied maze of unanswered questions. Giving in to a driving need to make sense of the recent events, she meditated, willing her mind into a clean slate that would hold all her questions. And the pitifully few answers she had ferreted out.

First was the wholly unexpected news that Jay had named her sole beneficiary in his will. That was disturbing in itself, but perhaps even more so was the unanswered question of why David Welton had felt it necessary to bring the news in person. Could his appearance be as simple and kind-spirited as it seemed? Had he come all this way to warn her that the police were bound to suspect her in Jay's unsolved death?

And Heather, with her quick and effortless explanations for every question Elisa posed. They'd been constant companions since Elisa's release from the hospital. When Jay's apparent suicide became public knowledge, why hadn't Heather voiced her suspicions about her employer's book-keeping methods? Why wait until now, when they were incommunicado and couldn't pass on the information to the proper authorities?

Thinking of Heather brought to mind the disk in her skirt pocket. With her eyes still closed, she tossed it on to the night table. She'd tuck it back between the mattress and box spring with the other documents later.

She was on the edge of dozing off when a soft tap sounded on the door. "Who is it?"

"It's me. Can I come in for a minute?"

Elisa sighed wearily and forced herself to be gracious. "Sure, Heather, come on in."

The lanky redhead slipped in and perched on the edge of the bed. "Feeling any better?"

"Just a little tired."

Heather smoothed the hair away from Elisa's face. "I can imagine—you've really had a tough time lately. Listen, 'Leese, I'm sorry I snapped at you earlier."

"Forget it."

"No, I can't. I must be exhausted, too—I never lash out like that."

Elisa managed a faint smile. "So why don't you go get some sleep? Everything will look brighter in the morning."

"Good advice, kiddo. With that very thought in mind, I filched one of your sleeping pills. Hope you don't mind."

"I didn't even know you'd brought them."

Heather shrugged. "I just grabbed a bunch of stuff out of the medicine cabinet. Good thing, too. Anyway, I'm so susceptible to narcotics that I'll probably crash on your bed in another minute."

She stood up and laid a plastic vial on the nightstand. "Ah, the infamous computer disk. You should keep it someplace safe. I understand they're easily destroyed."

Elisa smothered a yawn. "I'll be careful. I hate to be rude, Heather, but I'm about to zonk out. Do you mind?"

"No problem, just wanted to make sure we were okay."

"Fine."

"Then I'll see you in the morning. By the way, I put the sleeping pills next to the disk. You probably should take one. Might help you sleep through the night. Sometimes the wind sounds like a freight train coming through my room."

"Good idea," Elisa murmured. "I'll take one when I brush my teeth. Right now, I need a catnap."

"Good night, then." Heather softly closed the door behind her.

Elisa turned over and punched the pillow. But after ten minutes of restless tossing, she gave up. Her mind wouldn't stop fluttering from person to person, seeking a credible suspect.

She was startled to discover that she harbored vague suspicions of almost everyone. The Danzigers, for instance.

Instinct told her the sweet old couple were exactly what they appeared to be, but she couldn't forget that Miriam had been standing directly behind her on the staircase. She was heavyset, but Elisa nonetheless had witnessed the woman's physical strength. She hefted cases of soda as if they were marshmallows.

And Hank. He seemed like such a dear. But with Elisa's obvious inability to assess a person's true character, she couldn't trust her instincts. Was Hank's homey aw-shucks persona merely a blind? He'd been alone for hours cleaning and replacing the furniture in her room. It would have been a simple matter for him to rig the armoire so that it would drop on her bed sometime later. And he *had* been the first one to go into her room after the crash—the easier to remove any evidence he might have left behind?

The Bowmans—Mark and Betty. Were they really the middle-aged Ken and Barbie they appeared? Their conversations were giddy, pure fluff. And the constant "Yes, honey" and "No, dear" sweet talk between them felt artificial and forced. Then again, perhaps they were simply uncomfortable being marooned with strangers. Elisa decided to spend more time with the Bowmans tomorrow. If she talked with them long enough, perhaps they'd let something slip.

She sighed and climbed out of bed. Peeling off her clothes, she stuffed them in the wardrobe. She grabbed a favorite cotton nightshirt and kicked her sandals aside. A good night's sleep, that was all she needed. She'd feel better in the morning.

Picking up the small zippered bag that contained her toothbrush, soap and other hygienic paraphernalia, she trudged into the bathroom. As she splashed cold water on her face, Elisa reflected that it had been two full days since her last steaming shower. Her poverty-stricken childhood came immediately to mind. After her father's death, there had been too many occasions when her mother simply didn't have the money for the utility bills. Esperanza Montoya had been too proud to accept welfare or charity from her friends. As long as her children had shelter and food, she'd insisted on making her own way.

A bittersweet smile tugged at Elisa's lips. How many nights had they washed with cold water from a basin? Those same nights when they'd heated their beans and tortillas on a small hibachi on the balcony. And told ghost stories in the living room, spookily illuminated by a few candle stubs.

Those truly had been the best and the worst of times. Elisa had wanted something more for her future, for her own children. But her savings were rapidly dwindling, pushing her ever closer to that old life in the Los Angeles barrio.

Nothing she could do about her financial situation right now, she reflected as she tossed the damp towel onto the counter. There was Jay's will to consider, of course. Although if he had been involved in illegal activities, his estate could be held up for years. Even drained. Besides, he'd once mentioned that everything he had was tied up in his business.

She padded into the bedroom and pulled back the heavy spread. It was so hot, so muggy, she wanted to tear her clothes off and run into the raging surf. Then she recalled the furious battle she'd almost lost with the ocean the day before, and decided she could handle the heat one more night.

When she slid between the crisp, cool sheets, it occurred to her that there were still two people in this hotel that she hadn't considered.

Carey Howard, who owned those fishing boats and was Heather's *amour du jour*. When had they become so chummy? They'd known each other a while, Heather told Storm. If she was so interested in the pallid, mousy sportsman, why hadn't she ever invited him to the cabin, or even mentioned his name? On the other hand, maybe there was more to Carey than his mousy Milquetoast demeanor exposed. Carey could have instigated the relationship with Heather, instead of vice versa, as she had assumed. But what possible motive could he have for wanting to hurt Elisa?

What good were all these ridiculous hypotheses in the first place? The only thing that would help right now was a full, uninterrupted night's sleep.

Flipping onto her side, she slid her hand across the nightstand and picked up the sleeping pills Heather had brought. Elisa hadn't felt the need for one since her discharge. But tonight...tonight she would take all the help she could get.

She swallowed the pill and shoved the blue disk under the mattress. After turning down the wick to preserve fuel, she dropped her head on the pillow, wishing for an instantaneous blackout. The medication didn't work that way, of course, but she was getting desperate. But her mind simply wouldn't slow down and let her rest.

You're forgetting Storm, her subconscious chided. *What*

about the good doctor? Why is he so interested in your past? In fact, why is he so interested in you?

Try as she might to focus on these puzzling and vaguely disturbing aspects of the enigmatic F. Storm Delaney, Elisa's thoughts kept returning to the electric attraction that sizzled like a live wire when they were alone together. But, like that electrical current, they were either on or off. They either steamed the air with their barely containable desire, or they were facing off like punch-drunk boxers.

Except for this afternoon, when they'd talked, she reflected. In the parlor, and later, in the dining room, they'd had serious, meaningful conversations unfettered by antipathy or sensual appetite. Like friends.

She yawned and punched her pillow as the soothing medication began to work its magic. Friends. Her lips curved upward in a lazy, lusty smile. Close, *intimate* friends would be nice. Very nice.

Elisa was still smiling when sleep finally claimed her.

It felt as if she'd just dozed off when something— a sound, a disturbing noise—intruded. Bleary-eyed, she glanced at the luminous dial on the alarm clock. One-thirty! Damn this wind!

Flopping over, she dragged the other pillow over her head. Sleep, she wanted to return to peaceful sleep. But the meddlesome noise kept poking at her subconscious. Finally giving up, she threw the pillow aside and sat up. Listening.

It took a moment to identify exactly what had awakened her. At first, everything seemed the same. Room dark. Hotel silent. Wind blowing and—

That was it! The wind velocity had picked up considerably since she went to bed. Whistling and wailing, the gusts screamed through the brick building as if it were made of paper. Hurricane Jake was on the move again. Coming closer. Much closer.

She'd never heard or even imagined this kind of domination. As though a live, tormented being were screaming out its anguish in the empty night. She huddled against the headboard and yanked the blanket up around her neck. Shuddering ripples of pure fear undulated through her body, and crashed in her chest like the pounding surf.

Another horrendous gust whipped past, lashing the hotel with flying debris. She had badly underestimated the raw power of nature. This was so much worse than the earthquakes that rattled California. Earthquakes did their damage in minutes, even seconds, and then it was over. But this seemed to go on forever.

As her vision adjusted to the darkness, she frantically looked around, seeking a sign that the world was still in one piece. That wardrobe! Hadn't it just wobbled? What if it fell again?

Her head jerked toward the bathroom when something crashed to the floor.

The old hotel groaned and quivered beneath the storm's ferocity. Terrorized that the structure was breaking apart, Elisa grabbed for the kerosene lantern, knocking the box of matches to the floor in her haste. She had to be able to see! Otherwise, she'd never find her way to safety.

But there was no safe place. The world was coming to a brutal, horrific end.

Filled with a sudden fatalistic calm, she sank back and clutched the heavy lamp like a security blanket while she waited out her final moments on earth.

Like an evil trickster, the wind calmed a bit, giving her a moment's respite.

Creeeak! Elisa's eyes jolted open. She was startled to see her bedroom door slowly opening. A shadowy figure, either a ghost or someone in white clothing, stole into the room.

Elisa's heart leaped with hope. Storm! He'd said he'd come for her if they needed to move to the cellar. She tried to call his name, but her throat was so parched she couldn't speak. The figure turned and glided toward her bed.

Suddenly, the shadowy form loomed over her. It wasn't Storm.

This spectral body emanated malice and venom.

Terror flooded through her anew. The apparition leaned across her, and she could almost smell the evil. She licked her lips and tried to cry out. Just as a pillow descended over her face.

Gathering her wits, she tried valiantly to fight, but she was still weak from her long hospital stay. She reached out, but her grasping fingers found nothing but tangled sheets and clothing.

Her attacker was strong, vicious, and filled with purpose. The pillow pressed tightly against her nose and mouth, slowly but unquestionably closing off her vital oxygen.

A floating, desperate darkness surrounded her, and Elisa knew her life was fading.

She couldn't give up! The skinny Latina urchin from the poverty-torn streets of L.A. had fought too hard. For food, for education, for her art, and for her own identity. To have survived all that, only to surrender her life to an unknown assassin, was unthinkable.

If she died, so be it. But she would not give up.

With the ferocity of a nursing she-wolf, Elisa railed out at her enemy. Using her powerful dancer's legs, she kicked and bucked, until she heard her opponent gasp. Elisa jerked her head sideways, dislodging the smothering pillow. She gulped in life-giving air.

Her assailant screamed in fury and redoubled the attack.

She twisted to avoid the grasping hands, and felt the heavy kerosene lantern bruising her side. Kicking wildly in an effort to distract the killer, she thrust her hands beneath the blanket in a frantic search for the improbable weapon.

Her fingers finally found purchase on the brass bottom, and she raised it above her head like a bludgeon. "Get away! Don't make me hurt you."

Her attacker growled and leaped toward her.

Elisa swung the lantern with all her might.

It missed its mark, whizzing through empty space.

The killer's hands found her throat. And squeezed.

She swung again. The tinkle of broken glass showering the bed told her she'd made contact. But her strength was ebbing, and the savage fingers were closing ever tighter around her throat.

Knowing she might not get another chance, she gritted her teeth and grasped the exposed metal wick holder. Jagged shards of glass sliced her hand as she swung the heavy brass base.

It crashed against her attacker's head with a sickening thud.

As if this were a slow-motion scene in a violent movie, she felt the fingers that had been clutching her neck sluggishly releasing their hold. The would-be killer fell backward, smacking against the nightstand. Then sagged to the floor, landing in a silent, unmoving heap.

It was over.

But she didn't feel triumphant or brave. Waves of terror washed over her, and she began to tremble. She leaned against the headboard and shook until she felt her limbs would surely separate from her body and hurl across the room.

She should do something—summon help. Only Hurricane Jake could have lifted her from her bed. When the violent quivering finally began to subside, she tested her voice. Hoarse and raspy, but functional.

"Help!" she called out, but knew the puny sound would never carry through the clamorous wind.

She licked her lips and gulped deeply, filling her lungs with air and, she prayed, volume.

Then she screamed at the top of her lungs.

Chapter Eleven

Storm burst through the partially open bedroom door. "Elisa! Are you all right? My God, what's happened?"

"I—I'm okay. I think."

The weak, subdued voice murmuring from the direction of her bed told him otherwise. Cursing the downed power lines that robbed him of even minimal light, he inched toward her voice with outstretched arms flailing for hidden obstacles. When his bare toe smacked solidly against the footboard, he bit off the obscenity hovering on his lips and felt his way along the mattress.

"Storm? Is that really you?"

A huge fist of apprehension punched him in the stomach. He couldn't think of a single rational explanation for her peculiar question. "Yeah, it's me. Almost there."

His left foot nudged a bundle of clothing near the nightstand. Patting the mattress until he found an empty space, he lowered his hip on the bed. "Hey, Princess, what's up? Have a bad dream, or is old Jake giving you the willies?"

She breathed heavily, almost panting. A long moment passed. Then two. Finally, she said in a confused tone, "N-no dream. Not the hurricane. Well, yes, but… Oh, my God, Storm, it was horrible! Is—is he…still here?"

Convinced now that she *had* suffered a nightmare and was still having a difficult time breaking its spell, he leaned over and caressed her cheek. Her skin was cold, clammy, even though the hotel was uncomfortably warm and humid. His hand trailed upward, touching the silken strands at her temple. Her hair was so damp, he normally would have assumed she'd just stepped out of the shower. Except that with the generator turned off for the night there was no running water.

The apprehension heightened to dread. Something was terribly wrong.

Storm groped for the lantern on her nightstand. His hand skimmed across the wooden surface, but encountered only empty space. "'Leese, where's your lantern?"

She gasped and whimpered, pulling away from him.

Before he had time to absorb her unexpected reaction, the chaotic jumble of several voices resonated down the hall. Storm twisted around just as Hank stepped through the doorway, a Coleman lantern swinging from his upraised hand.

The older man stepped farther into the room, exposing the small band of onlookers behind his back. "What in thunderation is going on up here?"

Storm shook his head. "Don't know. Bring that lamp over here, would you?"

Hank turned to his entourage, his Southern accent more pronounced than usual. "Y'all stay right here till I figure out what's goin' on."

From the corner of his eye, Storm noted Carey Howard, David Welton and Betty and Mark Bowman. Now silent, they all looked fearfully around the deeply shadowed room, as if expecting Freddy Krueger to leap out of a corner.

Still holding the light high above his head, Hank slowly made his way past bedclothes and strewn pillows. He was almost abreast of Storm when the kerosene lantern wobbled crazily. "Oh, my heavens," he breathed, almost reverently. "What happened in here?"

That feeling of dread redoubled in Storm's gut as his gaze followed the lantern's illumination. His blood pumped violently through his veins when he finally saw what had demanded Hank's attention.

Only inches from Storm's left foot, Heather's inert body lay in a crumpled heap, in a widening scarlet puddle.

Leaping from the bed, he demanded, "Hank! Bring that light here, but watch your step! There's blood everywhere."

Hank took a few nimble steps forward before Storm grabbed the lamp and set it on the bedside table, automatically turning up the wick. Kneeling beside Heather's blanched face, he frantically probed her throat in search of her pulse. "Carey! Run to my room and get my medical bag off the dresser. Hurry!"

While he waited for his stethoscope and first aid supplies, Storm continued to move his fingers, searching for some sign of life. But there was no reassuring throb of pulse.

"Heather! Heather, can you hear me?" he shouted as he ripped open her black blouse and lowered his ear to her chest. *Come on, let's hear you beat. Beat, damn you!*

He swung his left leg over her body. Straddling her waist, he crossed his hands over her heart and began CPR. Without an electrocardiograph or stethoscope, there was no way to tell if he was having any success. Storm kept pumping.

Elisa leaned over the edge of the bed and cried aloud. "Oh, no! Not Heather! No, no. It can't be true. Not Heather, she's my friend." She broke off as a deep, shuddering sob ripped loose from deep inside. Still shaking her head, she whispered, "Oh, God, Storm, is she dead? Please say she isn't dead."

He couldn't take the time or breath from his resuscitation efforts to reassure her. Besides, he was fast coming to the conclusion that he'd arrived too late to help the injured redhead.

After a moment, Elisa rolled back to the middle of the bed, quietly weeping.

Carey Howard rushed through the doorway, stopping

suddenly when his eyes took in the gruesome sight. "Jeez, Doc, that—that's Heather!"

Nodding mutely, Storm nodded toward the bare space between his right leg and the bed. "Set it down."

Carey's hands were trembling as he dropped the medical bag with a thump.

Storm glanced up. "You know CPR?"

Carey shook his head, his pale blue eyes nearly invisible against his pasty complexion.

Damn! Someone had to fill in so he could get out his instruments and examine Heather more thoroughly. "Anybody?" Storm shouted.

"I do." David Welton stepped around Bowman and approached Heather's motionless body. "What can I do to help?"

"Get down here and take over."

Without hesitation, the normally dapper attorney dropped to his knees in the pool of blood. He flexed his shoulders, took a breath and crossed his hands. "Ready."

"All right. On four. I'll count."

His face a grim mask, the lawyer nodded.

"One. Two. Three."

At four, David slid his hands smoothly into position. Storm shifted his body into the tiny space beside the bed. Without missing a beat, the attorney took his place over Heather.

Relieved to find the other man so competent, Storm snapped open his bag. "Hank, you guys get over here and pull this bed away from me. I need room to maneuver."

When they'd moved the bed, with Elisa still huddled in the middle, Storm barked out orders. "Carey, go tell Miriam I need another sheet. Bowman, go on the other side of the bed and help Elisa. Get her out of here. Hank, I don't know what good it will do, but see if you can raise any emergency-service people on the shortwave."

All three hustled to perform their assigned tasks, leaving Storm and David alone with the motionless woman.

They worked frantically for the next forty minutes, to no avail. They were too late. Heather's death had been almost instantaneous. She'd suffered two heavy blows to her head. The first, just above her forehead, hadn't broken the skin and didn't look severe enough to have been fatal.

The second blow, however, had sliced a three-inch gash behind her right ear. A deep cranial groove beneath the injury strongly suggested that Heather had sustained a skull fracture, and was, in his opinion, the probable cause of her death.

Storm placed a hand on David's shoulder. They had alternated positions several times for the strenuous chore of administering CPR. Rivulets of sweat ran down David's face as he continued the frantic pumping. "David. You can stop now. I'm calling it."

The attorney shook his head and continued. "No, let me keep trying."

Storm gently disengaged his hands. "It's over. We've done all that was humanly possible."

David closed his eyes and wiped his forehead with the back of his hand. Rising from the dead woman's body, he avoided looking at her face. "She was only twenty-four. And too beautiful for her own good. What a waste."

Storm couldn't argue. Besides, David seemed to need to talk. "Did you know her well?"

"Not really." His face scrunched in a peculiar grimace. "I just can't help wondering, though, if her death wasn't somehow related to Jay Morrow's."

Storm's left eyebrow arched in amazement. "In what way?"

When David didn't respond, Storm draped a blanket over Heather and collected his bag. Both men rose to their feet in an unspoken accord. "What possible connection could tie their deaths together?"

David whispered as if he were in a cathedral. "What odds would you give that a man *and* his confidential secretary would both meet a violent death within a two-month period?''

"Coincidence, that's all," Storm averred.

"How can you say that, when we don't even know what happened yet?" Emerging from the shock of unexpected death, David slipped easily into his courtroom demeanor.

Not caring for the feeling of being cross-examined, Storm moved the lantern until its circle of light shone on the corner of Elisa's bedside table. "See that, where a chunk of wood is missing?"

David peered closely. "Yeah. So?"

Reaching into his bathrobe pocket, Storm held a thick splinter of wood up to the light. "I took this from the wound behind Heather's ear. The way I see it, she fell and smashed her head against that corner. I'd have to call it a clear case of accidental death. Wouldn't you agree, Counselor?"

David's gaze darted from the damaged corner to the sliver of wood. He shrugged. "Maybe. I hope you're right, Doctor. But there are still a lot of unanswered questions."

"Such as?"

"That's the inside corner of the nightstand, closest to the bed. It would be pretty difficult to fall from a standing position beside the bed and not hit the opposite corner. It would make more sense if Heather had been *on* the bed when she fell."

Storm considered his reconstruction. "More likely, I agree. But maybe she tried to break her fall or something. That inside corner is still very possible."

"I take your point."

"Was that your only concern?"

"No, I have several others." David momentarily shut his eyes and pinched the bridge of his nose. "Sorry, damnable headache. Anyway, granting that Heather could have tripped and cracked her head on that corner doesn't explain why she was in Elisa's room in the first place. Especially in the middle of the night."

"I'm sure there's an explanation," Storm answered, with more confidence than he felt. The lawyer had posed some significant and disturbing questions. Storm hoped Elisa held all the right answers.

IT SEEMED LIKE FOREVER before Storm and David came out of the bedroom. Despite the extremely dim lighting in the corridor, Elisa could still read their grim expressions well enough to understand the final outcome: Heather was dead.

Storm stepped forward and clasped her shoulders. "I'm so sorry, but there was nothing we could do."

Elisa gasped and drooped against his chest. Her exclamation wasn't one of shock, but of horror. Her mind was spinning so madly, she felt as if she were on a runaway centrifuge at the carnival. But just as the ride kept its passengers pinned against the wall, her thoughts whirled in dizzying concentric circles but held tightly to a single realization: Tonight, she'd killed her best friend.

Or at least the woman she'd *thought* was a true and loyal friend. But that had been before Heather stole into her bedroom and tried to smother her with her own pillow.

As the others gathered around, asking a dozen simultaneous questions, she raised her face from Storm's chest. Moving away from his comforting nearness, she asked in a quaking voice, "Wh-what happens now?"

"I need you to tell me exactly what happened, because I'll probably have to sign off on the death certificate."

A sudden hush fell over the small crowd as they edged in closer to hear her explanation.

How did she begin? Would they even believe her? She hardly believed it herself. She decided to skim over the odious truth until she could gauge their reaction. Licking her parched lips, she swallowed deeply. "I—I must have killed... I mean, she must've fell—" *No!* Her conscience censured her. *Heather didn't accidentally fall. You caused her death when you smashed in her skull.*

Carey Howard pushed past Miriam and stood inches

from Elisa's toes. His thin chest was heaving, and his pale blue eyes were alight with fury. "Which is it, Elisa? Did she fall or did you kill her? We want to hear the truth."

Storm stepped between them. "If you take that tone again, I promise the only thing you'll hear is the sound of my fist breaking your jaw. Got it?"

Carey didn't answer immediately, but turned and faced the others. "Doesn't this sound like a cover-up? We all know the oh-so-convenient doctor has the hots for Elisa. How can we trust either of them?"

Storm grabbed him by the shoulder, his fist cocked and ready to fire. "No, Storm!" Elisa tugged on his sleeve. "He's just upset. Let him be."

With a grudging snarl, Storm released the boatman.

Elisa thought her frayed nerves would surely snap if an argument or a brawl erupted. Besides, Storm was only trying to protect her, and she didn't need or deserve his defense. This was her responsibility, and she would face up to it and answer their questions.

Holding up her hand, she said, "I'll answer your questions if I can, but first, I need something to drink. Can't we go downstairs and discuss this like civilized people?"

Miriam rushed forward and draped her arm around Elisa's shoulders. "Good idea, honey. How about a nice cup of hot tea?"

"Sounds heavenly." She was doing her best to appear normal, to hold herself together. She was so weary of being weak and vulnerable. But Heather's death had devastated her, and she couldn't seem to fight her way out of shock.

"Good. Hank, go down to the kitchen and light some candles. Then get that camp stove fired up and put the kettle on."

His angular face looked even thinner than she remembered, and Elisa could have sworn new creases had etched his forehead since dinner. Her fault. Everything seemed to be her fault. Typhoid Mary had nothing on Elisa Montoya.

While Hank charged down the stairs eager to do his

wife's bidding, Miriam, who Elisa thought would have made a great drill sergeant, barked out more orders. "Mr. Welton, please escort these people down to the kitchen. Betty, would you go help that crazy old man of mine? He'll never find the kettle, let alone the tea bags and mugs."

"Sure," Betty breathed, and darted down the stairs.

She looked anxious to escape, and Elisa couldn't blame her. If that hurricane wasn't trying to level the hotel, she'd run away, too.

Miriam turned her attention to Carey and Mark. "I can't believe you two are still standing around gawking. Mr. Howard, why don't you go help Hank gather candles? Mark, fetch the shortwave out of the parlor and take it to the kitchen. We need to try to raise the authorities and report that girl's death."

After a last resentful glare at Elisa, Carey thudded down the steps, with Mark right behind him.

Miriam sighed deeply. "Well, thank the Lord that lot's gone. Bunch of ghouls. Oh, you poor child—standing here trembling in your little nightshirt. Storm, run downstairs to my bedroom and fetch another bathrobe out of my closet."

"No need," Storm uttered as he peeled off his own robe. Standing behind Elisa, he held it open for her to stuff her arms into the voluminous sleeves.

She snuggled into the terry-cloth robe, luxuriating in the residual warmth and intoxicating scent of his body. For the barest moment, the night's ghastly events faded into the background.

"Ahem." Miriam cleared her throat.

Plucked from her momentary sensory haven, Elisa lifted her eyes. Miriam's gaze was darting from the ceiling to the floor and back again as she scrupulously avoided looking at Storm. Elisa's pulse jumped as she wondered exactly what he'd been wearing beneath his bathrobe. Or not wearing, as the case might be.

But, like the older woman, she kept her head rigidly facing away from him. "Storm, maybe you should slip on some clothes before we go downstairs to meet the others."

"Absolutely not!" Miriam blurted. "I mean, of course he should get dressed, but I thought you two might want to wait a bit before coming down. Give the others time to get over their shock. Calm down a little."

"Good idea," he replied softly over Elisa's shoulder.

"Okay, I'm going downstairs and whip that bunch into shape." Miriam started to take Elisa's hands in hers, but stopped abruptly. "Honey, what on earth happened to your hand?"

Glancing at her open palm, Elisa was surprised to see that it was covered with blood. "Probably from Heather," she whispered.

"No, blood's still oozing out. You've cut yourself."

He stepped in front of her. "Let me see that."

After a cursory examination, he looked up. "You're right, Miriam, there are several cuts here. I'll take her to my room and get it cleaned up."

"You do that," Miriam said, and headed for the stairs. Her retreating footsteps were so quick and sharp, they sounded like gunfire.

"Now what do you suppose got into her?" Storm asked as he bent over to retrieve his medical bag from the floor.

"I can't imagine," Elisa lied, as she studied his tight backside, covered by close-fitting silk boxers.

He straightened up and took her elbow. "Let's look at that hand, and then you can tell me exactly what happened in your room."

Like a deflating balloon, Elisa's brief respite from the night's horror leaked away, plunging her once again into the black nothingness of despair.

STORM FINISHED wrapping her hand. "There were a lot of tiny glass slivers in several shallow cuts, but, fortunately, none of them looked serious. When you get back to the mainland, though, you might want to have your own doctor look at it—just in case.''

He'd taken a moment to slip on a faded gray sweat suit before he started cleaning her wounds. Although she'd found his former attire rather more...interesting, she was gratified by his sensitivity to the gravity of the situation.

He dumped the towels, along with the instruments he'd used, into a basin and carried it to the bathroom. When he returned, Elisa noted that he looked weary to the point of exhaustion. She could certainly relate to that. She was so tired she wanted to crawl under the covers and not come out until spring.

Unfortunately, her vengeful mind wouldn't stop spinning long enough for her to grab even a moment's rest.

Storm flopped onto his stomach beside her. He pressed his elbows into the mattress, then propped his chin on his upraised hands.

''So, you ready to talk about it?''

She had been dreading that question since they first entered his room. While she didn't fully understand her emotional response to Storm, she instinctively knew she would be deeply hurt if he thought badly of her. Or judged her too harshly.

She also knew the longer she put off talking about Heather, the more difficult it would be. Girding her heart against the condemnation she knew was coming, she told him the entire story.

When she finished, Storm stared at her, his dark brows furrowed in bewilderment. ''I must have missed something. You're saying that Heather Gellis, your roommate and supposed buddy, snuck into your room and tried to murder you?''

''I know it sounds unbelievable, but it's true!'' Elisa felt the hot scalding of tears pooling in her eyes. He *didn't* believe her! The shaft of pain thrusting through her heart was more excruciating than she'd imagined. Yet how could she expect Storm, or anyone else, for that matter, to believe her story, when she could hardly accept it herself?

He shoved his hands into his already mussed hair and rubbed his scalp in agitation. Sucking in his breath, he exhaled slowly. "Okay, so Heather tiptoed into your room, grabbed the pillow off your bed and tried to smother you. Right so far?"

Her teeth clamped tightly on her lower lip, she nodded.

"Then you fought?"

"Yes."

"And you managed to bonk her with the kerosene lamp from your nightstand?"

She nodded again, her black hair falling over her eyes. She pushed it off her face and stared into his intense gaze, urging him to believe her, to trust her. She held up her bandaged hand. "I remember the glass chimney broke. That must have been when I cut up my hand."

"Yeah, probably. So when Heather fell off the bed...?"

"She didn't exactly fall. The force of the blow seemed to knock her over. I mean, she tipped over onto her back and kind of slowly rolled off the bed. Her head hit the floor with a terrible crack. And then...and then she didn't move again."

Storm paced across the room, as if lost in thought. He leaned against the window frame and stared, unseeing, at the plywood sheet. The board popped and pulsated as it fought valiantly against the hurricane's fury.

Sitting on the edge of Storm's bed, Elisa closed her eyes and hung her head. Even if he refused to believe her, *she* knew Heather had attempted to suffocate her. Although Elisa had acted in self-defense, and knew that she'd truly had no other options, she couldn't dispel the sense of horror and guilt gnawing at her insides. She'd taken a human life—there was no denying that simple, ugly fact.

As if in an instant replay, her mind reran the film. Heather standing over her bed like the grim reaper, watching her intently. Then the slow movement as she reached over Elisa's motionless body to seize the other pillow. And then that awful choking feeling when she couldn't breathe! The film continued to roll. Now she was fighting back, showing a strength and will to live that she hadn't known she possessed. The film clip ended, and another image took its place: Heather's cold, lifeless body lying in her own blood, so like Jay's crumpled body, on the sidewalk far below his office window.

Elisa's eyelids flew open. But she...she hadn't ever seen Jay's body, so how could she know how he'd looked? She'd walked into his office after his death, but she'd never gone to the window. Never seen his broken and twisted corpse. Had she?

The flashing strobe deep in her brain chattered excitedly as fragments of her broken memory fit together like puzzle pieces, only to separate an instant later. This time, however, she retained a single distinct remembrance.

She *had* looked out Jay's window that night. The image of his broken body was too clear, too explicit.

But she surely had seen something else. Something so damning that Heather had believed she had to kill Elisa to ensure that her memory never returned.

Her feminine antennae on full alert, she somehow knew when Storm left the window. Appearing in front of her like a vision, he touched her chin. "You've had a hell of a night, Princess. Wish I could tell you it's over, but you still have to face the interrogation downstairs. Feel up to it?"

"No. But then, I don't think I'll ever feel up to anything again."

"Sure you will," he said softly. "Now let's go slay the dragons."

He kept a supportive arm around her waist while they made their way through the hotel and into the kitchen. Ignoring the empty chairs at the table, where the others were seated, she stopped just inside the doorway and leaned against a cupboard.

Storm hitched a hip on the countertop beside her. While

she was grateful for his bracing presence, she suddenly realized he'd never actually said whether he accepted her
explanation of Heather's death.

"Hi, sweetie, you feelin' better?" Miriam handed Elisa
a mug of steaming herbal tea. "Don't you two want to sit
down with the rest of us?"

"We're fine here," Storm said, as if he understood Elisa's need to keep a distance between herself and the others.

She didn't speak while she sipped the soothing tea. When
her mug was empty, she set it on the tile counter behind
her. Storm gave her arm a reassuring pat, and she turned
to the expectant group sitting around the table. Not knowing how to start, she simply plunged in.

"I can't offer a reason why, but Heather snuck into my
room around one-thirty."

She could see Carey bristling, eager to defend Heather's
reputation. Elisa rushed on with her explanation before he
could interrupt and sidetrack the others. "She, uh, took a
pillow from my bed and tried to smother me—"

"Now wait just a damn minute!" Carey leaped to his
feet, knocking his chair to the floor.

David reached up and snatched his wrist. "Sit down and
shut up."

Carey stared at Elisa for a long, hate-filled moment before he righted his chair and dropped onto it.

Trying her best to appear calm and rational, she eased
her hands behind her back and clutched the countertop for
support. She didn't dare look at Storm. If he trusted her,
believed in her, he would have told her so upstairs. But to
actually see the skepticism that she knew must be reflected
in his eyes would be too crushing to bear.

"Go on, Elisa," Storm urged softly, from the position
he'd taken right beside her. Her heart swelled at his show
of support.

Drawing strength from his gentle, blameless tone, she
continued. "There's not much more to tell. I, uh, somehow
grabbed the lantern on my nightstand and—"

This time it was David Welton who rose. "Stop!"

"What? What's wrong?"

He stalked across the room and stood in front of her, his feet wide apart, fists jammed against his hips. His voice, when he spoke again, was tense and low-pitched. "For your own protection, do not say another word."

"I don't understand."

Casting a sharp glance at Storm, he dropped his voice to a near whisper, as if to prevent being overheard. "This is going to be a criminal matter, Elisa. You're distraught and possibly suffering from shock. If you say anything that might be misconstrued by someone in this room, you will have to account for it later. Maybe in a courtroom." His grave voice told her he was offering a dire warning.

She turned to Storm to ask for his input. David put his hand against the side of her head, forcing her to face him. "Dr. Delaney is certainly who you should turn to for a medical problem, Elisa. But this is going to be a serious matter for the law to decide. And right now, I'm the only person who can give you legal advice. I'm urging you, begging you, not to say another word until you can consult with your own lawyer. Preferably a criminal lawyer."

Elisa blanched at the word *criminal*, but at least now she understood the jeopardy she was facing. It was possible that she might be charged in Heather's death. Remembering Carey's cold, scornful hostility, she was certain he, at least, would push the authorities for her arrest.

She still felt the high-priced attorney had an ulterior motive for coming to the island, but right now, she was convinced that she should heed his advice.

As if reading her thoughts, Storm flicked on his flashlight and said, "He's right. Let's go upstairs."

Buoyed by his apparent support, she gave Miriam what she hoped was a smile but felt more like a grimace. "Thanks for the tea." Murmuring a vague good-night to the others, she followed Storm through the swinging door and into the dining room.

Once they were alone, Elisa waited for him to comment. She needed his verbal support, as well as his physical presence at her side. She needed him to tell her not to worry, that everything would work out. That he'd be in her corner. But he didn't say a word as their footsteps echoed through the near-deserted hotel.

She had to hold his robe up high to keep from tripping on the staircase. She stumbled twice, as Storm's continued silence shattered her composure. Why didn't he say something, anything, that would express his faith in her?

When they reached the top of the staircase, she automatically headed for her own room.

"Wait!" Storm called. "You don't want to go back in there."

"Oh!" She stopped cold, and slowly turned on her heels to face him. His face was invisible behind the shining flashlight. "I—I almost forgot for a minute. I guess I should've asked Miriam for another room."

She could feel him slowly advancing toward her. That almost palpable sizzle of electricity whipped through the atmosphere, as his body radiated little sparks of lightning that bit her flesh with a gentle nip. When he was so close that she could smell his heady, masculine scent, he murmured, "No. I'd rest better if you stayed in my room."

Did that mean he was worried about her, wanted her company, or feared she would try to escape? His words and tone gave nothing away, and once again she felt the crush of despair pressing against her spine. Still, the only alternative to his suggestion was to venture back downstairs and face those curious faces again.

Silently acquiescing, she slowly passed him on the way to his bedroom.

Chapter Twelve

The moment her cheek nestled into Storm's pillow, Elisa wasted no time dropping into slumber. Although she slept straight through the pitifully few hours before morning, she remained eerily connected to her consciousness. As if she couldn't trust what might happen if she slept too soundly. She had a vague awareness of the bedroom door opening and shutting twice, yet she felt no alarm. Still later, she heard the sheets whisper when Storm slid into the far side of the bed, taking care not to touch or disturb her.

Yet the next morning, when the tide of wakefulness slowly flowed over her, she was surprised to find herself nestled in his arms. On his half of the bed. She turned her head to watch him sleep, and wondered anew about this complex and compelling man. That she was incredibly drawn to him on a physical level was a given. An immutable law of natural chemistry that couldn't be denied. She was human, after all. Given to the same instinctive urges that had plagued every living person since Eve developed that lust for Adam.

More disturbing was the way he got under her skin, into her very soul. Why had his opinion been so important to her last night? Why did she still crave his endorsement now? She didn't want the answer that she feared she might find if she searched her heart. She was willing to accept that, for this short period of her life, Storm Delaney was as important to her as her own lifeblood. His unflagging support in front of the others had been a life preserver, saving her from drowning beneath their skepticism. Saving her from doubting herself.

She watched him a few seconds longer. Her lips turned upward when his light snoring took on added volume. Then eased again when he wrinkled his nose.

She studied the lines and planes, noting a slight crease here, a faint line there. While she doubted he'd make it as a runway model—his face was too rugged, too unique— she preferred his craggy good looks to the life-size Ken dolls Hollywood kept churning out. This face belonged to a man who was dependable, competent, thoughtful and mature. It was also a face that had endured hardship, even tragedy. But it was in his eyes, those eloquent deep green eyes, that she'd seen his heartache and isolation.

Her fingertip hovered over his mouth—broad, firm, and decidedly masculine, with that tiny scar on his upper lip. Her finger lightly traced the outline of his mouth until he stirred in his sleep.

Not wanting to disturb him, she eased away from the warmth of his encircling arm and slipped into the bathroom. Automatically flicking the light switch, she was pleasantly surprised to discover that the generator was running. If there was light, maybe there would be a trickle of hot water left.

Stripping off Storm's oversize robe, she turned to hang it behind the door and was startled to find her own dangling on the brass hook. Her cosmetic bag and purse were on the marble counter. Another demonstration of his consideration. Why didn't she ever stumble on wonderful men like him in the real world? And why did he continue to waste his obvious skill in this tiny community?

She sighed as she twisted her hair into a knot and pinned it atop her head. Wasn't that always her luck? Lifetime city dweller Elisa finally discovers a sexy, exciting, mature and talented man, and, of course, he's hell-bent on living like a hermit on a secluded island.

SHE HAD JUST COMPLETED her morning's ablutions when she heard a frantic knock at the bedroom door. "No..." she moaned. "What now?" She fought a frantic urge to lock herself in the bathroom; she just couldn't handle any more trauma.

Her hand froze on the doorknob when she heard Storm moving about. A moment later, the murmur of excited voices drifted through the closed door. She couldn't make out actual words, only the animated tone.

Then Miriam Danziger's booming voice joined the others, and Elisa pressed her face against the door. This had to be a never-ending nightmare. But how much more bad news could any of them absorb?

After a few moments, the voices disappeared and she eased open the door.

Storm was facing the bureau, clad only in his gray sweats. Under different circumstances, Elisa knew, she would have stolen a few seconds' pleasure admiring his bronzed back and defined musculature. This morning, however, she tightened her sash around her waist and stepped into the room. "I thought I heard Western Union at the door. What's today's crisis?"

He turned and grinned. "Have you completely lost your sense of smell, or are you one of those tofu eaters that don't drink coffee?"

"No on both accounts." She strolled toward the dresser. "But I thought I might be hallucinating. Is that coffee I smell? Real perked coffee?"

In response, he held up a steaming mug. "Take cream or sugar?"

"Both, please."

He curled his upper lip in an exaggerated grimace. "And here I had you pegged as a purist."

She accepted the cup, tasted it and added another teaspoon of sugar. "No, a perfectionist. Now that's perfect."

"Perfectly awful." He carried his own mug back to the bed. Using the headboard for a backrest, he stretched out and crossed his legs at the ankle. "How'd you sleep?"

"Fine. But you're stalling." She settled into the easy chair in the corner across from the bed. "What grim news of disaster and peril was just delivered to our door?"

"Actually, our coffee was just delivered. I may have to bump off Hank and marry that woman." His teasing words fell flat, as they both suddenly remembered Heather.

"Guess that was kind of insensitive," Storm said.

She shook her head in response, and realized her hair was still knotted on the top of her head in a close facsimile of an old lady's bun. Setting her cup on the floor, she unpinned her hair and fluffed it around her shoulders.

Storm whistled appreciatively.

Embarrassed by his obvious appreciation, she growled, "Now *that* was insensitive. If you're not careful, I may have to report you to NOW."

He held up his hands in mock surrender. "Not to the dreaded feminist group! Oh, please, don't throw me in that briar patch. They might revoke my membership."

Elisa groaned aloud. It made a certain perverse sense that Storm would be an active supporter of the National Organization for Women, when she herself had never gotten around to joining. Giving up on that empty threat, she thought a change of subject might be in order.

"So, are you going to tell me what's up, or do I have to ask Carey Howard? I'm sure he'd be delighted to do what he can to really muck up my day."

He sat up and swung his legs over the edge of the bed. "The Bowmans stopped by with some good news and bad."

Elisa's pessimistic imagination swept into overdrive. The good news would be that they were still alive; the bad was that Hurricane Jake was heading right toward them.

"I'll give you the good news first."

She nodded. "Thanks. I appreciate your softening the blow."

Storm pointed to the boarded up window. "Listen."

Elisa perked her ears, but didn't notice anything unusual. She shrugged.

"What do you hear?"

"Nothing."

"That's the good news. Jake swept up the coastline during the night, but so far hasn't actually touched land."

Her head jerked up. "You mean it's over? The hurricane didn't hit us?"

"The eye didn't come ashore, but we took a lot of abuse from the storm's fringes. Hank and David are ripping the boards off the windows right now. Another hour or so and we can venture out to see how much damage the island sustained."

A warm gush of sheer relief washed through her body. But before she could truly savor the news, she remembered the other half and cautiously asked, "What's the bad news?"

"We still don't have any communication linkage with the outside world, and it'll be at least two more days before help arrives from the mainland."

Elisa jumped up and spread her arms like a triumphant eagle. "That's it? That's the bad news? Aw-riiight!"

She strode across the short space between them with every intention of giving Storm a high five. But things got muddled somehow. He rose to his feet just as she reached the bed. His arms were also spread, and the next thing she knew, they were ensnared in an embrace that could have loosely been described as a bear hug. If the bears were in mating season.

The next thing she knew, their bodies were pressed together and Storm's hands were tangled in her hair. And he was kissing her, evoking a crazy, light-headed passion that left her weak and trembling.

Tiny explosions of light, like holiday sparklers, fired off behind her eyes as his soft mouth savored hers. When she could no longer stand the torment, she pulled away, locking her hands behind his neck. "What a way to celebrate, Doc. I prefer your way to a magnum of Dom Perignon any day."

He winked and kissed her lightly on one of her eyelids. "We aim to please."

Elisa dropped her head to his shoulder, nuzzling against his neck. "I suppose we should go help the others dig out."

"I suppose," he replied, with more than a tinge of disappointment in his tone.

Releasing his hold, he stepped away.

She understood. If that kiss had lasted one more instant, she would have pushed him down on the bed and had her way with him. Even now, his nearness was almost too much to bear. Her agitated hormones were flitting through her erogenous zones like angry bees whose hive had just been plundered.

She took two steps in the opposite direction. "Let me find some clothes, and we'll go help."

"Over there." He hooked a thumb toward a space by the dresser, where her suitcase waited.

"You brought my clothes! Oh, thanks, Storm, that was so sweet." Fresh underwear, she thought. Hallelujah.

"Thought it was damned noble, myself," he grumbled. The obvious implication being that he'd prefer her unclothed.

Dragging out the suitcase, she poked around until she found a clean pair of shorts and T-shirt. He'd even brought her favorite tennies. "Be right back," she said, darting into the bathroom.

The brief time it took to slip off her robe, nightshirt and undies and reclothe herself was a welcome respite from Storm's powerful allure.

When she reentered the bedroom, he had taken the easy chair and was staring intently into space. He didn't move or acknowledge her return.

"Hello? Earth to Storm. Anybody in there?"

His head turned abruptly. "What? Oh, sorry, I was thinking."

A flip retort sprang to her lips, but she bit it back when she saw his somber expression. "Is something wrong?"

"Not really," he frowned. "But I wanted to talk to you for a minute."

"Okay." Elisa perched on the edge of the bed. "Sounds serious."

After a long pause, he cocked his head and stared deeply into her eyes. "First of all, I want to apologize for last night."

"Apologize! But you—"

He held up his hand, palm turned toward her. "No, let me finish. Last night, when you told me what happened, you were waiting for me to give you some feedback. Tell you that I understood that you'd acted in self-defense, that you bore absolutely no fault for Heather's death. And I didn't."

Elisa held her breath. This was when he was going to tell her that, drawn to each other though they were, he didn't believe her story. That he thought she was a murderer.

"I apologize for that," he continued. "I *did* believe what you said, from the very first word. I kept questioning you because it was Heather's sudden attack that I couldn't get a grip on. From what you've told me, she's been with you since the day you were released from the hospital, is that right?"

Elisa nodded, too taken aback by his candor to speak.

"So if she wanted to kill you, why didn't she try before now? Why wait until she's sealed up in a hotel with a half-dozen other people? You were alone in that cabin for several weeks—why didn't she try then?"

Perplexed, she raised and lowered her shoulders in a shrug. "I still can't figure out why she wanted to hurt me in the first place!"

"Maybe we can work that out. I'd feel better on your account if we were able to establish Heather's motive before the authorities arrive. It would lend a great deal of credibility to your claim."

Again, she could do nothing more than shrug. How could she help determine Heather's motive, when she was clueless?

Storm leaned back in the chair and drummed the arm with his fingers. "And you're sure you've told me all you recall about the night Jay Morrow died?"

"Yes. Except for one tiny thing."

He sat back up, suddenly intense. "What?"

"Nothing that would help establish Heather's motive, because I didn't remember it until after she...she died. When I saw her on the floor, I was struck with the similarity between the way she was lying and the way Jay looked on the sidewalk. Suddenly I knew, really *knew*, that I'd seen his body that night."

"Are you certain it was a true recollection and not just your imagination?"

"I'm positive. I can see every tiny detail, even down to the fact that he'd...he'd lost one shoe in the fall."

Steepling his fingers beneath his chin, Storm continued to watch her face. "I see. It's my belief that if one clear memory resurfaced, there's a good chance you can regain complete recall. If you'd seen something suspicious that night, something to do with Heather, surely that would give her ample reason to act first."

Elisa tossed her head, dismissing his theory. "But Heather left quite a while before I went into Jay's office. Besides, what could possibly explain her being involved in his death?"

"I don't know. But suppose for just a moment that Jay was already dead before you even arrived. You told me he was on the phone for a very long time before you decided to interrupt. How did you know he was still talking?"

A cold chill swept through her body, a portent of even

more horror to come. Storm had posed a suggestive and abhorrent premise. If Jay had died *before* Elisa's arrival, Heather's involvement was ensured. Licking her suddenly dry lips, she whispered, "The red light was blinking on Heather's console. Both when I came into the reception area and when I barged into his private office."

"Yet Jay obviously wasn't still talking on the second occasion."

"No, of course not."

He eased off the chair and knelt before her. "It all works out, 'Leese—Heather must have played some part in his death."

Elisa glared at him, refusing to believe his theory. "There's no way she could have pitched him out the window! And no one else was there."

"How do you know?" he asked. "You don't remember anything past opening the door. So how can you be so certain that you didn't see anyone else that night?"

She raised her hands and covered her face, as if she could prevent the appalling words from soaking into her mind. Clinging to her notion that Heather had been physically incapable of throwing a grown man out of a fourteenth-story window against his will, she whispered, "I just don't remember."

STORM HATED reopening her painful wound, but with this clear sign that her recollections of that night might return at any moment, it was imperative that they ferret out the entire story.

It *was* somewhat unusual that the disassociated fragments of memory would start to cohere after this long, but certainly not unheard-of. In his career, Storm had treated two similar cases. In both, the patients had suffered a more severe trauma to the brain than had first been diagnosed. After their brain swelling started to subside, previously unresponsive neurons had no longer been short-circuited, and the memories began to resurface.

It was his opinion that Elisa's injuries fell into the same category. With time, she should regain a complete awareness of that lost time.

But as wise King Solomon had once said, "With increased knowledge, comes increased pain." And she was sure to face a lot more emotional pain.

There was one other aspect of this situation that he was sure she hadn't yet considered. Obviously, Jay Morrow's "suicide" had been engineered by Heather, but he had no illusions that the woman had been acting alone.

Heather had been a slender woman, one hundred and ten pounds at the most. Surely she'd had an accomplice, a strong man to help hoist the securities broker's limp body out the window. It would have been a simple matter to accomplish.

Her boss wouldn't have been the least suspicious if Heather entered his office and wandered behind his back for some reason. She could have smashed him in the back of his head, rendering him unconscious—if not dead. Then she would have signaled to her accomplice to toss her boss out the window. Accomplice leaves, and Heather tidies up. She'd probably put his personal line on hold so that she wouldn't be interrupted by incoming calls.

That highly visible flashing red light would also deter anyone from unexpectedly entering his office.

She walks out, sees Elisa and points to the phone light. Then she skips out the door, leaving Elisa to bear the brunt of suspicion.

Yes, it all made sense, if a second party had been involved. But who? More important, would Elisa's returning memory also make her a threat to him?

Even worse, this tight knot deep in his gut told Storm that the other murderer was on this island right now. Perhaps in this very hotel.

Chapter Thirteen

After a subdued breakfast from which Carey Howard was conspicuously absent, Elisa and Betty offered to help tote the emergency supplies and foodstuffs back up from the basement. Storm, Hank and David had a murmured conversation in the corner and drifted back toward the dining room. Elisa assumed they were going to finish pulling off the window coverings. She had to admit it would be wonderful to live in natural light again.

With Miriam's explicit directives to guide them, the women completed the tiring task by midmorning. They'd just settled at the table for a refreshing glass of iced tea—with ice, since the generator had been humming for several hours—when Hank poked his gaunt neck through the doorway. "Hey, old woman. Come here a minute."

Miriam raised a meaty fist. "No, you listen, old man. You want to talk with me, you march your skinny behind in here."

He cast a sharp glance at the table and shook his head. "No, we need you out here."

Muttering under her breath, Miriam trailed behind him.

Although she was baffled as to why Hank had summoned his wife, Elisa knew instinctively that it had to do with her. Tired of keeping her head stuck in the sand, she drained her glass and hurried to the door. She was fed up with being a mousy little victim. That certainly hadn't been her style before the accident, and she'd liked the old Elisa better.

It was time to start reclaiming control over her own life.

Stalking into the dining room, she pursued the sound of Miriam's obstreperous voice. She paused just before the archway leading to the hall.

Miriam's broad backside was blocking the doorway, as she gave someone, probably Hank, the benefit of her organizational skills. "There's no way you're going to get that down those narrow back stairs," she insisted.

"Then you empty out the kitchen, so's we can lug it down the front way," Hank complacently countered.

Miriam's silver curls bounced furiously as she shook her head. "I don't like it. Hank, it doesn't seem right. Unsanitary, if not downright disrespectful."

While Hank argued that respectability would have to wait, Storm stepped into the fray. Elisa could see the top of his burnished hair over Miriam's. "You two can argue about this all day, but I guarantee that by tomorrow, Miriam, you're going to be sorry you didn't let us do it."

Overcome by curiosity, Elisa tapped the older woman on the shoulder. "Excuse me. Can I come through?"

Miriam stepped aside, and an ominous silence greeted Elisa as she stepped through the doorway. Besides the three people she'd already recognized by their voices, David Welton was leaning against the banister.

Forcing confidence into her stride, she sailed into the entry hall. The first difference she noted was that the protective plywood covering had been removed from the glass panels set into the front door. Beautiful, blessed sunlight spread its glory on the hardwood floor.

Then she caught sight of the other change in the foyer and felt the color leach from her skin. Shrouded in white cloth like an Egyptian mummy, Heather's lifeless body was lying at her feet.

The room began to sway, and she felt Storm's hand reach

out and grab her upper arm. "Steady, Princess. Why don't you go back into the kitchen?"

She jerked away. Anger rapidly replaced the brief moment of shock. "And why don't you stop treating me like a mental patient, or an emotional cripple? I was startled, that's all. Now what is it you were trying to do behind my back?"

Having the grace to look embarrassed, Storm lowered his eyes. "We, uh, need to move the body to the basement. No one was trying to patronize or belittle you. Since you'd been through so much, we were trying not to upset you."

Elisa knew they meant well, and under other circumstances, she might have appreciated their tactfulness. But she was already "upset." Only the passage of time would bring back her emotional equilibrium.

"Thank you, but I'm...fine. So why are you taking the...uh, Heather to the basement."

Storm looked away and spoke to the carved wooden pineapple that adorned the newel post. "We need to get her into the walk-in cooler."

It finally sank in. "Oh" was all she could say. But she was embarrassed and ashamed. In her zeal to regain her independent spirit, she'd marched right over their well-meaning efforts to share her burden. Before the "accident," she hadn't been too proud to accept help when it was needed. Why was she so harsh and defensive now?

Elisa nodded briefly, her cheeks flaming with shame. "What can you say when you just discovered you're acting like a horse's patoot—except 'I'm sorry'?"

A chorus of chuckles at her weak joke zapped the tension from the atmosphere. Storm beamed like a proud father at the way she'd defused the situation. "Why don't you wait in the parlor? This won't take but a few minutes, then I've got a proposition for you."

Her hackles rose for a brief moment at being told where to wait, but she was too intrigued by his "proposition" to be truly miffed. "Sure." Giving Heather's inert form a last sorrowful glance, she headed for the parlor.

Ten minutes later, she was placidly flipping pages in a year-old issue of *Newsweek* when Storm returned, swiping perspiration from his face with his forearm. "Hi, Princess."

She tossed the magazine aside. "Hi yourself."

Grinning like a naughty boy, he crossed the room. "We've done all our chores. Wanna go outside and play?"

Her eyebrows lifted. "Is it safe? To go outside, I mean."

"Should be. Electricity's been off a couple of days, so the downed power lines shouldn't be a problem, although we'll steer clear of them in case they still have reserved juice."

She was still hesitant. This hotel had become a haven of sorts, and she didn't know if she was ready to face the big, bad world. Although with Heather's death, the threat to her own life was gone. She no longer had any reason to fear.

Nor could she deny the jolt of excitement coursing through her veins at the thought of spending time alone with Storm.

The jolt easily won out. "Then what are we waiting for? Fresh air sounds wonderful. I was beginning to think I'd have to kill for a breath—" She stopped abruptly, appalled by her choice of words.

Storm reached down, grasped her upper arms and pulled her from the chair. Holding her face only inches from his, he said quietly, "It's just an expression. Don't go feeling guilty because you chose a phrase you've been using your whole life. You have to go on, Princess. Don't censure yourself, and don't start taking on guilt you don't deserve. Otherwise you're going to end up in intensive therapy. Trust me."

He always seemed to do the right thing, to know the perfect words to dispel the darkness that so often overcame her. It was hard to believe he'd been a part of her life for only a few short days. And in a couple more days, she'd be gone, leaving him behind.

Forcing a smile, she said, "Good advice, Doc. Now let's get going."

They still didn't leave the hotel for another twenty minutes. Storm insisted she change into slacks and sturdy shoes, because they would surely encounter mud and sharp debris. Knowing he was right, she trudged upstairs to don more sensible clothing.

When he finally unlocked the front door and they stepped out onto the verandah, she caught her breath. The wide street that ran in front of the hotel was literally hidden beneath the storm's detritus. Across the street, where the bait shop and souvenir store had been, it looked as if a giant had been playing pick-up-sticks. The collapsed buildings were reduced to chunks of wood, plaster and rubble.

Instinctively taking Storm's hand, they silently descended the wide steps, too appalled by the destruction that greeted them to speak. The entire block looked like a war zone.

As THEY STROLLED through the deserted village, stopping occasionally to pull debris off the road, Storm was surprised and pleased by another of the many layers of Elisa's personality. When he first met her, she'd been like a chrysanthemum bud, tiny, fragile in appearance, but tightly closed and defensive. Then she'd started blooming, opening up a bit, exposing layers of delightful petals. By turns, she was defensive, haughty, frightened, sexy, funny, charming, independent, willful, and even sexier. He couldn't wait to see what other hidden facets were exposed when she was in full bloom.

The Elisa he *thought* he knew, the graceful, sophisticated prima ballerina, would have tiptoed around the mud, refusing to dirty her feet. The real woman didn't hesitate to wade in and haul grubby branches off the road. Within ten minutes, her glistening white athletic shoes were coated with filth and mud. In more ways than one, the world-famous ballet star was a trouper.

She stopped suddenly, eyeing a small bungalow whose roof had completely vanished and whose porch drooped ominously. "Oh, look, Storm. That house is completely destroyed. How terrible, to lose your home like that."

He pulled her close. He had no doubt that her home in New York had been a luxurious ten-room apartment. Yet her empathy for the owners of this small dwelling was heartfelt and sincere. "If it'll make you feel any better, that place was owned by old Doc Otis. He passed away about six months ago."

She stepped away and whirled, taking in the two blocks they'd traversed. "But what about all these other places? So much destruction."

"Actually, there's far less damage than I'd imagined."

Elisa's eyebrows rose. "This is awful!"

"Everything's relative, Princess. According to the news report we picked up while we were tackling the windows, Jake finally touched land a couple hundred miles up the coast. Major damage. Millions of dollars."

"What could be worse than this?" she insisted.

"Look around. Other than those two cheaply built stores across from the hotel, everything is still pretty much standing. Of course, the vacation houses that were unoccupied probably took the brunt. With no one to board them up, I'm sure there's plenty of water damage. And we lost trees, light poles, sheds, even a couple cars. But since the hurricane only skimmed the island, looks like we got off pretty lucky."

Her gaze fluttered over a side road that was completely impassable for the debris. "It'll take months to clean this up."

Storm chuckled. "You've obviously never lived in a small town. Once the ferry's running and all the locals return, they won't lose a minute organizing work crews. They'll bring provisions and water with them. It'll be like a giant posthurricane party—a work party."

They continued to walk, clearing a path before them.

Elisa finally said, "In New York and Los Angeles, everyone waits for the city crews to clean everything up."

"With the wreckage on the mainland? We'd be waiting this time next year. No, small-town people, especially when they're isolated like this, help each other."

Once they left the village proper behind them, the road wasn't nearly so littered. Storm explained that since they weren't in a housing area, there hadn't been much to come down except trees and shrubbery.

They strolled for another half hour in companionable quiet. Occasionally they would comment on a small bush or a tiny flower that had miraculously survived the tempest. Mostly they just enjoyed the freedom of being outdoors again.

He had to admit that this trek was far more pleasurable in the company of a sweet-scented woman. Elisa spied something and ran ahead, allowing him to truly appreciate those fetching purple stretch pants she wore. Not too loose, not too tight. Perfect for showing off her firm little backside.

Storm felt his blood pressure start to rise. Now that they were out of danger, he couldn't seem to get his mind off the delectable possibilities she brought to mind. Every mundane movement she made caused heat to pool in his groin. Like now. Bending over to pluck that purple flower. Didn't she know she was driving him crazy? Of course, in his present condition, he'd found it titillating watching her haul slimy trash off the road.

Storm cursed his suddenly hyperactive libido. He wasn't a schoolboy who'd just found his father's stash of girlie magazines; he was an adult. A doctor. Besides, the middle of a muddy road would hardly be considered the optimum location for a tryst. Unless he could interest her in a little playful mud-wrestling.

To take his mind off his enticing companion, he set about naming all twenty-six bones in the human foot. It had been a long time since med school, and memorization hadn't been his strong suit back then. *Let's see, there's the...uh, longitudinal arch, and the transverse or mediotarsal arch, as it's sometimes called.*

He glanced at her narrow foot and suddenly couldn't remember any of the smaller bones. His gaze trailed upward, to where her purple stretch pants disappeared into her sneaker. That was right about ankle-level.

Even with the angry red scar, she sure had trim, sexy ankles. But he was getting off course again. Ankle, uh, tarsus.

Ankles curved up into glorious, muscular calves. That led to lush thighs that...

Giving up on that avenue of distraction, he went back to studying the littered pavement, occasionally kicking aside a piece of trash.

When they came to a low spot, now a pool of murky brown water, he took her hand. "Let's go over the ridge—no telling what's in the bottom of that puddle."

"Like what? Snakes?" Her snapping dark eyes widened. "I saw a special on someplace in Texas after a bad storm, and rattlesnakes were all over the place."

"I was thinking more of broken glass," he chuckled. "We're not known for our snakes. Might be a garter or two around, but I've never seen one."

She studied him with a suspicious glare for a minute. Shaking her finger, she muttered, "You'd better not be lying. I hate snakes, Storm. I mean, *really* hate them."

"I assure you, Princess, we won't run into a snake. A few rats and mice, maybe."

"Ugh!"

"Hey, snakes eat rodents. We don't have snakes, remember? Come on, let's take this road."

A brisk five-minute walk down the lane brought them to a clearing where a cozy beach cabin nestled on a ridge about fifty yards above the ocean.

"What a sweet little place," she exclaimed.

Sweet? Ramshackle, decrepit or rustic, maybe. But

sweet? He glanced around; fallen branches, uprooted shrubs and a few tiles missing from the roof. Otherwise, the place seemed to have survived the storm with little damage.

Elisa tugged on his arm and pointed to the ocean in the background. "It must have a wonderful view from the back side."

"This is Roundabout Cove. The cabin has a sunset view over the water. Fairly unusual on the East Coast."

She turned to him, excitement glittering in her brown eyes. "Do you think they'd mind if we peeked in the windows?"

"No, I don't think so."

Skipping ahead, her injured ankle giving her an odd but charming gait, she called from the front steps, "Can't you just imagine pots of red geraniums hanging above this porch?"

Actually, he'd never imagined any such thing. But then, he didn't consider himself a hearts-and-flowers kind of guy. When he reached the porch, she turned around, her lips in a slight pout.

"The windows are all boarded. I can't see a thing." Her disappointment was like that of a small child denied entrance to Disneyland.

"Then let's go inside, find a hammer and pry them off."

She frowned and shook her head. "I don't think we should. Wouldn't that be like...breaking and entering?"

He grinned and pulled a key ring from his pocket. "I know the owner."

"Storm, this is *your* place!"

"Guilty."

She whopped his upper arm with her small fist. "You were teasing me."

"So I was." He opened the door, covertly rubbing his arm. Wasn't a dancer's strength supposed to be in her legs?

Except for the shaft of light filtering through the open door, the cabin was pitch-dark. Taking Elisa's elbow, he guided her to the kitchen table. He lit the kerosene lantern first, then started coffee on a portable camp stove.

"Don't let it boil over," he warned as he hefted a large hammer. "I'll pry the plywood off the windows and be back in a jiffy."

When the enticing smell of perking coffee reached her nose, she turned down the burner. At home, of course, she used an automatic electric drip machine; she poured in water, dumped in the grounds, walked away and came back to a perfect brew. She'd never actually cooked coffee on a stove. But she'd watched Miriam and she knew the stuff had to cook a long time.

Speaking of time, taking down the window coverings was apparently a bigger job than he had thought. She could hear him moving around the cottage, the pounding and prying sounds occasionally punctuated by a muted curse.

While she was waiting, Elisa strolled into the living area. The front windows had been uncovered, and strong, warm sunlight bathed the open room. It was exactly as she'd imagined; wide planks of pine flooring, an enormous stone fireplace, and lumpy yard-sale furniture. Two doors opened onto the room, and beside the rustic stairs a small hall exposed two more doors.

Her eyes followed the staircase up to a large loft overlooking the living area below. A perfect cabin by the sea. If it was spiffed up a bit. She was mentally redecorating the downstairs when Storm's tread creaked across the wooden porch.

She turned around to find him silhouetted in the doorway. Millions of tiny dust motes flickered around him in a shower of silvery sparkles. His hands were raised, touching the door frame as if he were holding the structure erect. She couldn't make out his face, but her heart double-pumped at his commanding, self-assured stance.

"Coffee ready?" His voice was odd, strained and kind of croaky.

"I think so," she breathed. Her own words felt tight in her throat.

He followed her into the kitchen. She sat looking at her muddy sneakers while he gathered up the coffee fixings. "No real cream or sugar, just the artificial stuff."

"Blue or pink?"

"Huh? It's all white."

"I meant the artificial sug— Oh, never mind. It really doesn't matter."

"Whatever you say, Princess. So what do you think of my hideout?"

What she thought was that he'd unwittingly chosen the perfect word. "I like it a lot. It would be a great vacation home."

He sipped, lightly blowing on the steaming brew. "Works for me."

Slowly rotating a spoon in her own mug, she asked thoughtfully, "Why do you live here?"

"Pardon? Why do you live in an overpopulated, overpriced and dangerous city?"

She started to argue that she'd encountered more violence on this nearly deserted island than she'd ever faced in New York or Los Angeles, but realized he'd posed his counterquestion only to avoid having to answer hers. "Maybe. But how can you make a living here? Surely your skills would be better utilized in a larger community. A midsize town, if you don't like New York."

He took another sip before answering. "How long did you let this stuff perk? It tastes like burnt mud."

"Stop changing the subject. Why do you stay here?"

Setting his mug on the scarred wooden tabletop, he ran his finger around the ceramic rim. "Actually, I moved here from New York. In my former life, I was head of pediatric psychiatry at University Hospital. Worked mostly with troubled and abused children under twelve."

She covered his hand with hers. "That must have been so fulfilling. Why did you quit?"

"I left because I needed to make some changes. Listen, I've been thinking about the night Jay died. I think if we tried some hypnotherapy it might shake something loose."

Disappointment poured over Elisa like a cold shower. Storm's unwillingness to open up, to discuss any facet of his personal life, could mean only one thing. His interest in her wasn't personal, but merely professional curiosity. Hurt and furious at allowing herself to become so vulnerable, she lashed out. "That's all I am to you, isn't it—a complex intellectual puzzle to solve while you had a little free time on your hands? You never cared about *me* for a single moment!"

His hand slammed on the tabletop, causing her spoon to rattle. "Give your 'poor little me' act a break, Elisa! Okay, you've been through a lot of trauma lately. But, hell, you survived—you're here. But you don't want to start a new life. You'd rather cling to your misery. Poor Elisa, lost her career. Lost her boyfriend. Well, guess what, Princess? Lots of people lose everything and have to start over."

"So why don't you try it, Doc?"

"Because saving your life just seems like a higher priority right now."

"Now who's living in the past, Storm? Jay's dead, Heather's dead! It's over, remember?"

He pushed away from the table and stalked to the sink. Staring out the open window, he said quietly, "I don't believe Heather was acting alone. It only makes sense that she had an accomplice. I don't think it's over, Elisa, and if you don't face up to that, you might not live to get off this island."

She shook her head. "We've never really established that she killed Jay in the first place. Just a lot of useless theories. But even if she did, and even if she had an accomplice, I don't think he's here."

Slowly he turned to face her. Disbelief shrouded his eyes. "Why on earth not?"

Elisa paused. She didn't really know what she thought.

She only knew she wouldn't give in to his point of view again. Her days of being his psychological guinea pig were over. "Because if her accomplice was on the island, why wouldn't he have been with her last night? If he helped murder Jay, why not me?"

His hands clenched into fists of rage, he railed, "You are the most obstinate woman I've ever known! You simply refuse to accept the obvious, even at your own peril, just to spite me."

"That's not true," she lied, hating him for seeing right through her protective camouflage.

He took a step toward her, as if he wanted to shake her. Scrupulously avoiding touching her, he exploded. "You have to face the truth, Elisa! You can't hide from your memories forever!"

Stung to the quick by his cold, unfair appraisal, she stood up. Her voice was deadly calm, quiet. "Neither can you."

She turned on her heel and stalked out of the cabin.

Chapter Fourteen

Free from the stifling, confining space of Storm's cabin, Elisa stalked aimlessly along the edge of the beach rim, hiking and sliding over the occasional sand dunes blocking her path. After nearly a quarter mile, the ridge began a gradual slope to the sea. Taking off her sneakers, she rolled up her pant legs and sprinted down to the hard-packed sand at the water's edge.

Damn Storm Delaney. Even the majestic ocean, with its abnormally high surf, couldn't dissipate her boiling anger. He didn't hesitate to pry her open and yank out her bruised and bloodied soul. But ask him one simple question that breached the fortifications he'd built around his personal life, and he went ballistic.

Elisa was tired of men who kept secrets, men who wouldn't talk, wouldn't share, wouldn't trust. In fact, she was tired of men—period.

Making her way to higher ground, she picked a frond of sea grass and plopped on the ground. She poked the stem between her teeth. Despite her frustration with Storm's unyielding refusal to share his personal side, one thing he'd said kept coming back to her. Something about her refusing to see the obvious, despite her own peril.

Did he really believe that Heather's unseen coconspirator was actually on this island? And considered Elisa a threat? Although the sun was bright overhead, a cold chill raced through her veins, ending up as ice cubes in the pit of her stomach.

What if Storm was right? Similar thoughts had already plagued her own peace of mind. It was sheer obstinacy that had kept her from admitting it to Storm.

She stood up and took the easiest-looking path back up the slope. She'd been such a fool. Even if he didn't care for her in the way she wanted, he was still her only ally. The only person who might be able to help keep her alive until the authorities finally arrived on Double Dare Island.

Reaching the top of the embankment, she turned left, retracing the path she'd taken from Storm's cabin. She only hoped he was still there, still willing to help.

After fifteen minutes, however, Elisa began to doubt the route she'd chosen. She couldn't look for her footprints in the dunes, because the still-blustery wind continually swept them away. But something didn't feel right. If she recalled correctly, she should be able to see the ocean below her on the left from the top of this dune.

Picking up speed, she slogged up the sand drift. When she reached the top, she stomped her foot in dismay. All she could see to the left was more dunes. There was no doubt that she was well and truly lost.

She swiveled her head in the opposite direction. The dunes continued for another fifty yards or so, then dark green foliage dotted the horizon. Hmm. Could that be the marsh grove? If so, there was a shortcut to the village that Heather had shown her several weeks ago. She had never taken it by herself, though. For one thing, she generally exercised her ankle by pedaling her bike. Besides, a couple of sections of that grove were dark, spooky. Like the evil forest where Sleeping Beauty's hateful stepmother had hung out.

As she considered her options, she slowly became aware of the pulsing sensation just above her ankle. A sure sign that she'd overdone it, and unless she elevated that foot very soon, the excruciating throbbing that followed would continue for hours.

Without further balking, she headed for the debris-strewn path through the marsh.

Once she was a quarter mile into the swampland, she started having second thoughts. Alone, it was even spookier than she remembered. Ancient trees reached out for her with knobby arms, laden with dripping moss. Eerie calls from unseen birds screeched through the still, fetid air. Elisa crossed her arms over her chest, holding on to herself for comfort. She tried walking faster, but her ankle pulsated in protest.

A half-rotted log blocked her path, and she gratefully sank down for a moment's rest. Something skittered on the path behind her, and she swung around. Her eyes scanned the brush, the soggy ground around the cypress trees. She saw nothing but the dank, forbidding marshland. Yet the tenacious sense of another presence behind her, watching her, wouldn't pull its claws from her pounding chest.

Rising to her feet, she continued toward the village. She'd gone only a short distance when the back of her neck started burning as if she'd stepped in the path of a laser beam. She whirled around. "Hello? Is anybody back there?"

Only the swish of undulating marsh grass responded.

But someone, or some*thing* was following her progress.

She gulped, and broke into a light jog. Her ankle throbbed as if it were on fire, but she visualized Storm's vibrant green eyes and ignored the pain.

A small rodent scurried though the soggy leaves right beside the path, and she stifled a scream. A sudden memory of one of her dance mistresses came to mind. Madame Skelska. When a rehearsal went badly, or Elisa worked until the ragged edge of exhaustion claimed her, Madame Skelska had always exhorted her to consider the negative experience a challenge. A test of her emotional fortitude.

She breathed deeply and tried to spur her mind into taking Madame Skelska's advice. *Keep calm. You were the one who wanted your independence, to take care of yourself. Now you have the chance. Consider this a test of your emotional fortitude.*

Repeating the phrase as if it were a mantra, she trudged onward. *Keep calm. Don't let your imagination frighten you. Keep calm.* Then, breaking through the mantra like a sharp whip, she heard the clear sound of someone calling her name.

"Eliiisa! Eliiisa!" It was almost as if her name were being carried by the wind, as it whistled through the treetops.

Halting abruptly, she whirled to locate the source of the unearthly sound. But the high-pitched call stopped when she did.

"S-Storm?" she called. Then again, louder. "Storm, is that you?"

STORM PACED AND RAGED around the small cabin for a full half hour before he reached the conclusion that he'd acted like an intractable jackass.

She had been right on target. As usual. Why did he think he was entitled to an exemption from the rules that governed the human race? It took a lot of nerve to expect her to bravely confront her recent ordeal, and place herself in jeopardy, when he couldn't even face the two-year-old trauma of Karen's death.

No wonder she had been so incensed. He'd self-righteously tried to force her into facing reality, knowing he couldn't do so himself.

What if she'd really written him off this time? What if she refused to speak to him again?

Even more chilling, what if right now she was alone with the murderer?

Grabbing his shirt, he raced out the door. He had to find her. Had to. He only hoped he wasn't too late.

THE CRACKLE of a broken twig drew Elisa's attention.

She spun around. There! Her heartbeat stopped at the sight of a dark-clothed figure moving through the underbrush. Fear burbled in her throat.

That wasn't Storm. Couldn't be. He wouldn't play malicious games. Unless…unless *he* had been in league with Heather. It couldn't be, she wouldn't believe it, except…except that it would explain so much. If Storm *was* the accomplice, wouldn't it be clever of him to befriend her, worm his way into her confidence, her trust?

He could have pretended to dislike Heather; that way Elisa wouldn't have considered him as an accessory to Jay's murder. Very Machiavellian. But with Storm's agile mind, very easy for him to pull off.

In truth, she knew nothing about him. Not where he was from, the identity of his friends and family—nothing except the tiny tidbits of untraceable data he fed her from time to time. He'd played the role of burned-out psychiatrist to the hilt. Yet the only tangible proof he'd offered was an old business card. Anyone could have had it made at a stationery store. Or stolen it.

Had she played the fool with a loathsome killer who was cunning enough to carry off the role? *Oh, no, Storm,* her heart cried out. *Please, don't let it be true.*

But whether or not that was Storm stalking her through the swamp didn't really matter in the end. What mattered was getting herself out of the marsh. Alive. She'd deal with the heartbreak later, if she had to. If the truth didn't kill her.

The dark figure had disappeared from her view, but she heard the rustle of withered leaves as he circled around, placing himself in front of her on the path. There was no option but to turn around and go back the way she'd come.

Sucking in deep fortifying breaths, she dragged her sore ankle back down the winding path. The primeval wasteland was silent, but for her own heavy panting. No exotic birds called from the treetops. No small animals scampered through the underbrush. The swamp was soundlessly watching her life-or-death race through the gloom.

She continued to half run, half drag, her weary body along the rubble-strewn trail. Then a darting motion to her left caught her eye. *Oh, no. He was right beside her again.* Without an injured ankle to deter him, the stalker was having no problem pacing her.

So exhausted and terrified she could hardly think, Elisa faltered when she came to an unexpected fork. She couldn't take time to think, she had to keep moving. She chose the right branch, only because her pursuer was on her left.

After a few seconds, she no longer heard him rattling through the scraggly bushes, no longer sensed his presence. She allowed herself to slow down, to take in healing oxygen. Then she rounded a curve and stopped. She'd taken the wrong fork. This one was a dead end.

Her tormentor had boxed her into a corner. And he was between Elisa and the only way back to the beach.

STORM GLANCED at his watch. She'd been gone over an hour. He was just wasting his time. She had certainly gone back to the hotel; he wouldn't find her sunning herself on the beach.

He turned around and trudged back up the sandbank. She'd been plenty miffed; maybe he should give her time to cool off. He should go back to the cabin, draw some water from the cistern and clean himself up. She'd be more likely to listen to him if he didn't look like the wild man of Borneo.

When he reached the top of the ridge, Storm jogged over to a little trail that ran along the outside edge of the marsh. Even though that route was slightly farther from his cabin, the going would be a lot easier, and he'd make better time.

He yanked off his white T-shirt and draped it around his neck. What a scorcher the day had turned out to be. With all the storm clouds gone, the sun's blazing fury had been unleashed on the island. He hoped she was indoors by now.

Even with her creamy tanned complexion, she could still get a bad burn.

Walking along the edge of the two-mile-square swamp, he wrinkled his nose at the dank, decayed odor emanating out of the mire. He reached the small clearing leading to the path through the bog, a shortcut to the village that only the native islanders used. He hesitated. He wondered if Elisa knew about this shorter, but more arduous, way back to town.

Nah. Besides, she was a city girl—she'd never go into that dark, spooky place alone.

ELISA LOOKED AROUND, searching for something she could use to defend herself. The man in black hadn't reappeared, but she didn't delude herself that he was gone. Obviously, he knew this swamp, and all the paths that twined through it. He also knew she would reach a dead end and have to turn back.

Until she did, he could rest. And wait.

She spotted another downed cypress, just a few yards off the path. She gingerly made her way toward it, her sneakers squishing deeply into the saturated ground. She wondered if she was surrounded by quicksand, and stuck her toe into the soil before she took each step. When she neared the fallen trunk, she shuffled her foot through the mucky layer of decaying leaves blanketing the ground. There had to be a twig, a piece of wood, something…

Ah-ha! Just what she was looking for. She held up a sturdy limb, about a yard long and two inches thick. Brandishing it in the air as if it were a sword, she decided it might serve as a weapon. If it didn't break in half the first time it struck something.

Still, she thought, heading back down the path toward the main fork, it was more than she'd had for protection a moment ago.

Walking slowly to conserve her strength, she paused when she came to the sharp curve. What if he was right around the bend, waiting for her? She stood motionless for a full minute, listening. Relieved when her ears detected no unusual sound, she inched forward. When she rounded the arc, the path was clear all the way to the fork.

Releasing a huge sigh of relief, she stepped slowly, lightly, to avoid making a sudden noise that would expose her location. A yard, then two. The fork in the road, and relative safety, was only a dozen yards ahead.

"*Eliiisa!*"

She whirled around. The shadowy figure was only fifteen feet behind her.

Frozen in place, she stared at her stalker. Dressed in black from his feet to the top of his head, a black sweatshirt hood cloaking his face, the vile apparition moved slowly toward her.

"*Eliiisa... Don't be afraid, little Eliiisa.*"

Terror wrapped her in its folds, like the wide mantle of a vampire. She clutched the limb behind her back, praying this was a horrid joke—praying her trembling hands could hang on to the wood long enough for one good blow.

She had no alternative but to wait for him to step within striking range. If she tried to run, he'd overcome her in an instant. Her strength was nearly gone, and her foot throbbed unmercifully.

She knew her only hope was to will herself to stand still, to lull him into believing she was too frightened to move, and hope to take him by surprise.

He took another step and laughed—an evil chortle that sent shivers down her spine.

But her heart felt relieved on one count: This wasn't Storm. It couldn't be him. She would have sensed his presence.

The figure stepped forward. He was only ten feet away. Any moment, he would lunge forward and grab her. But her feet were welded to the ground. She wouldn't move until he was closer. Near enough for her assault to do some damage.

As if she were mesmerized by a dancing snake, she watched his progress, seeing every nuance of his clothing and movement, branding him deep in her soul. He held up his hands, as if he were preparing to clutch her throat. He wore dark work gloves with worn threads breaking loose like black hairs sprouting over his hands.

Glancing down, she noted his black tennis shoes, and the only color visible, fluorescent orange grommets behind his black laces. His somber black garb reminded her of a deadly black widow, with that single spot of color. The red hourglass to remind its prey that time was running out.

Without warning, she was struck by an explosion of forgotten memories. She was showered with unrelated images, like fragments of shattered glass. A drop of blood. A tiled corridor. A pair of black athletic shoes with Day-Glo orange grommets.

She'd seen those shoes before! But when, and why did the memory evoke as much fright as the reality coming toward her? So close, almost within reach.

Goaded out of her self-enforced paralysis, she shrieked like a banshee and reared back, swinging the heavy branch as if it were a nightstick. The wooden club struck him in the solar plexus, and he bent over, clutching his stomach.

Seizing her advantage, Elisa tore down the path. The pain in her ankle was burning with white-hot fire. She didn't know how long she could maintain the pace, but she wouldn't quit. The stalker might overcome her and force her to the ground, but she wouldn't willingly give in. Never.

Behind her, the brush rattled as he thrashed toward her, bellowing in rage. She'd almost reached the fork when the marshland suddenly stilled. Then, a shadowy figure appeared. Directly in *front* of her. Impossible. There was no way the killer could have gone around her, yet there he was.

Bracing herself for another battle, she poised to swing

her branch, just as the shadowy form stepped into a pool of sunlight. Storm!

STORM STOOD in the crux of the Y crossing. He should have gone straight to the hotel, instead of following his hunch. Even if Elisa *had* somehow taken this godforsaken route, she'd have reached the village a half hour ago. *Unless she was lost. Or hurt. Or…*

If he'd allowed logic to guide him, he would have gone straight back to the hotel. But the dark premonition that kept gnawing at his gut had told him she was in trouble. Needed him.

He'd already let her down once. This time, he had to make the right decision.

Although he heard no sound, sensed no movement, Storm felt prickles climb up his neck. Slowly, he turned, to meet the eyes he felt watching him, and saw her hobbling toward him. She must have been lost after all, but, thank God, she was all right. He would never have forgiven himself if anything happened to her.

She looked incredibly weary, and even from this distance he could see the fear etched on her face. She must have been running through this swamp, frightened and lost, since she left his cabin.

He rushed toward her, stopping suddenly, when he got a clear look at her expression for the first time. Her face was white with fear, the mindless horror of being lost in a dank, creepy marsh. He could understand that. But what was slicing his heart like a lance was the way she was staring, wild-eyed, at him. She was afraid of *him*. A sick, nauseating pain gripped his stomach.

The idea that he was somehow responsible for her terror hit Storm like a sucker punch to his diaphragm.

Chapter Fifteen

She seemed dazed. Disoriented.

Afraid to approach her, lest he frighten her more, Storm watched the play of emotions flicker across Elisa's face. As if she were seeing him for the first time, she studied him for a long, expectant moment. Then she seemed to reach some kind of decision. She blinked twice, and the frightened-doe expression on her face slowly evaporated.

She dropped the stick she was wielding like a weapon and lunged for him, hurling herself into his arms. Holding him so tight he thought a rib might break, she burrowed her face in his chest.

"Oh, my God, Storm, I've never been so afraid—"

"I know," he said soothingly. "This marshland is pretty hairy if you don't know your way around."

She pulled away and looked fearfully over her shoulder. "But I wasn't lost—not at first, anyway."

Wasn't lost? He'd seen her emerge from the dead-end trail.

"I noticed you were limping. Your ankle give out?"

"Yes, but..." Her voice trailed away as she took another wary look down the trail.

He suddenly realized his gut instinct had been right, after all. He tightened his grip on her shoulders. "What is it? What happened?"

She straightened up, wincing as she unintentionally put

too much weight on her sore foot. Catching her lower lip between her teeth, she kept casting nervous glances behind her as she haltingly told him about her flight through the swamp. And about the intimidating man in black.

The simmering anger that had been building in him for days boiled into a red, all-consuming rage. She had been through enough! He was going to catch this creep and beat him to a bloody pulp. He turned slowly, willing the stalker to show himself. But it appeared the coward only liked scaring defenseless women. Nothing would give him more pleasure than to track him down like the mad dog that he was.

"What if he's still back there? Watching us right now?" Her questioning dark eyes caressed his face.

He blew out a deep, frustrated breath. Yeah, he'd like to go after this punk. Right now. Except that to do so would leave Elisa alone and vulnerable.

Praying that he'd have another chance to vent his fury on this thug, Storm pulled her close and led her back to the beach path. Though she never complained, and only occasionally clutched his arm for support, by the time they hit the first dune he knew her ankle was putting her through eight kinds of hell.

Bending over, he slipped an arm beneath her knees and hoisted her to his chest.

"You don't have to—"

"Hush, and put your arm around my neck."

She complied, her small fingers feeling like soft velvet against his skin. Her voice was calmer now, and the color was slowly returning to her cheeks. "But I can walk. Really."

"Yeah, but I can walk faster. Longer legs. Besides, I'm expecting a hell of a tip for this highly personal taxi service."

Her head nestled in the crook of his neck and shoulder. "But I don't have any money with me," she murmured.

Storm laughed, hoping that was an intentional double

entendre. If so, it meant she felt safe now, safe enough to relieve her stress with humor. With that thought in mind, he teasingly replied, "No problem. I was, um, thinking of a different form of payment anyway."

"American Express?"

"Nope." He glanced behind them to make sure they were still alone. The stalker must have slithered back into the swamp with the other reptiles.

"No cash, no credit cards," she said, continuing the game. "How about trading beads?"

He could feel the tension easing from her body. This innocuous game of innuendo was working wonders to redirect her emotional focus. Besides, he was kind of enjoying it himself. "Nope. No beads."

Her mouth brushed against his chin, channeling a rush of heat so strong, Storm thought he might drop her. *Keep your mind on the next dune, Delaney. Where's that professional detachment you've always been so proud of?*

"Hmm..." she whispered thoughtfully. "I'm running out of ideas."

"Keep thinking."

"Oh! I've got it." She jiggled, twitching her sweet little butt against his arm. How much farther could the cabin be? "Wampum," she announced.

He swallowed. Forming words was a major undertaking. He had to keep reminding himself that Elisa was vulnerable right now. She could easily be swayed by any show of affection. As a therapist, he knew the warning signs. As a man who cared about her, he couldn't take advantage of her insecurity. "No wampum, either."

"I suppose you don't want furs or muskrat skins?"

"That's a definite no."

Sighing with mock frustration, she said, "Well, Storm. If you're not willing to accept any of the traditional exchanges, however will I satisfy the debt?"

Forgetting his vow of only moments before to stay emotionally detached, he threw his head back and laughed.

"You're a wicked, wicked woman. And, Princess, I'm not the least bit worried about either of us being satisfied. I'll take care of that part."

Elisa flicked the shadowy whiskers along his jawbone with a fingernail. "I'm *sure* you'll be up to it."

Storm choked, then chuckled again. He'd never seen this...playfully bawdy side of her before. Hell, he'd never seen it in himself. But he thought it was something he could get used to. In fact, he looked forward to it.

But if she said one more provocative word, they were going to finish this "discussion" right here in the sand. A man could take only so much.

Fortunately, Storm's cabin was right below the next dune, and he didn't have to concern himself with getting a sunburn on any of the tender parts of his anatomy.

When they reached the clearing, a new, and more disturbing, problem took precedence. What if the man in black had outmaneuvered them and was lying in wait in the cabin? Storm could be delivering her right into the arms of a murderer.

Slowly lowering her to the ground, he whispered, "Wait here while I check things out."

She opened her mouth as if to argue, but didn't follow.

The front door was wide open, but he'd left in such a hurry, he wasn't certain he'd closed it. The wooden porch squeaked if a mouse ran over it, so Storm knew a covert entry wasn't an option.

Sucking in several deep, fortifying breaths, he raced across the clearing, vaulted up the three steps and hit the door running. Half expecting the killer to smack him alongside the head with a crowbar, Storm hunkered down and rolled across the hardwood floor.

When he looked up, the room was empty.

He made his way to the gun cabinet. Pulling the key from his pocket, he pulled out his twelve-gauge shotgun and slammed five shells into the magazine. With the powerful weapon pumped and ready, he made a thorough search of the cabin, glancing out the window from time to time to check on Elisa.

After checking every nook and cranny, he knew the place was empty. He slid the loaded shotgun into the rear of the coat closet. He'd feel better if it was handy.

They'd outwitted the killer. This time. But Storm had no doubts he'd make another try.

"THE COAST IS CLEAR," Storm called from the porch.

Elisa's shoulders sagged with relief. He'd been inside for so long she'd started to fear the stalker had beat them back. She started limping to the cabin, but Storm met her halfway and hauled her into his arms again.

She was grateful for the opportunity to pamper her lame foot. But snuggling in his arms, drinking in his heady scent and feeling the slight tickle of his chest hair teasing her nose through his T-shirt, was starting to take their own toll. Her knees were wobbling so much she doubted she'd be able to stand upright.

Never in her life had she felt this...almost savage need for any man. She understood the cause, of course. She'd seen at least a hundred movies in which the hero and heroine had survived some terrible ordeal, then found release from the pressure in each other's arms. Still, even knowing that this overpowering sensual awareness was a physiological result of her near-death experience, she didn't know if she could trust herself alone in the cabin with him.

He carried her straight through the living area, down the hallway and kicked open a door on the left. It was a small room, dominated by a queen-size bed made of massive posts of peeled pine. An old-fashioned patchwork quilt, in a rainbow of colors, lay invitingly over the mattress.

"Can you stand for a minute?"

"Sure, I think so."

He slowly lowered her to the floor, and she leaned on her good leg to ease the pressure on her aching ankle.

Storm stripped back the covers, and helped her climb beneath the clean, cool sheets.

"Comfy?"

"Umm."

He strode over to the closet and brought back two more bed pillows. "Lift your foot."

When she complied, he carefully untied her sneaker and eased it off her foot. After studying the swollen joint, he removed the other shoe and patted her shoulder. "Looks pretty grim, swollen and bruised, but I don't think there's any serious damage."

She nodded. "My shoe felt so tight I was afraid it was cutting off the circulation."

He lowered his hip to the edge of the bed and fingered an errant strand of hair off her forehead. "I started to say you'd had a rough day, but your whole summer's been shot to hell."

Elisa smiled through her weariness. "I'd say that was a fair assessment. Storm?"

"Yeah?"

"I—I'm sorry about this morning. I know you thought I wasn't taking the threat seriously, but...I just wanted it to be over. And when you kept saying it wasn't—it just made me mad. Some kind of defense mechanism taking over, I guess."

He chucked her chin with his fingertip. "You're getting pretty good at psychobabble. At the risk of making you sound perfectly normal, you were rightfully ticked off because I kept hammering at you. Telling you what you should be doing. And that's my professional opinion, so don't argue."

Reaching down, he took her fingers in his and lightly rubbed her knuckles with his thumb. "Guess I've been passing out therapeutic advice so long I kind of let my mouth override my common sense. Chalk it up to that God complex—I think all doctors are supposed to have it."

She didn't know about that, but he *was* responsible for

a lot of wondrous things. Like the swarm of butterflies that had once more taken possession of the region south of her navel. But she couldn't let herself give in to these achy yearnings. Too much was at stake. She couldn't stand a broken heart right now.

He stood up. "I think I have some aspirin in the bathroom. Might help with the pain until I can get your medication."

"Thanks. And a huge glass of water."

"Sure thing," he called over his shoulder as he disappeared down the hallway.

Elisa leaned back on the pillow and closed her eyes. Storm Delaney was a kind, gentle and generous man. And he was quite obviously sexually attracted to her.

But she wanted more—or nothing. Her feelings for him had grown as swiftly as Jack's beanstalk over these few days. Maybe she was particularly vulnerable right now, and needed someone to fill the void. Perhaps she was simply reaching out for kindness, any kindness. She didn't think it was that simple, though.

He came back into the room and handed her two pills and an old-fashioned aluminum tumbler that was beaded with evaporation. She popped the pills and took a deep swallow. The water was crisp, free of additives and surprisingly cool.

"My cistern's connected to an underground spring," he said when she raised her eyebrows.

She finished the water and patted the edge of the mattress. Obediently he sat. "So what do we do now?" she asked. "We know for certain there's a second killer on this island, and I haven't the foggiest idea who he is."

He frowned thoughtfully. "Nothing about him seemed familiar?"

She thought for a moment and shook her head. "Nothing."

"And he didn't speak?"

"Actually, he did say my name a few times." Her mouth

felt dry and scratchy as she recalled his eerie voice wafting through the swamp. "Even told me not to be afraid, at the same time he was doing his best to frighten me to death. His voice was high, like he was talking through a tin can or something, and weird. Almost supernatural. No, he didn't sound like anyone I know."

He rubbed her forearm, as if he were polishing fine marble, and rose from the bed. "We'll work it out later. Right now, I'm going back to the hotel and collect some of our stuff. I imagine Miriam's worried sick about you by now."

Raising her head off the pillow, she struggled to sit up. "I want to go with you. I have no intention of facing that creep again. At least not without a gun—a *big* gun."

His large hand pressed against her shoulder, easing her back onto the pillow. "You're staying here. Doctor's orders. In the first place, I can make better time alone. Besides, I'm afraid you're going to inflict some muscle or nerve damage if you don't give that foot a rest."

"But—"

He touched her lips with his index finger. "Secondly, I shouldn't be gone long. I think we cleared a wide enough path that I can get the Jeep through. Finally, I have no intention of leaving you without a gun. A big gun."

Stepping into the hall, he came back with the biggest, most ferocious-looking firearm she'd ever seen. It looked like a small cannon.

"I don't think I could *lift* that thing, much less fire it."

"I doubt you'll have to."

He pointed the muzzle toward the floor and kind of pumped a wooden cylinder along the part of the barrel. The distinctive ratcheting sound it made caused her stomach to clench in fear. Elisa cringed and knotted the edge of the sheet between her fingers.

Storm set the safety on the powerful weapon and lowered it to the floor. "You know that reaction you just had? That's one of the most recognizable sounds in the world.

And, believe me, no man in his right mind wants to come up against a woman with a loaded shotgun.''

She shook her head, doubt written all over her face. ''I was really thinking of something smaller. Like a .357 Magnum.''

He pointed to the doorway, about six feet away. ''Someone's who isn't familiar with firearms could be right where you are, aim for that door and miss it. Easily. But if that bastard's anywhere in the *house* when you fire that twelve-gauge, you have a good chance of getting him. More important, he'll know that and will probably hightail back to the swamp.''

Against her better judgment, Elisa let him talk her into keeping the shotgun. He spent another twenty minutes showing her how to work the weapon. When he was finished, he laid it on the bed beside her.

Although she still didn't like the evil-looking beast, at least she was fairly certain she could defend herself without blowing off her own foot.

After warning her several times that he would lock all the doors behind him and call out loudly upon his return, Storm left for the half-hour hike back to the hotel.

She kept her hand on the smooth wooden stock and listened for unusual noises. The old cottage creaked and groaned as the wet wood siding started drying after the storm's ravages.

The hurricane was past, and she was truly grateful, but the aftermath of moist, hot air was almost unbearable in the small guest room. And she didn't dare open a window.

Looking up, she spied a narrow strip of compact windows running along the edge of the ceiling behind the bed. Since they were far too small to allow a grown man entrance into the house, she cautiously stood up in the bed and eased one open. Soothing fresh air billowed into the room, along with the tangy scent of the ocean.

Ah... She drank in the salty fragrance. Better. Much better.

Once she settled back against her pillow, her sharp hearing picked out the magnificent sound of the waves crashing into the rocks that lined the shore. She sighed. What a wonderful, completely peaceful spot he had chosen for his refuge. But a strong, vibrant man, with his desperately needed talents, shouldn't be imprisoned on a lonely island. He should be back at work, using all the impressive skills he'd trained so hard to develop. Too many hurting children needed his help.

But Storm wasn't ready to let go of the hurt he'd been nursing for so long. He was so raw that the pain oozed openly from his wound, but still he wouldn't share his heartache. And she wouldn't settle for a man who couldn't share his pain, as well as his happiness.

Intimacy between lovers shouldn't be confined to the bedroom. A hot flush glowed on her cheeks when she realized how easily she'd thought of Storm as her lover. Her subconscious hadn't said, "if" they became lovers; the thought had burst forth like an accomplished fact.

Elisa was so lost in her troublesome thoughts that she scarcely noticed the passage of time. Suddenly, she sat up, startled by a metallic clicking sound from the front of the house. Her heart thumped wildly, keeping time with the pulsing blood in her ankle.

Easing her hand around the stock, she pulled the shotgun onto her lap.

The front door creaked open, and heavy footsteps echoed on the hardwood floor.

Her hands trembling like small leaves in a gale, she raised the weapon, trying to remember the exact spot between her arm and chest where Storm had shown her to position the shotgun. Tiny rivulets of perspiration ran down the side of her face. She didn't want to have to fire this weapon. Didn't want to take another life. But she wasn't willing to surrender her own, either.

Heavy masculine footsteps reverberated across the hardwood flooring in the great room.

She snicked off the safety.

"Oh, my God! Elisa, it's me! Don't shoot. Can you hear me?" He sounded more frightened than she was. "I forgot to yell from the door. Put the safety back on and lay down the shotgun. Gently!"

More than happy to comply, she gently lowered it onto the bed. "I heard you," she called. "The gun's down. I was afraid to unpump it, though."

"Elisa?" He peeked around the door frame.

She smiled. "Just call me Ma Barker. Boy, you were sure right. Just the *sound* of this gun is enough to scare a pack of thieves. You ought to see your face."

"I'm not sure I like the comparison, but you did exactly what I told you." He stepped across the room and disarmed the weapon, keeping the barrel pointed to the floor. When he'd finished, he stuck it inside the closet.

Crossing back to the bed, he examined her ankle and the two bruised lumps on her head. After pronouncing her nearly healed, he said, "Now that you've had a couple days of Miriam's wonderful food, are you ready for some real simple grub?"

Her stomach growled in timely response. "Right now I think I'd settle for a seaweed salad."

"Don't set your expectations so high. I'm a miserable chef—can't even manage a barbecue. But I'll see what I can scratch up."

While Storm was whistling like Happy the dwarf in the kitchen, Elisa limped into the bathroom. Because his cabin had its own cistern, there was plenty of water. None of it, however, was hot. He'd mentioned earlier that it was best to keep the gas turned off until the power company gave the okay.

Still, after sweltering in this unseasonable heat for the past few days, the cool—actually chilly—bathwater was a welcome treat. After freshening up, she dabbed on a touch of makeup, wrapped her long hair in a chignon and donned the flower-print sundress he'd brought back from the hotel.

She caught her reflection in the mirror and grinned. Elisa looked and felt like a new woman.

Opening the bathroom door, she was immediately caught up by a wonderful aroma started wafting down the hall. Obviously, Storm had downplayed his culinary abilities. Following the tantalizing aroma to the kitchen, she paused at the door. Still whistling, he was chopping radishes and tossing them into a wooden salad bowl.

He looked perfectly at home performing the small domestic chores, unlike most of the men she'd dated in the city. Most of them thought romaine grew in salad bars.

"Smells wonderful," she said.

He tossed a grin over his shoulder. "I warned you, don't get your hopes up."

Despite his dire predictions, the simple fare of steamed crab legs—compliments of Miriam's freezer—and tossed green salad was delicious. Her stomach was already protesting when Elisa dunked a last succulent chunk of crab into the drawn butter. Wiping her mouth on the paper towel he'd provided, she declared, "Enough! I couldn't hold another bite."

Storm glanced at her empty plate, and at the saucer heaped with crab shells. "Glad to see you could choke it down. How about some coffee? Or would you like more wine?"

Actually, she'd gotten the tiniest buzz from the two glasses she'd already had, and she wasn't ready to give up the soft, glorious feeling. "Maybe another drop of wine, but that's my limit."

He gathered up the empty plates. "I'll make a deal with you. You go find a CD or cassette that plays nice, relaxing music, and I'll bring your wine in the living room."

"You got a deal."

Count Basie was tinkling the ivories in the background when Storm carried two glasses and a fresh bottle of chardonnay into the living room.

"I only wanted a drop," she protested.

"How am I supposed to get you drunk and have my wicked way with you if you won't cooperate?"

"Guess you'll just have to get creative."

He pointed to the sofa. "Why don't you lie down right there?"

"Uh, I know I said creative, but could you add subtle to your repertoire?"

He chuckled and grabbed a couple of throw pillows off the floor. "Actually, I want you to elevate that ankle some more."

"Oh," she said, with a hint of agitation. Keeping her back turned, so that he wouldn't see the disappointment on her face, she climbed onto the sofa and stretched out her legs.

Storm seemed willing to take the game just so far before withdrawing. His continued strategy of advance, then retreat, kept Elisa off balance and confused.

After propping Elisa's newly wrapped ankle on a throw pillow, he handed her a glass of the golden wine and hunkered down on the floor next to her. As he sipped slowly, his fingers plucked at the worn tweed fabric of the sofa. She felt as if he was trying to broach something important, but couldn't find the right opening words.

Finally he set his glass on the chunk of burled redwood that served as a coffee table. He cleared his throat and kept his eyes on the frayed thread he'd been picking. "This morning you said that I had no business telling you to face up to your past when I couldn't do it myself."

"But I was mad, I—"

He held up his hand, shutting off her protest. "You were right. So I thought maybe I could tell *you* and...unload a little."

When she didn't reply, he continued. "Anyway, I think I mentioned that Karen and I were living in New York. We'd just moved from Baltimore, where I had a pretty good deal at Johns Hopkins. But when I was offered the position as head of the children's psychiatric section at University

Hospital, I leaped at the chance. I'd finally be able to focus on the very issue that had led me into psychiatry in the first place—abused and troubled children.''

Elisa sipped her wine. ''I can certainly understand. Nothing is more satisfying than being able to fulfill a lifelong goal.''

Storm nodded. ''Karen certainly didn't understand. She was unhappy with my decision, although, like the perfect wife she'd always been, she let me decide for myself. Actually, Karen wasn't into making decisions. She didn't like heavy responsibility. Anyway, once we moved to New York I was so wrapped up in my new job that I didn't notice when her depressive symptoms developed. She had the disorder for years, and was treated by an excellent doctor in Baltimore who kept her episodes pretty much under control. I'd *assumed* that she'd hooked up with another clinic in New York, but...''

Elisa finished for him. ''But she didn't.''

''No. I *knew* how she hated change, how she'd put off making the smallest decision until it was impossible to avoid it any longer. I should have taken the initiative myself. Except she never wanted to be treated by someone I recommended. It made her feel too vulnerable, like she thought we'd discuss her case or something.''

Elisa set her glass on the coffee table, and looked down at Storm's tousled chestnut hair. She longed to take him in her arms and comfort him, but knew this was something he had to do alone. Purge his pain, once and for all. ''What happened then?''

''After a few weeks, even I noticed the signs. She wouldn't get out of bed all day. Wouldn't shower unless I made her. Textbook symptoms of acute depression. Anyway, I got a referral for an excellent doctor who wasn't affiliated with our hospital, and made Karen an appointment. She didn't keep it. But I didn't find out until much later. I was furious with her.''

''I can imagine,'' she said. ''It's frustrating when someone could help themselves so easily, but won't make the effort.''

He nodded. ''I've never really worked with adult depression or bipolar disorder. The few depressed kids I see are usually that way because of their situation. It's more hopelessness than anything else. But with Karen's illness, she was too far gone to help herself. Anyway, I made a second appointment and blocked off time from work so I could take her myself.''

Elisa was silent, feeling instinctively that he was finally approaching the heart of the matter.

''I was too late,'' he said, his voice breaking with unshed tears. ''When I went home that afternoon to pick her up, she was lying in bed. Cold. She was so cold. I guess she'd hoarded pills for years. She'd swallowed about a hundred and fifty different narcotics and over-the-counter medications.''

''Oh, Storm, that's just awful. I'm so sorry.''

''Yeah.'' He laughed ruefully. ''I'm sorry, too. But my wife is still dead.''

''But that wasn't your fault! You did everything possible to help her.''

''That's what I'd tell you if you were a patient, but it simply doesn't hold true for me.''

She reached down and cupped his chin, tilting his face upward. ''That's not fair! You can't set up a second standard, a much higher standard, for yourself than you would for anyone else. Give yourself a break, Storm. It *wasn't* your fault.''

But she could tell he wasn't ready to give up the guilt that was ground into his soul like shards of glass.

''What kind of doctor wouldn't notice his own wife's mental deterioration until it was too late? Answer that, Princess.'' The quiet anguish in his voice brought tears to her eyes. He'd suffered so long, absorbing and hoarding guilt that wasn't his to take. But nothing she could say would ease his burden unless he was ready to lay it down.

What kind of doctor was he? At least ten answers came to mind, but she didn't offer any of them. He was so intent on blaming himself that telling him not to wasn't going to make a difference. For now, she was pleased that he trusted her enough to share his pain. Maybe time would help him erase this dark, ugly blot from his soul.

When she didn't answer, he unfolded his legs and strode into the kitchen, returning with the half-empty bottle of wine. He topped off his own glass and poured the remainder into hers.

He lowered himself to the floor and sat, cross-legged, facing her. "Confession's supposed to be good for the soul, but I feel like I just upchucked."

She laughed. "Oh, Doctor, I'm afraid you're going to have to chew on some more of your own advice. Remember telling me that purging was *good?* Like getting your stomach pumped and removing all that poison from your system?"

"Yeah, yeah…" He swiped at the air, dismissing her teasing remarks. "So let's talk about you for a while, Princess. How did a beautiful *señorita* from the Coast become a world-renowned prima ballerina?"

"I don't know about the 'world-renowned' part, but mostly it was just pure hard work."

"I'll bet. You must've paid some heavy dues."

"Not just me. My mother, especially. When my dad died, we didn't have much money, so Mom worked two, sometimes three jobs to take care of us. She was determined that we wouldn't run the streets, wouldn't get sucked into the gang influence, so she kept shoving us into after-school recreation programs."

"Smart woman," Storm said.

"One day some dancers from a visiting company came to our school and performed for us. They took my breath away. Dancing on air, wearing glamorous costumes, looking like fairy princesses. That night I ran home and begged my mother for ballet lessons. We couldn't afford it, of course, but I didn't really understand that at the time. So I kept bugging her.''

Storm laughed and finished his chardonnay. ''And finally wore her down.''

''You guessed it. She started taking in laundry to pay for my lessons. Later, I got some help from different Hispanic organizations and even won a couple scholarships. But it was never enough to pay for everything, so my mom continued to work day and night, as well as doing other people's laundry.''

''She sounds like a wonderful woman. I'd like to meet her someday.''

A warm, glowing smile softened Elisa's face. ''She'd like that. She was always so proud of me. When I had my first professional performance, she went up and down the street telling everybody that her daughter, her *chica,* was going to be a big star. I had a dream, you know, that I could pay her back someday. Buy her a fine home. Hire someone else to do *her* laundry.''

''And you were well on your way to accomplishing that when you had…the accident.''

Tears welled up in Elisa's eyes, and she knuckled them away in agitation. ''Now I'll never be able to repay my mother.''

Storm reached up and caressed her forearm. ''In her eyes, I'm sure you already have.''

''I feel so robbed, so cheated. It's not just losing my career, or my full mobility, or even my memory. But I lost the power to earn the kind of money I needed to buy that home for my mom.''

He eased up onto the sofa beside her and drew her into his arms. ''Something else will come along. Trust in yourself. You were smart enough, strong enough and determined enough to claw your way to the top of the dancing game. You can accomplish anything you set your mind to.''

She was quiet, and he hoped she was absorbing his

words. With a face, mind, body and determination like hers, she could rule the world.

He quietly got up and checked the fire. Her eyes followed him back to the sofa. Those ebony-dark, exotic, entrancing eyes. "How's your foot?" he whispered, trying to remember exactly what vow he'd made to himself that afternoon. Something about not taking advantage...

Elisa shrugged. "I think it's numb. This is the first time since the accident that I've had more than one glass of wine."

Oh, great. Not only did he have his stupid vow to contend with, now she was pleading intoxication, and he'd never sunk so low as to seduce a woman in her cups.

If only she didn't look so lovely, so beguiling. She'd changed into a flimsy summery dress that skimmed her hips and floated when she walked. The hem normally fell just below the knee, but now it was hiked up onto her thigh, exposing her slim, silky legs to his appreciative view.

Scrupulously keeping his hands from touching her alluring limbs, he carefully unwrapped the makeshift binding around her ankle. Miriam Danziger's sheet supply must be precariously low by now, he thought inconsequentially.

The swelling had gone down considerably. By morning she'd be good as ever.

His eyes trailed up her leg again, lingering on the dark and forbidden area at the top of her thighs. A guilty thrill shot through him, until he looked up and saw her watching him. Her eyes were issuing an invitation, but he had to refuse.

"'Leese, you know that I...I would like to...more than anything in the world. But it's unethical for a doctor to, um, you know, with a patient."

"I'm not your patient, Doctor."

"Not in the strictest sense of the word. Still, I know how vulnerable you are, and—"

"Right now I'm about as vulnerable as a she-lion. I'm a big girl, Storm. I'm not asking for any commitments."

"That's good! See, because I'm not ready for another relationship... What I mean is—" Tugging his fingers through his unruly hair, he floundered, trying to find the words that would convince her that he wanted her, *really* wanted her, but just couldn't...

"Storm?"

"Mmm?"

She wiggled her index finger. "You think too much. Shut up and come here."

"There?" Now that was a direct order if he'd ever heard one. All his vows, all his intentions, disappeared like morning fog as he moved upward, anxious to do his lady's bidding.

Her slow, languid smile drew him to her lips. Heat fanned through his groin as he stretched out on the sofa facing her. His shoulders touched hers, his chest was seared by the delectable mounds of her breasts. Her soft place pillowed where he was hard.

Elisa's hands wrapped around his neck, and she moaned when his tentative fingers sought and cupped her breast. Her nipple perked beneath his touch, but he had to feel more, closer. Pulling back, he unbuttoned the front of her sundress. Arching slowly, provocatively, she helped him slide the dress over her hips.

She had a beautiful body, as he'd known she would, but it was the beauty of her spirit and her soul that held him spellbound.

A moment later, her bra and panties were disposed of and she lay there, a glorious goddess, and it was his pleasure to serve her. He slid to the floor, and lowered his head over her tempting breasts. His tongue flicked and suckled until she squirmed and moaned with passion.

He'd never known a woman like Elisa Montoya. A woman who could thrill him, challenge him, frustrate him and cherish him, all within the space of a few moments. If only he could stretch this night into forever. But it was too late for happily-ever-afters. For Storm, there was only to-night.

Vowing to give her enough sensual bliss to last a life-time, he happily set about pleasuring her. His mouth trailed downward, over the smooth, exquisitely sensitive flesh just above her waist. Lower, darting and probing in the deli-cious area around her navel. "Oh, Storm, please. I'm ready."

"Not yet," he whispered. "There's lots more of you I haven't kissed yet. Haven't loved yet."

A shudder rippled down her body, urging him to con-tinue his journey. He rained flicking, moist caresses down her stomach until he found the sweet, dark mound at the crux of her thighs. He raised slightly, placing his hands on her hips until he tilted her toward him. She was like a fabulous feast, and he wanted to savor each and every bit of her.

The heat of her fingers singed his back, massaging his taut muscles. "You have to stop," she whispered, her hips writhing beneath his hands. "I can't stand any more."

He ran one hand up the flat of her stomach, along the silky-hard tip of her breast, up her throat until he found her mouth. Tracing the shape of her slightly pouty, sultry lips, he lowered his head and drank in the sweet nectar of her pulsing femininity. "Oh!" she cried aloud, her fingers tan-gling through his hair, urging him on. Her mouth opened, and she took his finger between her lips, suckling him as he was her.

At last he drew away, and kissed her inner thigh. "I think we'd be more comfortable if we finished this in the bed-room," he murmured.

"You're the doctor," she whispered in a ragged, breath-less voice.

Storm once more scooped her into his arms, but this time there was no danger. Only a mutual yearning. A need that had to be filled.

He'd never had a woman like Elisa. Wild. Wanton. As

giving in her lovemaking as she was in every other aspect of her life. Although he would have called himself an experienced lover before tonight, he knew now that he'd never loved a woman before. Or been loved so well.

When they reached the bedroom, he gently lowered her onto the bed. The room was dark, with only the moonlight illuminating his solid, hard body as he stripped off his clothes. She reached out and touched the firm, conditioned muscles of his thigh. He was like a living statue, with sinews taut and sculpted. Her searching fingers found the strong evidence of his arousal, and she stroked him, his passion fueling her own.

She could feel his muscles tense as he gasped with pleasure. After a while, he eased into the bed and lowered his body to cover hers. She looked into his eyes—they were glittering gemstones in the moonlight—and was filled with a sense of completeness. No matter what tomorrow brought, if she never had another night with him, Elisa knew she'd spent her entire life waiting for this moment.

Closing her eyes, she begged him to take her away, away from fear, away from solitude, away from the world.

Storm took her. And she cried aloud as waves of pleasure shuddered through her body.

Chapter Sixteen

Elisa rolled over and stretched, feeling fuzzy and contented. She reached out and touched Storm's pillow. His empty pillow. Sitting up, she shoved her rumpled mass of jet hair out of her eyes and frowned. Then smiled when she heard Storm moving around in the front of the cabin.

Last night had been incredible. An exhilarating, sensuous feast that left them hungry for seconds. And thirds. This morning she felt sated, completely filled with his essence, as if they had been melted down and reformed into a single being. She blinked and sucked in her lip, startled by her giddy thoughts. *She sounded dangerously like a woman in love.*

Her heart thumped at the word. The deep, pervasive sense of completeness soaking into her bones *felt* the way she'd always imagined deep, unwavering love would feel. But she couldn't fall in love! Not now, and not with him. Her life was in a terrible upheaval, and Storm lived this hermit's existence, and...and he hadn't said a word about love last night.

Neither of them had ever spoken of their feelings. They'd spoken only of the sexual fascination that had beguiled them from the moment he towed her out of the ocean. They'd both also made it perfectly clear that they weren't looking for any kind of commitment. Only a night's respite from the loneliness that stalked them both for so long.

No promises, no regrets. Those were the rules they'd played by, and she couldn't change them now, at the end of the game.

If she strolled out of the bedroom, murmuring sweet nothings and love talk, Storm would run for the beach and *swim* to the mainland. He'd also be embarrassed, appalled and full of pity. And she'd rather die than endure his pity.

No, she had to keep up the charade, never let him glimpse her true feelings. Pretend last night had been sinfully delicious and stress-relieving. And nothing more.

The pleasure she found in his arms had momentarily shut out the horror. At least for a while. And for that, Elisa was grateful.

Sliding out of bed, she visited the bathroom and slipped into her clothes. Pasting a casual smile on her face, she slowly ambled down the hall.

He was in the kitchen, and the fragrant aroma of coffee and bacon wafted out to greet her. She suddenly realized she was famished. Why not? She'd certainly worked up an appetite during the night.

"Morning," she called cheerily as she reached for a mug.

Storm grinned over his shoulder. "Hi yourself, Sleeping Beauty. Get enough?"

"Sleep, I presume you mean," she asked bluntly, taking a sip of the steaming brew. His offhand, slightly raunchy comment served to solidify her theory. He saw last night as a thoroughly delightful romp between two consenting adults. This morning, their roles were to be those of casual lovers. So be it.

He turned off the burner and turned around. Resting his rump against the countertop, he frowned. "Everything okay? Thought I detected a note of...sarcasm. Even anger."

Shaking her head, she dragged out a chair. "Nothing's wrong. I'm always a little edgy when I first wake up—no big deal."

Now it was his turn to delve for an ulterior message in her careless remark. What did she consider to be "no big deal"? Her moodiness in the morning, or the very special night that they'd shared? Because he considered last night a *very* big deal. A life-altering experience.

He'd hoped they could talk openly this morning. See where they wanted to take this fragile new gift. Storm had existed for the past two years in a vault of guilt and broken dreams. He'd tried to bury his heart with Karen. But Elisa had saved him from that cold, dark existence.

He had planned to lay his feelings out in the open for her to accept or reject as she would. But now, with tension radiating from her like sonar waves, he decided to bide his time.

Turning back to the propane stove, he cracked four eggs into the skillet. Maybe her odd mood had nothing to do with him, with the perfect union they'd found last night. She couldn't know that his greedy masculine ego needed to know that she, too, considered last night a special event. Beyond the scope of merely scratching a sexual itch.

Elisa's level, matter-of-fact tone broke into his thoughts. "Do you think it's safe to go back to our—I mean, my cabin?"

Suddenly he understood. The specter of the killer had taken center stage again. If he'd been thinking more about the threat to her life than about his own fragile ego, he would have realized the fear would attack her again this morning.

He had to believe that her detached mood wasn't because of him, because of her disappointment in him. "Taking a look at the cabin is a good idea. Maybe we'll find something in Heather's things that will help identify her partner. *After* we eat. I don't know why, but I woke up with a raging appetite."

"Me too," Elisa said shyly.

Not wanting to read too much into her comment, he

dished up a steaming plate of bacon, eggs and hash browns and set it in front of her.

"You expect me to eat all that? I don't eat that much for breakfast in a full week."

Storm rubbed an imaginary bruise on his side. "And that's why your bones almost did me serious damage last night. Eat."

She managed to pack down nearly a third of the portion he'd given her before she shoved the plate aside and patted her tummy. "I'm going to explode if I eat another bite. If I hang around you very long, I'm going to end up fat."

He wiped up a bit of egg yolk with a slice of bread. "As long as you're healthy, who cares if you're fat? Although the very idea boggles the imagination."

She stood and started carrying the plates to the sink. "What should I do about hot water?"

He wiped his mouth and stepped behind her. "Let's leave them till later. I'll have to boil some water."

Waving off her dire warning about the ravages of dried egg on china plates, he grabbed his keys. "Let's go check out your cabin. Just in case Heather left any incriminating bits of information lying around."

Although he seriously doubted that the redhead had left a diary detailing her part in Jay's death, along with the name of her compatriot and their motivation. Lucky breaks like that only happened in the movies.

TWO HOURS LATER, they'd found nothing to disprove his theory. They spent the first hour pulling the plywood coverings off the windows so that they'd have enough light for their search. Their neighbor, Brian McPherson, must have nailed them up after he finished his own place. They would have to go next door and thank him when they were finished.

Storm wondered what Elisa was feeling when they finally breached the sanctum of Heather's bedroom. At first she resisted opening drawers and closets, as if prying into her former friend's belongings were more reprehensible than the part she'd played in her death.

With a little nudging, she gave in and inspected the dresser while Storm tackled the closet. They quickly discovered that Heather's personal effects were unbelievably *im*personal. Clothes, makeup, a couple of glitzy novels and a box full of beauty magazines.

They rooted under the bed, mattress and dresser. Elisa tore apart the bathroom while Storm scoured the attic. Not a letter, photograph or even a bill turned up. At last they gave up and returned to the main living area.

Completely stymied, they stood in the middle of the room, facing each other. She had a small, dark smudge on her chin, and he leaned over to wipe it away with his thumb. Instinctively she jerked away, as if to allow his touch would breach some inner bulwark. Puzzled and disheartened, he marveled at the change in her demeanor since last night.

"What do we do now?" she asked, her arms folded defensively across her breasts.

Storm's hand fell to his side. What he *wanted* to do was talk this out, but his wounded feelings weren't the highest priority right now. A killer had to be unveiled before he got to Elisa again.

Dragging his fingers through his hair, he clasped his hands behind his neck. "I suppose we should go back to the hotel and start asking questions. If our culprit's there, maybe he'll slip up."

Elisa hesitated. Storm knew she was dreading facing Carey Howard again. Although she'd acted in self-defense, the lovestruck man was filled with rage at his loss. It was easier to take his anger out on Elisa than to face the truth about the woman he'd cared for.

"I can't think of anything better," she admitted as they headed out the door.

Brian McPherson was standing on his porch, as if wait-

ing for them. Elisa waved as they trudged across the sandy
lot.

"How's the arm, McPherson?" Storm called as they approached the big man's porch.

He twisted his forearm dismissively. "Good as new.
Thanks, Doc. So what're you folks up to this fine mor-
nin'?"

"Just checking things over," Elisa replied. "Thanks for
finishing boarding up the place, Brian. That was very
thoughtful of you, although I don't know how you managed
it by yourself."

He scratched the reddish stubble along his jaw. "Well,
you girls have been pretty good to a lonely old bachelor
this summer. Especially Heather, always bringing me left-
overs."

Elisa blanched. "Oh, my God!"

Both men stepped forward, as if to catch her. She waved
them away. "No, I'm not sick or dizzy. I just remembered,
Brian doesn't know yet—about Heather!"

"Yeah, I do," he said glumly. He opened his screen door
and beckoned them to follow him inside. When they were
seated in the dim, and noticeably cooler, great room, Brian
wiped his eyes. "Hank Danziger was making the rounds
of the island yesterday, making sure everybody was okay,
and stopped by and told me. Saddest damn thing I ever
heard of."

Storm and Elisa murmured their assent.

Brian leaned forward and focused his pale blue gaze on
Elisa. "What happened? I thought you two were such good
friends."

Storm saw her eyelids flutter at Brian's mild reproach.
He wished he could take her pain, her undeserved guilt,
and carry it on his own soul for a while. His protective
instincts demanded he step in and stop McPherson's interrogation. But Elisa was her own woman and needed to
answer for herself. So he kept his counsel and waited, with
Brian, for her reply.

"I thought we were friends, too, Brian. That's why we're trying to find out what happened. Did Heather ever say anything...odd?"

"About you?"

"About anything," Storm added.

Brian's huge fingers grazed his beard again. He stared into space, as if lost in thought. Finally, he shook his head. "Nope. Nothing that I can recall, anyway. Heather was always...real special, you know?"

There didn't seem to be much left to say. Storm and Elisa rose to their feet. "Thanks, anyway."

"Anytime," he said, as he followed them to the door.

The door to a study off the great room was standing open, and Storm noted an impressive array of computer equipment. "Whew! You could open your own computer store. Use all that in your work?"

Brian nodded. "Thanks to computers, modems, faxes and the Internet, I was able to leave the city and keep my job."

"What line are you in?" Storm asked.

"Crunching numbers and information," Brian answered vaguely.

The man was obviously still too grief-stricken to engage in polite conversation, so Storm took advantage of the lull to make their exit.

Elisa was still unusually quiet. Ignoring her remoteness, Storm took her hand as they walked away from Mc-Pherson's place. The only sound in the soundless mid-morning air was their feet crunching on the mixture of sand and crushed seashells that created a path of sorts between the beach houses.

"By the way," Brian called out as they climbed into the Jeep, "according to Hank, the ferry'll be running again in the morning. 'Course, no telling how long before the power's restored."

Storm waved an acknowledgment and started the engine.

When they drove away, Brian was standing on the porch again, his sad eyes following their departure.

They rode in silence over the rutted and littered road to the village. Storm considered the ramifications of renewed ferry service to the mainland. Those stranded on the island would be free to leave in the morning. If he and Elisa failed in their efforts to identify Heather's accomplice, a killer might very well go unpunished.

A second, even more disturbing, thought surfaced. What if Elisa chose to take that ferry? Her life was in the city, and surely that was where she'd return at the first opportunity. Would she go back to New York, or return to her mother's home in California?

It didn't really matter, he reflected. Either place would take her away from him.

In more ways than one, time was running out.

ELISA GLANCED across the bucket seats to where Storm was staring out the windshield, looking as though his mind were a thousand miles away. She knew he was thinking about the ferry; so was she. When that boat arrived in the morning, she and the others would no longer be confined to Double Dare Island.

But, unlike the others, she was torn. Her mind told her to run for safety, run back to her friends and family. Her heart told her to stay. Explore the wonder they'd started to discover last night.

But what did Storm want?

As if feeling the searching heat of her gaze, he swiveled his head to face her. "Before we reach the hotel, I think we should come up with a game plan."

His husky voice was impersonal, detached. She locked away her troubled heart. He was right; they should stay focused on finding the killer. Only a few hours remained between the murderer and freedom. And once she left the island, Elisa knew, she'd be on her own against him.

Forcing a layer of aloofness into her tone, she asked,

"How do we go about questioning them? One at a time, or as a group, à la Agatha Christie?"

"Individually, I think. Since neither of us are experienced investigators, if we have too many people to keep track of, we may miss some gesture or nuance."

Actually, Storm was quite experienced in interrogation, she thought. His years of studying and evaluating patients would prove invaluable in ferreting out the truth. But if their quarry was one of the hotel's occupants, they'd already spent considerable time in his company without feeling any vibes. Anyone who could kill so brutally wouldn't flinch at telling a few well-chosen lies.

They pulled into the hotel drive and Storm eased along the side to the parking lot in the rear. Hank, Mark Bowman and David were dragging vegetation and refuse into a huge pile at the edge of the concrete pavement.

"Why don't you go on inside?" he said. "I want to talk to Hank for a minute."

"Sure." Feeling like the unwanted thirteenth guest at a dinner party for twelve, Elisa slid off the high bucket seat and onto the ground.

Tears stung her eyes as she hurried up the back steps and entered the quiet, deserted kitchen. For once, Miriam had abandoned her usual post, and Elisa had the comforting room all to herself. She took a soft drink from the cooler and sank into a chair at the kitchen table.

The tears felt hotter now, more imminent. And she didn't even know what she was crying about. As usual, Elisa's inner voice knew when she was fudging the truth. It wasn't the frustration, fear, guilt or despair of this long ordeal that was wearing her down. Her tears were for the lost intimacy she'd had with Storm last night.

The soul-satisfying tenderness that no other man would ever be able to evoke in her. The tenderness that had been missing this morning.

Sighing deeply, she mentally closed the book on any future with Storm Delaney. She stood up and arched her back. She might as well go upstairs and gather the rest of her things. Later, she'd have Storm drop her off at her cabin so that she could finish packing. Tomorrow, she would take the first ferry off the island.

She heard the murmur of voices in the parlor, and treaded softly as she crossed the foyer to the staircase. The last thing she wanted—or needed—was another shouting match with Carey Howard.

Luck was with her, for she didn't encounter a soul on the short journey to her room. She hesitated outside the door. Her return to the scene of the crime. If she closed her eyes, she could still see Heather's body, lying in a pool of her own blood. Every tiny detail was crystallized in her mind. The way Heather's leg had crooked. That strand of red hair across her face. The smear of crimson where her bloody head had touched the dust ruffle.

Blanking her mind to the abhorrent memory, Elisa pushed open the door.

For the first time, she saw the bedroom in natural sunlight. The pale wallpaper with tiny pink cabbage roses was a perfect complement to the diaphanous white sheers at the window. The brass bed was dressed with a new coverlet, in pale mint green. It was a lovely room, decorated with gentility and taste. The sort of furnishings she might have chosen for herself.

If not for the utter devastation.

Her room had been ransacked. The perpetrator had been thorough and chaotic. The mattress was off the bed, its ticking ripped to shreds, bedsprings poking through the damaged covering. Every drawer had been rifled, and her clothing was strewn about haphazardly. Her favorite silk blouse was on the floor, trampled by muddy feet.

Nothing had been spared. Even bath and cosmetic items in the bathroom had been opened and dumped on the floor. The plastic file with her personal papers had been ravaged, its contents ripped apart and discarded.

The incongruous scent of spilled cologne and bath powder wafted through the room.

Who, she wondered, could have done this? She knew *why.* The person who combed through her belongings had been looking for one thing: the computer disk. It was the obvious key. So far, it had caused the deaths of two people. People she'd cared about.

But who knew she even had it? Unless Heather had told her confederate, Storm was the only other person who knew it was in Elisa's possession. That detested niggling doubt wormed its way into her mind again. *Storm* had been at the hotel yesterday. Saying he was picking up clothing for her had given him the perfect excuse for being in her room.

She clasped her hands over her mouth to keep from crying aloud. It *had* to be Storm. Or Heather's vague, ghostly accomplice, who seemed to be everywhere at once. *If* he even existed. The idea of Heather having a partner in her crime had been Storm's. And Elisa had been so quick to believe him.

She rubbed her palms up her cheeks, stretching the supple flesh as if she could somehow flex her mind. If only she could recall the rest of that night, then she'd know for certain.

Leaning against the door frame, she strove to sort out her contradictory emotions. One minute she was falling in love with Storm, the next she suspected him of murder. He was right on one account, at least. She obviously needed professional counseling.

But as she relived the events of the past few days, the wonderful, generous, caring and exquisitely sensual side of Storm Delaney won hands down against her vague mistrust. He was no more capable of deliberate, cold-blooded murder than she was. He'd literally saved her life. He'd stood beside her when the others abandoned her. He'd even shared his own heartache. How could she have hoped for his love, when she hadn't been able to give him her trust?

Her hand slowly dropped to her waist, and she pulled up

the edge of her T-shirt. Tucked into her waistband, where it had been since Storm retrieved it after Heather's death, was the much-sought-after disk. Proof positive the killer wasn't Storm. He'd known that blue floppy was with Elisa at his cabin. He hadn't needed to search for it.

Shame filled her at the realization that she'd needed his innocence verified, confirmed beyond a doubt, while his confidence in her had never wavered.

She sank to the floor, just inside the doorway. She'd absorbed one too many shocks; one too many terrors. One too many ugly self-realizations. She'd reached the end of her emotional tether.

STORM HAD BEEN WAITING for Elisa nearly a half hour when he finally climbed the stairs in search of her. Rounding the landing, he saw that her bedroom door was open. The distorted shadow of someone's upper body and head was clearly visible on the hallway carpet. Unlike a human form, however, the shadow wasn't moving, not even minutely. His steps quickened.

"'Leese? Are you all right? What's going on?"

He reached the doorway and halted abruptly. She was sitting on the floor, her back to the doorway, her head bowed as if in prayer. Glancing past her, Storm saw that her room had been ransacked. And by someone who enjoyed destruction.

Dropping to his knees behind the unmoving woman, he lightly touched her shoulders. "Elisa? It's me, Princess. Everything's going to be okay now. C'mon, let's go downstairs and have lunch."

Slowly, as slowly as honey dripping through a pinhole, she lifted her head. Twisting her neck slightly, she faced him. "Guess I zonked out. Sorry."

Sorry? The man who'd destroyed her things and was dead-set on destroying Elisa was the one who was going to be sorry.

Storm's jaw clenched until his muscles ached. He'd

never been angrier in his life. If he could get his hands on this bastard for just five minutes...

Right now, though, Elisa was more important than his own feelings of inadequacy and powerless rage.

Rising to his feet, he took her limp wrists and drew her upright. He ran his palms up her bare arms, over her shoulders and up the smooth dusky column of her neck. Cupping her face, he leaned close and whispered softly, "You have nothing—do you hear me?—nothing to be sorry for."

"I feel like such a weakling. Like I'm always falling apart and you have to patch me up again."

He shook his head in wonder. "Elisa Montoya, you're the strongest person I've ever met. I spent two years locked away in my own guilt, my own self-pity, until you drew me out."

She didn't comment or raise her eyes to meet his, but he sensed that his words were penetrating her despair. Tilting her chin until she was forced to look at him, Storm continued, "In the past two months you've gone through more emotional and physical havoc than most people face in a lifetime. And you have the nerve to call yourself weak? Give me a break, Princess—you make Schwarzenegger look like a wimp."

A tiny smile cracked her frozen expression. "A female Terminator, huh?"

Relief washed over him. Once again, she'd found the emotional strength to pull herself out of shock. This woman was like a velvet-wrapped blackjack. Soft and fuzzy on the outside, with a forged-steel interior. Lightly kissing her forehead, he led her into the hallway, quietly pulling the door closed behind them.

"Come on, Arnold, let's go downstairs and terminate those suspects."

BUT THEORY proved easier than practice.

Carey Howard flatly refused to discuss his relationship

with Heather. "You're only trying to muddy the waters, Doctor. The murderer is standing right beside you."

His baleful eyes tossed a scornful glance at Elisa. "Go ahead and keep trying to cover up. You're not fooling anyone. All the smoke and mirrors you can drag out won't erase what really happened to Heather. Believe me, the truth will come out soon enough when the police get here."

With that, he slammed his door in their faces.

Was his refusal to discuss the matter a sign of guilt or of a broken heart? Storm couldn't tell. He only knew Carey Howard was at the top of his list of suspects.

The Bowmans agreed to speak only if they could remain together. Storm didn't consider them serious suspects, although it was possible Mark and Heather had been having an affair behind Betty's back. But Jay's death had occurred at the height of tourist season on the island. Mark Bowman swore he hadn't been ashore for more than a half day since April. Betty nodded her agreement. Unless she was covering up for him, Storm was ready to scratch him from the suspect list.

Nor did Hank and Miriam provide any worthwhile information. Like the Bowmans, the hotel kept them firmly in place from late spring until fall. Miriam *had* gone to Norfolk for two days for dental work in early June, but since then, the Danzigers declared, they hadn't left the island. The hotel demanded so much of their time, they even ordered groceries and cleaning supplies by phone.

"Listen, you two," Miriam said as they rose from the kitchen table. "I'm just an old country woman who didn't get much schooling, but I know one thing. Evil is stalking this island right now. Steer clear of whoever this devil is. Don't let him get his clutches into you kids."

Storm ran his knuckles along her withered cheek. "You ever decide to leave that old man of yours—" he winked at Hank "—you look me up."

"I'll do that." She tittered, twitching her shoulders like a schoolgirl. "Where are you two headed now?"

"We want to talk to the others," Elisa said.

"Then we're going back to my place," Storm added. "I think Elisa will be safer there."

Hank drummed his fingers on the wooden tabletop. "Don't know, son, you're a far piece away from town. You might be a better target out there alone. Reckon you two ought to stay here tonight?"

Storm chuckled. "You old miser, you just want two more nights' rent."

"That would be fine, too," the old man agreed.

Miriam's ever-present dishtowel snapped.

"Ouch! What's wrong with you, old woman?"

"You let these kids stay where they've a mind to. They'll come back for dinner. Won't you?"

Storm glanced at Elisa, as if waiting for her answer. "I, uh, don't think so, Miriam." The idea of Carey Howard's hate-filled eyes staring at her across the table would ruin everyone's meal.

But Miriam wouldn't accept no for an answer. Hank was going to fry his infamous Southern-style chicken, and she'd already made coleslaw and baked beans. Miriam allowed as how she was even considering frying up some hush puppies. "So you just have to come," she concluded. "This is our last night. We have to celebrate surviving the hurricane. It's tradition."

Elisa refused to show her ignorance by inquiring what manner of food a hush puppy might be. She tried to think of an excuse for declining the invitation that Miriam would understand. Finally, she settled on the truth. "I just don't want to get into another wrangle with Carey. It's not fair to anyone."

Miriam swallowed her in a fleshy embrace. "Why, bless your soul, child. He's just upset. Carey doesn't mean any harm. Besides, it's such a pretty evening, we're going to set up picnic tables on the patio. You won't have to be at the same table with anybody, if you don't want to."

Unable to come up with a valid rebuttal, Elisa gave in.

Storm stepped forward to rescue her from Miriam's smothering bear hug. "I think I just saw David in the parlor. Come on, 'Leese, we'd better get in there before he disappears."

"Don't forget—six o'clock!" Miriam shouted as they escaped through the swinging doors.

Once they were seated across from him, Storm broke the ice by asking if David could tell them his whereabouts on the night of Jay's death.

The lawyer was obviously amused by their amateur efforts at detection. Folding his left arm across his stomach, he tapped his lip with his right index finger, doing a poor impression of Jack Benny. "Well... Let me see. Where was I on the night of my client's death? Why, I was at a dinner party, I do believe. With about five hundred of the mayor's closest friends."

He slapped his hand on the end table. "This is an insult. To my professionalism, my humanity and my intellect. Don't you think I was questioned by the police about this affair? All of Jay's friends, business associates and casual acquaintances were checked out. The police even questioned his barber. Now that Jay's death has been ruled a homicide, the police will find the killer!"

Storm cocked his head. "Why is it you don't seem to want Elisa to clear herself? Maybe if she's arrested the police will stop delving into his business affairs. Is that what you're hoping, *Counselor?*"

Shaking his head, David pointed an accusing finger at Storm. "You self-serving jerk! I don't know what you're trying to imply, Delaney, but my business dealings will withstand any scrutiny."

"Then why are you so opposed to Elisa searching for the truth?"

David laughed dryly. "What arrogance! To think you can uncover the truth about Jay Morrow's death, when the entire New York City police department couldn't."

Storm hesitated, considering the attorney's words. If

Welton had an ironclad alibi for the night Jay died, that let him off the hook. So why was he so defensive and angry? Because he thought they were casting aspersions on his reputation? Or because he had something to hide and thought they were getting too close to his secret?

Deciding to let the matter rest for now, Storm rose to his feet. "The NYPD may have the greatest force on earth, for all I know. They certainly have awesome support—computers, manpower and forensic facilities. Elisa and I have one small advantage, though."

Storm paused, and stared unrelentingly at the lawyer. "The New York police also had some eight million possible suspects to sift through. But there are only a handful of people on this island right now, and one of them is guilty."

Chapter Seventeen

"Well, that was sure a waste of time," Elisa commented. She leaned back against the bucket seat. "No one was so overcome with guilt that he sobbed out a confession. Nor were any of them were wearing black tennis shoes with orange grommets."

Storm swerved around another pothole. Glancing at her, he arched an eyebrow. "Not giving up already, are you?"

"No, but—"

The four-wheel-drive vehicle bounced as it cleared a wrist-thick tree limb. Storm kept his gaze fastened on the rutted lane. "But what?"

Elisa twisted toward him as much as her seat belt would allow. "But what if we're just chasing our own tails? What if Heather somehow acted alone, or Jay really committed suicide? If he had been pilfering money from client accounts, maybe Heather wanted to pick up where he left off. Maybe she thought that disk would tell her where the funds were hidden."

Storm hesitated for a long moment. "Those are some good points, but...still, I think we were on the right track. Heather said she was computerphobic. Was that true?"

"Don't know," Elisa shrugged. "She had a PC on her desk at the office, but I only remember her typing on her IBM Selectric. Jay used to tease her that the Smithsonian kept asking for it. A relic of times past, that kind of thing."

"Let me play the devil's advocate," Storm said, as he turned onto the narrow trail that led to his home. "What if that was all a cover-up, so no one would suspect her?"

"Possible," Elisa admitted. "But she still could have been acting alone."

Stopping in the graveled parking area, he turned off the engine and yanked up the parking brake. He swung around and faced her. "I know you want to believe that, 'Leese, so you can feel safe again. But *someone* chased you through that swamp."

Her brief hope visibly deflated, she climbed out of the Jeep. He hated that he couldn't ease her fears, instead of adding to them. Right now, though, her feelings had to be sacrificed, if they were to stand a chance of apprehending the murderer. Because if he still considered her a threat, this evening might be his final opportunity to quash Elisa's returning memories. Forever.

Inside the cabin she kicked off her sandals and flopped down on the sofa. If her brain didn't stop spinning in this vicious, endless circle, she was going to lose her mind. She needed to think about springtime. About practicing at the barre. About succulent Dove chocolates. Anything but this terrible, indecipherable puzzle.

Storm took the opposite end and pulled her bare feet onto his lap. At his touch, her thoughts ran off in an entirely different direction.

"Seems to me that we keep hammering away and not making much progress," he said.

"That's what I was trying to tell you in the Jeep," she grumbled. "You said we had a lot more information than when we started."

"We do. For instance, now we know definitely that we're looking for a man. That eliminates Miriam and Betty. We know he had on black running shoes with orange grommets—"

"And he knows I still have the computer disk," she said, interrupting him. "So what does all this 'knowledge' do for us?"

Ignoring her cynicism, he trailed an aimless fingertip along the top of her foot. "We know we need more data."

She sucked in a breath, as he began to slowly knead her foot. "And...and...where do you propose to find this data?"

"From you."

"Me?" she squeaked, lifting her head to glare at him. "I've told you everything I know, and that amounts to zilch."

"You know more," he insisted.

She shook her head in disbelief. "Are you calling me a liar?"

He grinned and flicked her big toe. "Why do you always assume the worst? I was referring to those memories you can't access yet."

"What's left to try? Brain surgery?"

"Not tonight," he chuckled. "Actually, I was thinking more of hypnosis. Did the doctors try any hypnotherapy while you were in the hospital?"

"You mean like levitating me off the bed?"

"I'll take that as a negative response. Are you game to let me try?"

Instinctively Elisa edged away from him. Let him inside her brain? To question and probe her innermost thoughts without her even being aware of it? Absolutely not. She'd seen a hypnotist on television once. He'd made some of his victims think they were chickens, and they'd clucked across the stage. She'd been embarrassed and humiliated on their behalf.

How could Storm ask her to give him that kind of power over her mind? The very idea was unthinkable.

"No," she whispered.

"I understand," he hastened to reassure her. "You're thinking about those entertainment hypnotists that make women jump into strange men's laps, and old people take out their teeth in public. Aren't you?"

She nodded mutely.

"Therapeutic hypnotism is nothing like that. You'll be

completely protected and, trust me, no one can make you do anything against your will.''

"Then how did that guy make those people flap their arms like wings?''

He laughed—a dry, mirthless sound. "The chicken cluckers? They *wanted* to be on that stage. They wanted the attention, the notoriety. He didn't *make* them do it, he just planted the thought and they volunteered.''

"But how can I be sure?''

Slowly, patiently, Storm explained how he helped his patients through hypnosis. It was a particularly effective tool in recalling lost and repressed memories. On some level, Elisa would be aware of everything that went on around her. If an emergency were to occur, she would instantly awaken. And to further reassure her, Storm crossed to his desk in the corner and brought back a small tape recorder.

"I'll turn this on when we start, and keep it recording until you come out of the trance. You can play it back and listen to every single word.''

She was still wary of the hocus-pocus nature of this experiment. But Storm was an expert, a professional therapist. Earlier today, she'd made up her mind to place her trust in him. The way he never waffled, firmly believing in her innocence. Now was the time to prove to him, and to herself, that she could loosen the stranglehold of control. Now was the time to show her faith in *him*.

"Okay, let's go for it.''

"You might be more comfortable in the bedroom.''

A flip retort came to her mind, about his true motivation being a desire to get between her and her knickers. But somehow, the flippant remark died on her tongue as she silently led the way into the guest room.

Leaving the overhead light off, he tested the recorder and flipped on a small lamp on the dresser. The soft glow was comforting, tranquilizing. Elisa lowered onto the bed and closed her eyes. He put a pillow behind his back and sat against the headboard, keeping his body several inches from hers.

"Comfortable?" he asked.

She could feel the warmth of his body radiating across the small space between them. "Mmm... Very."

"Okay, now, I want you to let your mind go blank."

His slow, soothing voice poured over her, like cool rainwater on a hot summer afternoon.

"Focus on the gray nothingness that fills the empty space."

In her mind's eye, she saw a viscous gray haze that whirled and circled through her synapses. Calming grayness. Relaxing.

"Concentrate on each tiny molecule that makes up that gray void...."

But she couldn't concentrate on anything. Her mind had drifted into some plane of existence she couldn't quite see. She was vaguely aware of Storm's voice, droning in her ear. Like the peaceful buzzing of a fly.

She could hear herself answer his questions, but the sound didn't seem to come from her throat. Nor did the answers come from her consciousness.

"Okay, that's fine. You just stepped into Jay's office. What do you see?"

"Papers. Blowing everywhere. The window is open. There used to be a safety grid, but it's not there now."

"Go on."

"Jay's not on the phone. Heather said he was but he isn't. Jay? Where are you? Why don't you answer?"

"You're doing just fine. What did you do when you saw the office was empty?"

"I went to the window. It was July, but the air was cold. So cold." She crossed her arms and shivered. *"Someone should close that window before all Jay's papers fly out. I tried, but it seemed stuck. A piece of material, fabric, was caught on something. Then I looked down and...and saw him."*

"You saw Jay?"

"I didn't know it was him at first. It was awful. Grue-some. He was a long way down, and there was a lot of blood. But the more I stared, I started to pick out things. The dead man had the same color hair, and was wearing a suit just like Jay's. The gray one. And he had on a red tie. Jay always wore a red necktie. I knew it was him. I felt it."

"You're doing just fine, Elisa. What happened next?"

"I heard a noise and spun around. The office wasn't empty! Someone was hiding behind the filing cabinet. I screamed and he jumped out at me. I was so scared."

"He can't hurt you now. There's no need to be fright-ened. Did you see his face?"

"N-no. It was too fast. Too scary. I just ran. He was so close. I could almost feel his hands on my neck. I managed to reach Jay's door a few feet ahead of him and slammed it behind me. It locked automatically. It—it took him a while to figure out how to open it, I guess, because I ran down the hall. The elevator! I pushed the button, but it didn't come. Jay's door just opened. Come on, come on! But no matter how many times I punched the button, the elevator didn't come."

"Shhh. Take it easy. Let's rest for a moment." Storm could see her heart pumping wildly beneath her thin cotton T-shirt. Taking her hand, he probed her wrist for her pulse rate. It was too fast. Erratic.

Elisa was no longer remembering. She'd stepped back into her own past to relive the torment of that night. If there was any way to access those memories without subjecting her to this anguish, he'd do it. But there was no other way.

Gently stroking her damp forehead, he said, "Just relax. Think about the gray space, the soft, safe gray space. The man can't hurt you now. He's in the past. You're just re-membering, that's all."

When her pulse rate slowed to near normal, he continued. "You're safe, Elisa. But let's remember that night again. You were waiting for the elevator, and he came out of Jay's office, is that right?"

"He's playing with me. Somehow he knows the elevator won't come. He must have jammed it or something. Because he's walking so slowly. Like a cat stalking a wounded bird."

"Can you see him yet?"

"No. Too many shadows. But he's getting closer. God, what am I going to do? Where's the damned elevator! He's in front of the next office. There's still a light under their door. Maybe if I screamed. But my mouth is so dry. His shoes! I can see his black shoes, with orange thingies around the laces. But his face is still in shadows. Run. I've got to run! The emergency stairs!"

"Shhh. Take it easy. You're getting away from him now. Is he still following?"

"Yes! I hear him clumping down the metal stairs, but I'm faster. Two flights. I can hear him breathing. He's not in good shape. I can run forever. The tenth-floor landing. Ninth. He won't give up. But he's panting now. Eighth floor. Seventh. Sixth. Is the guard still in the lobby, or should I go to the parking garage and try to reach my car? He's way behind now. Gasping for breath. Fifth floor. Fourth. Third. I'm running out of steam. I danced last night, and my legs are aching. Second floor. Lobby. Should I hope for the guard? No! He might be on his rounds. I can make it to the garage. He's not following. He's resting. I can do it!"

"You can, Elisa, you're going to get away. Have you reached your car yet?"

"No. My feet are echoing like thunder on the concrete. He can follow the sound, he doesn't have to run. My keys! I have to be ready. Damn this purse! Why didn't I clean it out? Wait—I feel them. There's my car! Ten more yards. Got 'em. Eight yards. Oh, oh, the door just clanged open. He's here!"

"But you're far away, Elisa. He can't catch you. Open your car door. Lock yourself inside."

"Yes. Hurry, hurry. Key won't fit. Come on, come on. He's standing by the doorway, looking around. Thank God!

I'm inside. The motor won't start, it's cold. He hears me. He's coming this way! Hurry. Hurry. Start!"

"You're safe, Elisa. The car door's locked. Isn't it?"

"No! It locks automatically when I put it in gear. I forgot. How do I do this? Oh, dear heaven, he's only a few feet away. Click. It's locked. Try the engine again. I have to get away. He might have a gun. Start, oh, please, start."

"Calm down. You're going to make it. I promise."

"Ohhh, thank God! It started. Calm down. Slow down. Take it out of gear. Ease off the brake. What's he doing? He's standing right in front of the car! I'll have to run over him to get past. I can't. I just can't."

"Keep driving toward him. He'll move. You can't stop, you can't let him win. He killed Jay, remember?"

"He'll move. He has to. Three feet. Two. Why doesn't he— Oh! He jumped out of the way. I'm safe. But I have to drive slowly, I'm too scared. My hands and knees are shaking and I don't want to hit anything. He might catch me. He's still following the car. He just stepped under a light."

"Did you see his face?"

"No. Just his hair shining under the security lamp. There's the exit! I'll have to open the window to put my pass in the slot. He knows it. He's running again. Up the ramp, right behind me. Okay, the pass is in the slot, the gate is supposed to open! Hurry. Why won't he give up?"

The terror was starting to build in her voice again. Obviously, she had made her escape. And she had never seen the killer's face. There was no point in torturing her any longer. "Look, Elisa—the gate's lifting. You're pulling out now. He can't chase you any longer. You're safe."

"Safe." Her numb voice echoed his.

With infinite slowness and care, Storm brought her out of the trance and pulled her damp, exhausted and shivering body into his arms. He'd been so certain that hypnosis would cure her memory lapses. So arrogantly sure that he'd put her through that hellish experience all over again. And for what? They'd learned nothing new.

The killer had no way of knowing that Elisa had never seen his face that night. She'd turned and looked at him a half-dozen times. Yet luck had been on his side that night. But he didn't know it, and he was determined to silence her before her lost recollections resurfaced.

But who was he? David Welton, Mark Bowman or Carey Howard? Or, God forbid, someone they'd overlooked. Heather's partner could be holed up in a shack right now on the far side of the island. He could be a complete stranger to Storm and Elisa. Someone they'd never suspect. Hell, it could be Hank Danziger, for all they knew. That rustic, good-ol'-boy facade would be a perfect camouflage.

Heather had known almost every local resident.

Any of them could be the murderer.

WHILE the first hypnotherapy session failed to clear Elisa's blurry memory, it did seem cleansing, in a way. Immediately after Storm brought her out of the trance, she fell into a deeply luxurious sleep. When she awoke, she felt better than she had since the accident. Alive. Rested. Filled with energy and determination.

Of course, her spirits were buoyed when she opened her eyes to see Storm intently watching her. "How do you feel?" he asked softly.

She cocked her head, considering. Relaxed, rested, somehow lighter. As if she'd laid down most of the heavy load she'd been shouldering for weeks. Even her mind felt...clearer. As if the murky charcoal cloud were slowly fading away. Raising her eyes in surprise, she smiled. "I feel fine—great, actually."

"That's exactly like you're supposed to feel." He beamed like a proud papa.

Elisa raised up on her elbow. "We didn't learn anything new, did we?"

"Not that I could tell right off, but we'll listen to the tape later. Maybe between us we can pick out some detail that will help."

"Sure," Elisa murmured doubtfully.

Kicking off his shoes, Storm stretched out beside her. He turned on his side, facing her. "Let's leave that subject alone for a while."

She nodded. Frankly, she was utterly weary of thinking about Jay's mysterious death, Heather's betrayal, and the rest of the dreadful chain of events that had dragged her to this low point.

His finger trailed a squiggly pattern down her arm. A tiny tingle followed in the wake of his touch. Oh, no, Elisa admonished her lusty appetite. Hadn't last night taught her a lesson?

But the imprint of his touch was still warm on her soul. This *morning* might not have turned out the way she wanted, but last night...last night had been magical.

Yet she couldn't forget his casual let's-still-be-pals attitude this morning. As if their deeply satisfying bond had never happened. His heart hadn't been transformed like hers, so he couldn't know how badly he'd wounded her with his bland indifference.

She edged out of reach of his magnetic field.

He inched closer. "I did want to talk about something else, though. Last night."

Her heart skipped, and she blurted out the first thing that entered her frazzled mind. "I don't like to talk about sex, I'd rather do it."

"Okay, if that's the way you want it." He nonchalantly reached down and unsnapped his jeans.

"No!" She sat up and pushed her hair out of her eyes. "That's not what I meant. I meant that it makes me uncomfortable to talk about delicate, er, sensitive—"

"I understand completely," he reassured her, lowering his zipper.

In self-preservation, she rolled off the bed and glared at him. "You're not listening to me, Storm. I didn't say that I wanted to—"

"No, you weren't listening to *me*." He grinned and sat upright. "I said I wanted to *talk* about last—not make love, although that would be a fine alternative. And while I appreciate your...enthusiasm...for our lovemaking, I have to remind you that wasn't the only thing that occurred last night.''

Elisa frowned and gingerly lowered her hip onto the bed. ''Now I'm totally confused.''

He patted the mattress. ''That's what I wanted to do—clear up any confusion. Any misunderstandings.''

A mixture of dread and anticipation filled her as she eased onto her side. ''Okay. You go first.''

Tugging his fingers through his hair, Storm paused, as if collecting his thoughts. ''I want to know why you seemed so different this morning. So, I don't know, unfazed by what happened between us last night.''

''Me! You're the one who was whistling around the kitchen like Joe College right after he scored with a hot chick. Not a kiss, a hug, or even a warm glance.''

''I made you breakfast!''

Elisa raised up and glowered. ''I didn't want eggs. I wanted to hear that I mattered. I wanted a little emotional intimacy.''

Storm blew out a deep, frustrated breath. ''Life sure has a way of turning around and kicking you in the butt when you're not expecting it.''

Elisa shook her head, confounded by his apparent subject change. ''What?''

''You said 'emotional intimacy.' Do you know how many times I tried to explain that concept to Karen? A hundred—maybe a million. But she believed that sex was sex and love was love. If I wanted to show her love, I could fix a meal. Buy a small gift. Take her out to dinner. But sex was for the bedroom.''

Her heart lurched in sympathy. What a cold, empty marriage he'd had. A despondent wife who couldn't make decisions or adjust to change. Who compartmentalized the pieces of their life as if she were storing buttons. The love button in this box. The sex button in this one. The financial button goes over here.

No wonder he hadn't known how to react to a woman's

emotional needs. He'd been programmed not to recognize them. Nor was it any wonder that he found sanctuary in helping children. They were so open, so free, so willing to show their love and affection on all levels.

Elisa reached over and cupped his face in her hands. Slowly, with infinite tenderness, she kissed his lips. Then each eyelid, and finally the scratchy stubble on his chin. Drawing back, she whispered, "I'm not Karen, and you're certainly not like any man I've ever known. So we need to find our own comfort zone, make our own rules."

"Sounds fine to me," he breathed, his voice heavy with bubbling passion.

"Here's my first rule—I want, no, need, to be intimate on all levels. Can you handle that?"

He thought it over for a moment. "You may have to help me."

"My pleasure."

His left arm snaked around her waist, drawing her softness against him. "So let's start with a clean slate. Right now." Storm tangled his fingers in her hair and pulled her face to his, and kissed her. A long, slow, shuddering kiss of tantalizing promise.

When they parted for air, she whispered, "You have quite a bedside manner, Doctor. Teach me some more."

And so he did.

WHEN THEY PARKED behind the hotel, Elisa was ready to face down a man-eating tiger.

This was her favorite time of day. Although the sun had lost its sting, it hadn't yet sacrificed its place to nightfall. Even the blazing-hot wind had melted into a balmy breeze, drifting like silk over her bare arms. She was wearing the flowered sundress that Storm liked so well, and had left her hair free to drift down her back. The early evening was marvelous, and Elisa thought smugly that she looked and felt pretty marvelous herself.

Thanks to Storm, and his double dose of "therapy."

"Hey, kids, glad you could make it." Hank's voice floated down to greet them.

Elisa looked up and waved. Hank and Brian McPherson were on the back-porch roof, replacing shingles that were ripped loose during the hurricane. Brian was like that, Elisa thought. Always ready to jump in and lend a hand. He'd even helped Heather rework her stock portfolio after some of her investments took a nosedive.

Despite the dreadful events of the past few days, there were a lot of nice, decent and caring people on the island. Her head cocked to take in Storm's firm, stalwart profile. Some exceptional people, in fact.

"Need some help?" he called.

Hank poked two nails between his teeth and waved aside the offer. "Nah. We've about got it. You look like you're dressed for an ice cream social, anyway."

Glancing down at his aqua striped cotton shirt and white duck Bermudas, Storm grinned sheepishly. "Been taking fashion tips from that lawyer. We're going to work on accessorizing next."

"He just wants to show off his legs," Brian muttered, his grim expression not showing a hint of humor.

"You guys are just jealous. To show my goodwill, I'll buy you both a drink when you come inside."

Hank raised his hammer in a salute. "And we just might take you up on it."

Storm clasped Elisa's elbow as they climbed the rickety porch steps. "It's show time," he whispered in her ear as they stepped into the kitchen. "Ready?"

"Mmm." She squared her shoulders, but her confidence in their plan was already evaporating. When they first came up with the scheme, she'd thought it had a fair chance at success. Now that the time for implementation was at hand, she couldn't believe the killer wouldn't see right through the tissue-thin ploy.

But they had no other options. Only twelve hours remained before the first ferry arrived. If they hadn't uncovered his identity by then, they'd never have another chance.

As expected, Miriam was at the stove. The mouthwatering aroma of sautéeing onions filled the air. Her head swung around when they crossed the room. "Elisa! You look wonderful, honey. You must have gotten plenty of rest, or something."

"Or something," Storm uttered under his breath.

Poking him with her elbow, Elisa peeked over Miriam's shoulder. "I feel a lot better, thanks. I know you're going to refuse, but can't I help with something?"

The back door opened, and Hank and Brian trudged in and headed directly for the stainless-steel sink. Miriam evidently had everyone on the island well trained.

Lathering his hands with a grainy bar of industrial soap, Hank called over his shoulder, "That ornery woman don't think nobody else is fit to mess around in her palace, Elisa. No sense wasting your breath trying."

Storm broke in, saving them all from the Danzigers' warmhearted but long-winded version of "The Bickersons." "Where's everybody else?"

Miriam grabbed a carrot and started scraping it clean. "Reckon they're all in the parlor. I told them drinks were on the house tonight."

"Except for one," Hank declared. He reached for a paper towel and handed Brian the soap. "The doc here is buying the first round for us working men."

"Humph. Working men. Another hour, you'll be hollering for a heating pad and liniment."

Giving his indomitable spouse a lusty kiss on the cheek, Hank made his escape, beckoning to Storm and Brian to follow him.

Brian paused in the doorway. "What about you, Elisa? Buy you a drink?"

"Not yet, thanks. You guys go ahead. I'll join you in a bit."

She directed a pointed, but covert, glance at Storm. He dipped his head in a fractional nod of understanding and disappeared into the dining room.

Chapter Eighteen

By the time Hank and Brian had finished their drinks, and had had their fill of ragging Storm about his legs, the other hotel guests had settled in for a pleasant evening. The prospect of being able to get on with their real lives seemed to have given their spirits a boost.

As a special treat for their last evening, Hank had used his emergency stash of fuel to fire up the generator. The overhead chandelier twinkled, adding to the cocktail party atmosphere. To an outsider, the group would have appeared to be vacationers, enjoying the bonhomie of like-minded travelers. Their expressions didn't give away the fact that they'd been living under black and deadly shadows for the past several days.

David Welton was swapping deep-sea-fishing tales with Mark Bowman while Hank entertained the others with his fabled stories of peculiar guests the hotel had housed over the years. Miriam was keeping a sharp watch on how much beer her spouse was imbibing, while talking quietly with Carey Howard.

Only Elisa was missing, but, perhaps being sensitive to Carey's feelings, no one asked about her.

The stark panic that swept through the hotel after Heather's death seemed to have subsided. A reserved calmness had replaced strident alarm, although Storm sensed in them an undercurrent of guarded tension, as if they were underlings at the boss's posh cocktail party. Expecting someone to spill his drink on the carpet—hoping it wouldn't be them.

Everyone was in place. Not much longer now.

When Hank started spinning yet another outlandish yarn, Storm took advantage of his attention lapse to move quietly to the archway. Blocking the opening to keep anyone from leaving this little gathering was part of his role in the upcoming play.

Glancing around to make sure no one was looking, he reached up and flipped off the light switch.

"Hey! What happened?"

"What the hell?"

"Not again!"

The chorus of voices carried a sharp edge of trepidation.

Storm waited a moment, while their eyes adjusted to the sudden darkness. Then he flicked the switch again, and stepped forward, standing just inside the chandelier's spotlight.

A second later, they all stared at him, blinking against the sudden invasion of light.

"Did you do that, Delaney?" David leaned forward as if to attack.

Storm held up his palm, and the lawyer slowly sank back into his chair. "Just wanted to make sure I had your attention."

Carey jumped to his feet. "What's this all about? I'm sick of you and your parlor tricks."

"You don't have to put up with me much longer, so just sit down and listen."

When he had their still and undivided attention, Storm reached into his pocket and pulled out the bright blue computer disk. Holding it above his head, he waggled it between two fingers. "Anybody here interested in this little jewel?"

As he expected, no one stepped forward to stake a claim. "Oh, come on. *Someone's* been pretty anxious to get their hands on it. Heather even tried to kill Elisa for this disk."

Betty Bowman gasped and scooted closer to Mark.

Carey Howard slammed his drink on a side table with an audible clunk. Bourbon sloshed over the side of the cut-glass tumbler, its pungent smell pervasive in the confined room. "Now see here, Delaney! What kind of garbage is this? I should've known you'd lie, cheat or steal to help your high-and-mighty girlfriend. But I never thought you'd stoop to slandering a dead woman."

When Storm moved slightly toward him, Carey's tirade abruptly ended, and he slumped back into his chair.

Storm slowly stared at each face in turn. No one broke eye contact. A sign that they were all innocent? Or did one of them have molten steel running through his veins?

Playing his last card, Storm walked around the room, holding the blue disk in front of him. He watched as each pair of eyes circumspectly stared, mesmerized by its sinister portent.

"Take a good look now," he said. "Because first thing in the morning, this little piece of plastic, and all the information it contains, is going to be turned over to the police. Someone in this room, a man, understands the importance of that information. Because Jay Morrow left the evidence that's going to put him in prison. For life."

Still, no one cracked.

David looked bored. Mark Bowman confused. Carey Howard arrogantly disbelieving. Hank stared back, his wrinkled face screwed up in a disturbed frown. Brian McPherson took a sip of beer and set the glass on the mantel, his expression bland and indifferent.

A hushed quiet ruled the tense space until Elisa stepped through the archway. Holding them up like trophies, she carried a large black running shoe in each hand. The light reflected off the sneakers' Day-Glo metal grommets, like tiny orange moons.

She stood just outside the chandelier's reach, where the light didn't touch her face. Her gaze hidden in shadow, Elisa could have been accusing any of them.

Suddenly, she tossed the shoes into the circle of light. "You certainly can't deny these!"

Heads snapped downward as all eyes were suddenly riveted on the black running shoes.

"I saw them when you chased me through the marsh yesterday. And I saw them the night you killed Jay Morrow. These shoes will convict you."

Carey rolled his eyes. "I don't know what you're trying to pull, but those shoes don't prove anything. They could belong to anyone."

"But they don't. They belong to Jay Morrow's murderer. And lab tests can confirm who wore them. Feet sweat, don't they? And any body fluid, even sweat, leaves enough DNA for a positive identification. Isn't that so, Counselor?"

She turned to David Welton.

Fingering his upper lip, he slowly nodded. "Yes. I'm no expert, of course, but I'd say Elisa's absolutely right. The owner of these shoes could be positively identified."

Mark Bowman unfurled his arm from his wife's shoulder. "So one of us owns running shoes—so what?"

Storm cut in from where he'd been quietly standing by the doorway. "These shoes tie in with one more piece of information Elisa hasn't shared yet."

"What's that?" Brian McPherson asked, his tone reflecting only casual interest.

Elisa stepped into the light, but kept her head bowed, so that only the crown of her blue-black hair was fully illuminated. She wanted the killer to wonder, to squirm. He had to make the first move, or all was lost. "Oh, I forgot to mention that, thanks to Storm's hypnosis therapy, I have my memory back. You were hoping I didn't see you, but I did."

Betty Bowman crossed her legs, and the silky sound of her nylon hosiery sounded like firecrackers in the taut atmosphere. But still the killer's composure hadn't cracked. Even though Elisa knew his identity with absolute certainty, she had no tangible evidence. Only a shard of memory. But it was him, and he *knew* he was guilty.

Fractionally raising her voice, she played her trump card. "Don't you remember running behind my car while I was driving up the ramp? You ran out of breath and stopped under a light.''

The morbid anticipation was almost palpable. Elisa could feel the breathless expectancy as every eye watched her with rapt interest.

Taking another step forward, she raised an accusing finger. ''And that's when I saw you. Standing there in your black sweatshirt, with those shoes. But you were tired, weren't you? So you shoved back the hood of your sweatshirt, remember? And you know what? Your red hair really caught the light, *Brian McPherson!*''

He reacted with more speed than she'd expected from a man his size. In a single movement, like a striking rattler, he leaped from the fireplace and lunged toward Elisa.

Storm was only a split second behind him, but he was too late. McPherson jerked Elisa sideways, pinning her in front of him. His powerful forearm wedged under her chin. He could break her neck with a simple twist of his arm.

Or he could simply pull the trigger of the nine-millimeter Beretta whose barrel was prodding her temple.

Storm backed off, holding his arms out, trying to defuse McPherson. ''Take it easy, guy. You don't want to hurt her. It's all over.''

His ruddy face bloodred with rage, he snarled, ''Not yet it isn't. Once I'm off this miserable sand dune, no one will find me. Now hand over that disk, Doc, or I'll turn your girlfriend into a real airhead.''

''There's no way off this island. A full cadre of police will be stationed on the ferry. It's too late.''

McPherson's left arm was still tightly clamped against Elisa's throat. Nudging her with the gun barrel, he inched toward the incriminating shoes. ''Not yet. I told Heather to stop taking chances and get rid of her. Elisa was a walking time bomb. But would Heather go ahead and do it? Hell, no. But I'm not going to prison because that silly bitch was a coward.''

Elisa took a measure of comfort from the fact that Heather hadn't wanted to harm her. If she'd gotten her hands on that disk earlier, none of this would have transpired.

Storm stepped toward them, and McPherson shoved the barrel tighter against her flesh. "Don't! I'm warning you, Doc, one more move like that and your girlfriend is history."

"Let her go, McPherson. You have the disk. Take one of Carey's boats and you can be long gone before the cops arrive."

McPherson laughed. That same vile chortle she'd heard in the swamp. "Nice try, but no dice. As long as she behaves herself, this little dancer is going to be my Get Out Of Jail Free pass. Now keep out of our way."

Yanking his forearm even tighter across her throat, he growled, "Let's go. This way."

Elisa gagged from the lack of oxygen, and he eased the pressure slightly. Forcing her feet to move, she allowed him to guide her toward the archway. But she couldn't go with him, wouldn't go. She had no doubts that the moment he felt safe Brian McPherson would eliminate any loose ends—namely, her.

Slumping, so that he would have to support her entire weight, she waited for her opportunity. She couldn't move her head, but she could sense Storm following her every move with his eyes. Elisa knew she had to act before Storm allowed his fury to blind him.

The others had huddled together against the far wall, paralyzed by fright.

Just as they reached the doorway, McPherson glanced over his shoulder, dividing his attention for an instant, unwittingly releasing the pressure on her throat. Knowing this might be her only chance, Elisa feinted downward, breaking his hold, then spun around.

"Wha—?" McPherson's reactions were fractionally slower than hers, and that was all the advantage she needed.

Raising her good leg, Elisa flexed her toes, incredibly strong toes from years of carrying her body weight, and kicked upward. She caught Brian under the chin. The clunk of her foot striking bone echoed in the silence.

At that instant, Storm sprang forward. Wrapping his arms around McPherson's waist, he threw the large man to the ground. The Beretta went skittering across the hardwood. Both men scrambled for the weapon.

Storm's fingers were almost touching the cold steel when McPherson grabbed his ankle and slid him backward over the slippery floor. Kicking furiously, he had almost escaped his grasp when the larger man ducked his head and bit deeply into the flesh on Storm's leg.

Yowling with pain, Storm redoubled his attack. But McPherson managed to touch the hatched grip of the gun, and sent it skidding farther away.

Elisa wanted to jump in and help, but was afraid of adding confusion. Storm's pant leg was hiked up, and blood was oozing from the vicious bite mark. She had to help—somehow.

Then she remembered that they'd brought a fearsome equalizer.

Rushing into the hallway, she grabbed the twelve-gauge from its hiding place in Miriam's umbrella stand and dashed back to the parlor. "Stop or I'll shoot, McPherson." For emphasis, she pumped the shotgun.

Storm had been right. That deadly sound would stop any man in his tracks. McPherson hesitated just long enough for her to cross the short distance and prod him in the back with the barrel.

Rolling over, Storm fished the Beretta from under a table and rose to his feet. "It's all over, McPherson. Get those hands in the air. That twelve-gauge has a hair trigger and Elisa's a little nervous."

McPherson's hands shot into the air, and the room broke into chaos.

MIRIAM HAD FETCHED a length of clothesline and Hank had tied his indignant former friend into a kitchen chair. The sailor in the group, Carey Howard, had double-knotted the rope. McPherson wasn't going anywhere.

Nor was he willing to spill his guts. He kept demanding his rights, but David Welton patiently explained that they were civilians, and Miranda rights only applied to government-sanctioned authorities. He was under citizen's arrest and had no rights until turned over to the police.

Elisa knew the moment the police arrived McPherson would scream for a lawyer. He knew enough about the law to refuse to answer any questions. She doubted they'd ever know the real story.

Holding the bright blue disk in her hand, Elisa sighed. "If only we knew what Jay was trying to tell us."

Mark Bowman stepped forward. "If you want to retrieve some data off there, I can probably help."

"You can?" Elisa's eyes widened in amazement. "But we don't have a computer. And I thought you owned a restaurant."

Mark chuckled and took the floppy. "I have a laptop in our room. Everybody uses computers, Elisa. Come out of the Stone Age. Tracking food, sales, supplies, payroll—you name it, my computer does it for me."

Betty rushed upstairs and retrieved her husband's laptop. It took him a while to understand Jay's system, but between what he found on the disk, and what Elisa and Storm had already put together, they were able to piece together a viable scenario.

With McPherson's help, Heather had been skimming money from Jay's securities clients for several months. McPherson had set up a program that she used to transfer funds to a dummy account set up in his name. Because they kept the account on Jay's books, when he ran his totals, the final sums had always been right.

In a short period of time, the cyberthieves had managed to accumulate over a quarter-million dollars in the dummy account. McPherson had warned her not to get greedy; it had almost been time to transfer the money to an offshore account and move on. He would leave a computer trail that pointed to Jay Morrow as the culprit.

But a few days before the planned transfer, Jay must have noticed something in the books that worried him. Heather had overheard Jay talking on the phone to a consultant, an accountant who specialized in finding "discrepancies." He would be in the office in two days to start.

Panicked, Heather had phoned McPherson to come to New York to speed up the transfer. They'd been in the office that Friday evening. Jay had been gone most of the afternoon, so she'd thought he'd left for the day; she'd known he had plans with Elisa for a late dinner.

Brian had still been downloading information he needed to complete the offshore transfer when Jay walked in and caught them. They'd overwhelmed the slightly built securities broker and tossed him out the window.

Elisa assumed they'd chosen that method because it was quick and expedient and could be made to look like suicide. She could well imagine Heather's surprise when she'd strolled into the office, almost catching them in the act.

The kicker was that Jay had suspected Heather all along. His other co-workers had been with him for years; Heather was the only new element with access to his computer. While waiting for the accountant's report, he'd taken the precaution of freezing his accounts. The numerical sequence code needed to reopen those accounts was on that blue disk.

So after committing fraud, theft and murder, Heather and McPherson had been no closer to the money than they were in the beginning. They'd had to have that disk.

Carey leaned forward, elbows on his knees, his lean face a study of rapt attention. "But I don't understand why you suspected McPherson in the first place? I mean, without the information on this disk, what made you suspicious?"

Elisa shrugged. "Several small things. First, his friendship with Heather, of course. But that gash on his forearm really raised alarms."

Miriam frowned. "Why?"

"He *said* he'd cut his arm at home, but the bloody towel came from this hotel. Of course, he could've taken a...souvenir sometime before, but when Hank found that broken window in the basement, it all fell together. McPherson cut himself breaking into the hotel. He grabbed one of Miriam's towels so he wouldn't drip blood all over the place."

Storm, who'd been helping fit the pieces into a coherent puzzle, picked up the story. "They thought Jay might have gotten the disk to Elisa. By Heather's attaching herself like a limpet, she would know if Elisa's memory returned. If she knew anything about that night's events, Heather would have been the first to know. That's why she was in no hurry to eliminate Elisa. Too messy. Too many coincidences to explain."

Elisa grimaced. "Thanks. I'm so glad that I was too much trouble to kill."

He wrapped an arm around her shoulder and kissed the top of her silky black hair. "Me too, Princess, me too. But what I don't understand is how you got hold of McPherson's shoes. I've been with you every minute, and there was no way you could have gone to his cabin and snooped around until you found them. It's not like he was staying here at the hotel."

In reply, she disappeared from the parlor, returning in a few moments. She held up her hands. One contained an empty bottle of black shoe polish and the other a bright orange flask of fingernail polish. "Sorry, David, your new running shoes were about the right size. So I gave them a quick going-over with the shoe polish and, thanks to Heather's rather flamboyant taste, added her nail enamel. And voilá! The incriminating evidence."

Storm burst out laughing and bundled her in his arms, swinging her around until she called for mercy. "You are one fantastic woman, know that, Princess?"

"Mmm. Just keep telling me that."

"That was quite a chance you took. What if he hadn't taken the bait?"

Elisa shrugged. "I know that a guilty conscience makes a person susceptible to accepting blame for almost anything. I was counting on Brian's guilty conscience."

THAT NIGHT, they lay on the floor in Storm's cabin, watching the log crackling on the hearth. It was too warm for a fire, so they opened all the windows and doors. Atmosphere, according to Storm, was far more important than comfort.

"You've taught me a lot these past few days, 'Leese."

Uh-oh, here comes the old brush-off. She took a sip of wine to camouflage the sudden brightness in her eyes.

"You've taught me it's time I stopped feeling sorry for myself and got on with my life."

A life without me.

"But I'm not ready for New York yet. I'm thinking about going into private practice. What are you thinking of doing?"

Storm was a louse, but he was still a nice guy. He wanted to make sure she would be all right before he dumped her. How thoughtful.

Elisa shrugged. "I guess I'll go back to Los Angeles, maybe open a ballet school."

He leaned back and toyed with a strand of her glossy black hair. "Good idea," he said thoughtfully. "Or…or you could come to Baltimore with me. I've been thinking that modified ballet dancing might be just the thing to help disturbed kids regain their self-esteem. It certainly helped nail a murderer. What do you think—like to move to Baltimore?"

Elisa's heart sang with joy, but her old, fearful self wouldn't quit. She'd never been to Baltimore, didn't know a soul there.

Storm lightly yanked on her hair, demanding her attention. "Come on, 'Leese, follow your own prescription. Take a chance. Live dangerously. Live with me. I'll keep you on those lovely toes." For emphasis, he hauled her into his arms and settled his warm, enticing lips on hers.

He was right, she thought, just before her thoughts faded to visions of stars and moonbeams. Baltimore was a good town. She'd meet people, nice people. After all, Storm would be there, and she knew *him*. And she had definite plans to keep him busy, for years and years to come.

Take 4 bestselling love stories FREE

Plus get a FREE surprise gift!

COMING NEXT MONTH

#437 FATHER AND CHILD by Rebecca York

43 Light St.

Zeke Chambers needed a wife in 24 hours. But could he ask Elizabeth Egan, the woman he secretly loved, to marry him for a pretense, to put her life in danger? But Zeke had no choice: He had to save the life of the child he just found out he had.

#438 LITTLE GIRL LOST by Adrianne Lee

Her Protector

After a fiery crash five years ago, Jane Dolan and her infant daughter were given a new beginning and new memories. So how could she believe reporter Chad Ryker's claims that her family is in hiding and that her precious daughter isn't her child?

#439 BEFORE THE FALL by Patricia Rosemoor

Seven Sins

Wrongly indicted, Angela Dragon is out to find who framed her—even if that means confronting the mob…and escaping a dimple-flashing bounty hunter. Mitch Kaminsky has problems of his own: When Angela learns the truth, will she still want him, or will pride keep them apart?

#440 ANGEL WITH AN ATTITUDE by Carly Bishop

Avenging Angels

To mother an orphaned baby, Angelo's one true love Isobel had turned mortal. Now with a killer on her trail, Isobel needed protection, and Angelo could trust no one with her life. He'd let her down once before; he wasn't about to lose sight of her again.

Look us up on-line at: http://www.romance.net

As Seen on TV!

Free Gift Offer

With a Free Gift proof-of-purchase
from any Harlequin® book, you can receive
a beautiful cubic zirconia pendant.

This stunning marquise-shaped stone is a genuine cubic
zirconia—accented by an 18" gold tone necklace.
(Approximate retail value $19.95)

Send for yours today...
compliments of ◆HARLEQUIN®

To receive your free gift, a cubic zirconia pendant, send us one original proof-of-purchase, photocopies not accepted, from the back of any Harlequin Romance®, Harlequin Presents®, Harlequin Temptation®, Harlequin Superromance®, Harlequin Intrigue®, Harlequin American Romance®, or Harlequin Historicals® title available at your favorite retail outlet, together with the Free Gift Certificate, plus a check or money order for $1.65 U.S./$2.15 CAN. (do not send cash) to cover postage and handling, payable to Harlequin Free Gift Offer. We will send you the specified gift. Allow 6 to 8 weeks for delivery. Offer good until December 31, 1997, or while quantities last. Offer valid in the U.S. and Canada only.

Free Gift Certificate

Name: _____

Address: _____

City: _____ State/Province: _____ Zip/Postal Code: _____

Mail this certificate, one proof-of-purchase and a check or money order for postage and handling to: HARLEQUIN FREE GIFT OFFER 1997. In the U.S.: 3010 Walden Avenue, P.O. Box 9071, Buffalo NY 14269-9057. In Canada: P.O. Box 604, Fort Erie, Ontario L2Z 5X3.

FREE GIFT OFFER   084-KEZ

ONE PROOF-OF-PURCHASE
To collect your fabulous FREE GIFT, a cubic zirconia pendant, you must include this original proof-of-purchase for each gift with the properly completed Free Gift Certificate.

084-KEZR